Life's Defeat

Life's Defeat

Life's Series: Book One

Rebekah Raymond

Tesmur Publishing

Life's Defeat © 2015 by Rebekah Raymond

Editor: T. Morgan Editing and Writing Services

Cover: April Volition

Printed by CreateSpace, An Amazon.com Company
Available from Amazon.com and other retail outlets
Available on Kindle and other devices

First Printing, 2015

ISBN 978-0-9948698-0-7 (Paperback)

ISBN 978-0-9948698-3-8 (eBook format)

ISBN 978-0-9948698-1-4 (pdf)

Tesmur Publishing
4 Range Place NW
Calgary, Alberta CANADA
T3G 1P6

Acknowledgements

I cannot express enough thanks to those who supported me through the process of bringing this novel to life.

To Paul Absher—without your insistence that I join NaNoWriMo I never would have revisited this once-short story. Thank you for your encouragement, your military knowledge, and your excellent literary banter.

To Megan Rio and Kimberly Henry—for listening to me through this process, reading my work, giving criticism, and aiding me with social media. You are awesome ladies.

To Taija Morgan—your critical and informative editing helped shape this amazing piece into what it is. Thank you, for never letting it be "too much".

To my parents, family and friends who supported my funding campaign and followed my steps from fledgling writer to published author. You know who you are—I am thankful for the belief you had in me.

To my children—my daughter whose interest in learning to write kept me going, my son whose frequent waking at night allowed me a lot more writing sessions.

Lastly, to my husband, Chris. Without your support I could never had continued and finished this. You have been my best friend on this unforgettable journey of both our life and my writing. Many more years to come, CB.

When getting older, no one ever tells you what it's like to die.

No one ever expresses the angst one feels as the life drains from the body, the rising challenge to resist the inevitable.

But then I suppose that's because they are dead.

I am not.

By some cruel twist of fate I managed to experience this interminable hell and come back, taking a deep gasp into lungs that burned from disuse, my joints stiff and sore from rigor, my voice raspy and vision blurred.

I came back, again and again.

To be sure, it was not a path I would have chosen. And if you wish to take one thing from my experiences let it be this: when you see that bright light, run toward it. Run as though your life depends on it. And it does. For if you come back, everything changes.

And it's not always in a good way.

To Start

The first time I went up against the man with the cigar personally, it was by mistake.

I remember being young, the tender age of sixteen, and newly made a soldier. We had finished a mission, my comrades and I, sabotaging an act of corruption so deep there was a good chance we had saved many people within a village from a devious fate. Drug production and prostitution were averted, women and children free to return home unharmed while the men worked, feverish, in the mines of the hills.

For all that I lacked in experience, I was disciplined and well-trained—I knew I had proven myself well. Still, I was unprepared for the outright menacing act of the madman. As my team prepared to leave, I turned, witnessing the criminal step from a secret door out of the warehouse.

I called out for my teammates, but the words fell on deaf ears as the blades of our helicopter created a small windstorm in the dusty alleyway. Turning back, I stepped toward the man with the cigar's large black vehicle, seeing him pause before disappearing behind the opened door.

He stared at me, the faintest of smiles tugging at his lips as he removed his cigar. He threw it, smoldering, to the ground, his pocked-face lightening as his eyes pierced into my soul. I didn't look away, my youth betraying a defiance I thought I needed to express authority.

The gods know I was a fool then.

As he stepped into the oversized SUV, I saw the vehicle dip with the weight of the robust criminal and his accomplices. The doors closed, and still I stared. Then he was there, leaning forward from the front passenger seat, his face again looking at me as his smile became a grin. He gave an order, and the vehicle lurched forward.

To this day I am not sure why I didn't act, why I didn't run back to the helicopter and request help, why I didn't at least pull my gun when I first saw the man and shoot him in the brain.

It could have saved so much pain, so much heartache.

Instead, it took me a moment to realize that the man had ordered my execution—the SUV was headed straight for me at a breakneck speed. Two choices flew through my head then, to dive out of the way or to try to take down the men. Stupidly, I chose the latter.

Time seemed to slow as the engine of the black beast roared with its speed. I reached beside me, pulling my gun, and with a flick of the safety began to shoot. The bullets ricocheted off the windshield with appalling speed, their target shifting as I attempted to find a sweet spot in the glass, any vulnerability at all.

There was none.

By the time I figured out the vehicle was impenetrable, it was too close. Despite the speed with which I turned and raced for my own team's mode of escape, I wasn't fast enough.

When the vehicle hit, there was a massive shove, sounds of crunching as the front grill imprinted into my back. I spun around as I fell to the ground. The vehicle bounced as I created a speed bump, both sets of tires driving over my arm. I lay there on the ground, my eyes closed as I reminded myself to breathe, the air coming in short gasps from a pain within my lungs.

Bursts of immense irritation emerged then, throbbing stabs of agony from my arm and leg, wetness spreading across my head and limbs. I cried out, tears escaping my already swollen eyelids. I heard the engine slow as the vehicle did, felt a tremor within the loose ground as it skidded sideways to a stop. I shifted, my body protesting with pain as I fought to sit up, my eyes opening to focus on the helicopter. They had noticed me, my captain running in my direction now, yelling something I couldn't catch.

Rolling over slowly, I forced myself to my uninjured knee, hoisting myself up somehow onto a foot that was shaky at best. I had no choice—I couldn't stay in the street, and I feared the vehicle would come back if I lay there long enough. My only choice was to get back to the helicopter, no matter how.

I glanced at the SUV, my neck mobile enough for slight movement, and caught the eye of the man with the cigar. His face peered out the window with a look of contemplation. He nodded once as I straightened my back, my spine blossoming in a pain I barely knew possible. The window rolled up as the vehicle took off once more. This time, it drove away.

It was my first experience with a major injury, my first real meeting of the man with the cigar. The largest incident that would shape my life into what it would become years later.

I would heal, as my body was a glutton for punishment. It took time, for sure—days of traction and weeks of casts and therapy marking what had been a sort of rite of passage within my military faction, the first near-death. I bore it well, I think, saving my episodes of pity and self-loathing to when I knew I was alone and could cry without an audience.

Those times of loneliness were when I would think, wondering at my own intelligence.

Why hadn't I just run away?

Why had I stood my ground when I knew it was futile?

Most importantly, I wondered about the criminal and his interest in me. At first I had thought it was a matter of being in the wrong place at the wrong time. But the man had stared at me—he had looked happy to give the order of my death, as though he had a personal vendetta. And there was the nod.

What was that look?

Beginning and Ending

When I left what had been my home, holding the few meager belongings I owned, my rucksack on my shoulders, I had no idea I would wish that I had chosen wiser in my life's decisions. But no change in course would have prepared or defended me from my fate. To understand that is to know the beginning.

It started with a car crash.

My father, I am told, was an excellent driver, especially with my mother and me in the car.

That night the road was slick.

My father swerved at the wrong time, sending the vehicle into a spin along the still streets of the city. Minutes passed by in a blur. Something was hit. The car began to roll.

I don't remember much else, being that I was a young child. My memories of the event now are a mix of tidbits of my own truth and that which was told to me. I do know that when the car came to rest we were upside down, the vehicle's panels crunched, the roof dented, glass shattered.

My parents were dead, their bodies mangled messes. I remember the blood streaming down my mother's head, dripping onto the inverted roof. My father's open eyes held a surprised expression, a large piece of metal from some part of the vehicle sticking out from his chest.

And I, I was fifteen feet away, huddled on the cold concrete and whimpering, my fingers clenched around my bloody dress. My long brown hair was disheveled, the ribbon keeping it tied long lost, my tights shredded, bare legs covered in nicks. My arms were wrapped tight around my bent legs, their surface a collection of cuts and gooseflesh.

I was never told how I got out of the wreckage. Shiny black boots approached—a man with a kind but weathered face knelt on the cold sidewalk and offered his hand. After a last look at the carnage and what should have been my fate, I took the hand and followed the man away to my new life.

It was explained to me that my parents belonged to a fellowship of sorts. They were always watched, always in contact, so it had not taken long for the news of their accident to spread. Always anticipating the worst, they had been smart with their money, investing and saving and living within their seemingly meager means. But that intelligence had meant a large inheritance for me, something well-needed later in my life.

The man who had taken me from the wreckage was another of the fellowship. By apparent coincidence, he was headmaster for a private boarding school which took in the elite as well as promising middle class and poor children sponsored by the state.

Just as I trusted him that first night in the street, I trusted that he told me the truth about my parents' fate.

I had no reason not to.

The school was an odd juxtaposition within the confines of the city. Surrounded on either side by office buildings, the three-story, rock-faced school took up an entire city block. Encompassed by a massive concrete and metal wall, the complex looked like an office building from a distance, its outside drab and dark, its windows tinted black.

When one entered the outer wall, the place transformed, a typical grassy lawn unfolding before the building. Thin, leafed trees thrived somehow within the compound, as did flowers, all stretching tall to reach the limited sunlight that fell through the breaks in the surrounding buildings.

Behind the school lay a massive field, serving both recreational and scenic purposes, and beyond that a forested area that separated the grounds and the massive wall. Looking up one could see large clear plates high over the wall, acting as both windbreaks and an extra security system should the need ever arise.

The school itself was built to look like an old

English stone structure, although it was unclear if the outer wall and city had grown up around the three-story monument or if the materials had been brought in and weathered to appear ancient. Either way, vines grew up the side of the walls to emphasize the solidarity of time.

Large inviting windows and beautiful double stained-glass doors adorned the entrance to the school, opening up into a grand entranceway and rich polished-oak wall paneling and bamboo floors. Chandeliers sparkled from the ceilings, both functional and opulent in their beauty.

A massive staircase led upstairs and what appeared to be the back of the school lay across from where I stood, down a long hall, unexpected bright light coming in through the door on the other side. Despite this, the school's overall small appearance was deceiving again—within the confines of a maze-like hall system learned over time was a full contingent of private, shared, and bunk-style sleeping quarters for students and teachers alike, kitchens, classrooms, gymnasiums, lounges, and doors to areas smaller children such as myself were not privy to.

Surprisingly, there were others there near my young age, and after being treated for minor wounds at the infirmary I was washed up, put in a tidy uniform and given a bed in a bunk room with eleven other children. While there would always be one or two bullies within the several-hundred-child student body, tolerance was emphasized and I quickly made friends, although I held most at a cautious distance.

I started classes immediately, an interesting combination of standard curriculum sprinkled liberally with diplomacy, language, and international interests. Athletics were added, then arts and culture as I grew older and stronger in my academics. I thrived on learning and my education became paramount to me, someone with nothing beyond what was within the outer walls of the school.

Mr StPatrick, the headmaster who had saved me, watched with interest from behind closed doors, always aware of my progress with strange fascination. An active participant in the daily running of the school, StPatrick made it a point to visit classrooms and learn about each student. But with me I felt him watch in anticipation. It was as though he were waiting for a butterfly to emerge from a caterpillar's chrysalis.

I could not have possibly known at that time how the school, with its hidden agendas and secret standards, would mold me into what I became so distinctly.

As I began my ninth year at the school, StPatrick gave me a choice: continue with my current curriculum, or join a group of students who had been specially selected for advanced schooling. I knew of the group he spoke—they wore a different garb than the usual uniform and walked with an air of deserved superiority.

I thought about those students, whose eyes shone in dangerous defiance, their knowledge vast in the subjects they helped the younger students with and shuddered. They had an edge of mystery held between them when they were suddenly called away during class, frowns and determined brows replacing smiles.

I chose.

I was immediately given a new room assignment, more private with only two roommates, and a new uniform. My new classes began that day.

Had I known the extent of the new life to which I had agreed on taking, I am unsure whether I would have made the same choice. On one hand, it was what destiny had sought me to become for years. On the other, I could have been blissfully ignorant. I could have lived out my life with my parents' money, oblivious to the dangers life around me possessed. I could have gotten married, had children of my own, and died peacefully an old woman.

Of course, I also could have ended up like my parents, victims of an unfortunate and devastating accident.

My new courses were invigorating, meant to integrate us young soldiers so smoothly into any environment that we could literally travel anywhere without being noticed. I asked once if we were spies. My new friend, Tomlin, a kind, sandy-haired boy three years my senior, shook his head but said nothing more. It was an answer only I would be able to come up with, and not until I had experienced this new life fully.

By my fourth month of training I was fluent in three languages, proficient in marksmanship and drilled in the necessity of silence and obedience. Apparently, I surpassed expectations. Even Tomlin was surprised when a call went out to his team, a gun placed in my hands.

When I stepped outside the school for the first time in twelve years, I hesitated before loading into an armored vehicle with my hard breastplate fastened and gun sitting ready in the holster at my hip. I thought I had understood. It wasn't until we were at our destination, the elder students going first to silence any opposition, and not until I saw the four diplomats strapped to chairs and gagged—their wide, pleading eyes gazing back at me—that I really got it.

We were no longer students.

We were a unique squad of few, meant to bring about resolve through justice, by whatever means necessary.

History Combined

During the last World War two hundred fifty years past, the nation's government had given up on regulated security, pulling funding from all organized military stations. The first two world wars, one hundred years prior to that, had been a show of weaponry bragging and racial intolerance. The third was merely a retaliation and struggle for domination.

It failed horribly.

After the horrors of the war, the committee decided it would no longer support the vast fortune it took to run the operation and could not justify the meager rewards. It left the country disorganized, filthy, and unprotected.

Still, that nation and the world at large did not go to crap as most thought it would. Some attributed the minor success at staying alive to the meagre reforms put in place: the restrictions on population, the productivity of assigning jobs to those without. In truth, these actions helped the people not starve, but did nothing for their ability to thrive. We, however, did.

Vigilante groups sprung up across the nation, taking matters into their own hands as the lowest scum sought purchase on the land, the people, and the profits both held. The vigilantes had no official name, no way to decipher them as one unit, except for the common grey-black garb and the fact that they were very good at what they did.

Ex-military, air force and navy, soldiers, mechanics, technicians, all forcibly unemployed when the government made its ruling, they all came together to become a united force. When they became incapacitated or too old to continue, they taught the next generation, now without the benefit of government-regulated training but skilled nonetheless. They taught the next and the next.

Our faction, made up of such young teenagers and young adults, was an anomaly within the vigilante effort. There were few places where the young were being trained to arms in the name of the cause, fewer examples still where the efforts actually thrived. And among all those schools that tried to create what we had, we were one of the few who did it well.

The majority of the nation or the world had no idea their more or less peaceful existence was owed to these people, these secret groups who wiped out crime and violence before it became out of control.

A few, like us, did.

We felt the responsibility of peace weigh heavily on us every time we donned the grey-black garb, every time a technician placed a gun in our hands. We relished in the moments of success after a calamity was averted, felt personal loss when one of our own didn't return.

Once I came to terms with what we were, I began to embrace all that we could do. When not on a mission, we were students, finishing what academics we required, both traditional and operational. But we were there as leaders as well, helping the younger students and acting as aids to the teachers. As part of our training we were taught to be kind and compassionate to the students, respectful to the teachers. But when a call came in, our wrist watches vibrating in a familiar rhythm, our efforts were politely abandoned and we left for those secret doorways I had so wondered about as a young child.

Once in the school's underbelly, we were briefed. We suited up in our grey-black pants and shirts, military boots and bulletproof vests, guns in our holsters and knives in our sheaths.

Within one night we could travel halfway across the world to assist in an international crisis. It seemed we could do anything as a team. In a few hours I could change my attire and hair, or add lipstick, mascara, and blush, and saunter confidently into a high-end nightclub or casino and be served drinks without a moment's hesitation at my young age, infiltrating a ring of the worst type of scum. Or, within moments of a mission beginning, we could find a hidden door in the back of a shady establishment and save numerous enslaved children or malnourished and overworked old women in a cocaine operation.

As soldiers of the cause, we fought hand to hand, aimed our guns and pulled the triggers with immediate discretion, and used our youth to deceive and betray those who we knew lived to the detriment of others. They were criminals, all of them, slavers and drug dealers, killers and narcotic producers. Their work was to put mankind into a slump of despair and dependence.

Ours was to take them down.

And once in the school's secretive military faction for some time, what I learned StPatrick had told me long ago was a brotherhood, I learned a truth about myself. I was very good at what I did. Too good.

It was both thrilling and terrifying.

I left the school on my nineteenth birthday, not because I didn't enjoy what we did but because I had seen too much. I had been with the team four years and in that time we had accomplished things I could before only dream of.

I had grown as a person, embracing my duties both in and outside the school, and by then knew of my parents' money and the possible opportunities it posed. Mostly, I wanted a break from the gory advancement of the field. We had lost eight soldiers that year, and while the violence had elevated to a point of necessity, it was too much. I was then a team captain and tired of sending youth to their deaths.

So, with quiet goodbyes to a few friends and fellow soldiers, and a knowing nod to StPatrick, who had tried to convince me to stay, I stepped outside the school's outer walls. I had no armor, no team, no weapons to protect me.

I travelled.

With nothing holding me back I drew on my funds, stocked my new rucksack and made last minute decisions on which flights to take, trains to ride, boats to partake of, and where I would sleep and eat.

It was the best time of my life.

I learned new words, experienced different cultures, received ceremonial tattoos and piercings, danced with children and elders, helped deliver babies and goats alike, smoked with shamans, ate in expensive European restaurants, and shopped within the height of fashion. I travelled the world, living off the plains of Africa, observing the statues of the islands and world wonders in Europe, feeling sand between my toes in deserts and beaches.

Still, the school was on my mind.

It had been a hard time living with the team, but it had given me purpose. It was when I was enjoying a breakfast of a baguette and fruit in a small café and saw on the news that the school had been attacked again that I made my decision.

I would return.

I stepped out of the cab, rested from the long sleep on my flight, and handed a few wrinkled bills to the driver, glancing at the imposing fortress-type wall of the school as I did. I tried to figure out how long I had been away, but time was not important when one was enjoying the world freely—I hadn't even brought a watch. I shouldered my rucksack and pressed on the metal doors, heaving the heavy outer entrance open slightly so I could step through.

Somehow, from the outside, my childhood home seemed smaller, not in size, but in comparison to the expanse of the world. I took a few steps inside the complex and stared at the classic brick architecture, the green moss winding its way up the sides, the trees that were beginning to change color with the new approaching season. I took casual steps toward the school, taking it in visually as I approached the long path to the front.

I glanced up as I walked and halted only thirty paces from the building, seeing the flames coming from the main bay window. Months of inaction had dulled my senses and it took a moment for what I was seeing to register. I stood there, shocked, not comprehending what I knew was happening.

The window blew out, shooting shards of glass and wood framing from the structure. I dove to the ground, my rucksack filled with treasures heavy on my back, protecting me from the worst of the onslaught.

I felt small slices along my bare arms and legs, and

my hands as they covered my head. My ears pounded from the boom. I wondered if I had gone deaf for a moment, then little echoes began to reach me as I shrugged off my sack and got up to a kneeling position, observing the tiny cuts along my fingers and above my knuckles.

Running footsteps came from the building and I struggled to stand, grinning when I saw who was coming. Tomlin, with a handful of other soldiers approached, their faces black with soot but otherwise seeming unharmed. He had changed in the time I was gone, losing the last of the late-teen boyish looks, his face becoming leaner and features more defined. Now, at the age of twenty-three, my old captain was finally what he aspired to be: a man. Clad in his mission-oriented, grey-black, long-sleeve shirt and pants, Tomlin looked up from his run. Confusion crossed his eyes.

No one had known I was returning.

He slowed his pace and motioned for the others to flee. Ensuring they were past us, he grabbed my arm, motioning the same. He was yelling at me, his voice coming in and out like a damaged stereo speaker. I heard only parts of words, my blast-shocked brain slow in reading the young man's lips, a skill I had once possessed.

Had it really been that long?

Another voice came through, clearer now, deep and rich in tone, and the two of us gazed up in alarm. The blood drained from both our faces. The man with the cigar—someone we had fought so many times— walked toward us, tall and imposing. He never hesitated to use others to his advantage, and thought their lives dispensable if it served his purpose. We had lost many a good soldier to him. He was a man who believed thoroughly in the idea that taking was a right, and that good and evil were a moot point. Evil always won.

He had pursued us endlessly for as long as I could remember being with my fellow soldiers, this man whose name we didn't even know. The most malicious of the criminals we had ever faced, we had sought him as well, hoping for just one chance to stamp him and his organization out. But every chance we got, he was there one step ahead of us.

I remembered he had once tried to kill me, specifically.

The tall, stocky man came to a stop, his glossy, brown-black hair slicked back, his hands on the hips of his finely tailored pants, his usual long animal-pelt jacket draped like a cape over his shoulders. He was surrounded by his own small group of militants armed with an assortment of knives and guns. Many of the blades were in-hand and poppy-stained and I hated to think how many children and soldiers had met their end.

The man was smoking his thick cigar, like usual, his chubby pocked-face expressing glee as he took us in. No doubt capturing a captain of a vigilante group, as Tomlin had been for years, would be a great accomplishment. He spoke and I struggled to hear, inadvertently leaning forward while Tomlin held me back, his fingers digging into my sliced flesh. He grit his teeth as he replied, "You'll have to kill me first."

That, I heard clearly, and I glanced to the usually calm-headed young man in surprise at the bold response.

The villain motioned sideways, cigar still in his mouth, light-grey smoke puffing out the side periodically. One of his men approached, holding what I thought was a gun. When he stepped around the others into the open I saw how wrong I was.

Similar to a crossbow, the weapon possessed the mechanics of a grappling-hook launcher, something we had used many times ourselves. The hooks were pressed flat, however, making it appear to be an arrow. The lowlife took off the safety and grinned through his boss' smoke as he aimed at Tomlin, then me.

Tomlin immediately argued, and the words, though still not complete in my dazed state, gave me enough of his message. He told the man that I had left the school a year ago, that my mind had been swept clean before then—a false claim. Such things were possible, but wholly unreasonable unless absolutely necessary, the procedure dangerous to both the patient's mind and life. The hook moved as he spoke, aiming once again at the boy—now man—I worked with so many times before.

The man with the cigar considered this. He grinned. His eyes sparkled as he insinuated we were lovers, that Tomlin was only trying to save me. In a move I knew spelled trouble, the man took one last puff of his cigar and threw it down, letting it smolder in the gravel.

His lackey pulled the trigger.

Tomlin realized the device was aimed at me before I did. Even then, it was too late for him to pull me away. The hook came out faster than either of us could have anticipated.

The arrow punctured my midsection. Searing pain entered my upper stomach. The tip of the arrow exited my back. Within seconds, the arrow stopped. It jolted still by a small section at the base meant to prevent it from passing completely through its target.

Another moment passed. I felt the tip of the arrow pop open and anchors dig into my back, catching me within the confines of the weapon. I doubled over from the impact. A burning and fullness occurred from the steel lodged in me.

I looked to my friend as realization dawned and saw his expression, one of horror with eyes wide and mouth hanging open. My hands reached around the rod of the thing just above my belly. There I could feel warm, thick liquid, viscous as it oozed from my wound, though not as much as I would have expected.

Tomlin reached out to me, his fingers resting on my arms, trailing down to my own hands for what felt like an eternity. His hand became slick with my blood as I cringed, feeling a pull from the cable connected to the rod. Looking up, my vision again started to blur. I could see the man with the cigar grin toothily as he reached over the launcher and began to pull in the cable hand over hand.

With no choice, I looked back at Tomlin once more, my words halted by a moist metallic taste in my mouth. As the cable pulled taut I cried out, stumbling forward, pain jolting through my stomach and spine as the rod and hooks shifted and bit in further. With each movement I felt more blood escape, now trailing down my tank top and shorts, running down my bare legs and into my socks and hiking boots. Five feet away, sensations began to disintegrate, and by two the twinkling of a blackout threatened. Finally to my inadvertent destination, the man with the cigar took me by the shoulders and leaned in to whisper.

My eyes grew large in response before the darkness overcame and my life ended.

Wonderment

The hazel eyes of my father, a man I had never really known, stared back at me with both sadness and pride in the shiny reflective surface of the captains bars I held. I had finally made Captain, a goal I had been working toward for three years. Today was the first day I got to wear my bars.

Three years. It seemed unbelievable that I had trained that long, that I had plodded through missions as only a cadet, then a private and lieutenant, for the better part of thirty-six months. But, I had finally done it. Of course, my promotion came at a price, owed to the death of another, a fresh-faced captain, only seventeen years old. *He* had only lasted two months before his demise at the end of an incendiary device lodged in the ground. He had been stupid, careless—we all knew to check for such things.

This was the stepping stone I needed, I craved. It was the promotion I needed to have and hold well for the chance to obtain my final goal: the vigilantes.

I longed to be part of them, to be invited to join

their ranks once my time at the school was done. I knew the chance was slim—they only brought in the best of the best, but I also knew I had a better chance than most. Unlike their other prospects—chosen from untutored talents from around the world, activists and do-gooding unfettered adults whose efforts to make the world a better place had *not* resulted in their deaths by some miracle—I came trained. I came from one of the few places where that talent had been nurtured and hardened and harnessed into the strict code of military perfection they demanded.

The fact was that I had earned my new title only because of this young man's stupidity and because our commander had a preference for four captains at any given time. I didn't feel remorse about it. I didn't feel I deserved the rank any less.

Someone else could have been chosen for the honour.

With a renewed sense of pride, I glanced down over my appearance, my above-ankle military boots spit-polished to a shine, dress pants pressed and wrinkle free, shirt buttons straight, the bottom tucked at my waist. My belt was new, the black leather-looking composite gleaming and unscathed by the rub of knife and gun holsters.

I caught the hazel eyes in the reflection once more, those eyes that were mine and yet not. As I lifted the bars, I wondered what my parents would have thought of my promotion, my lifestyle choice.

StPatrick had implied my mother and father had once been with a vigilante faction, what he had once called a fellowship. If that was true, and I had no reason to suspect my headmaster and commander played me false, then I liked to think my parents would have been happy to see me finding purpose with my life, even if that meant fighting and bloodshed and near-certain death.

Nothing would make me happier than to know that I had made them proud. Except, perhaps, my own pride the day I hoped to step out with my own vigilante team.

A girl could dream.

Perhaps it was the fact that I lay in death that I relived the day I had wondered most about my parents. It could have been the connection we held then, all of us held in the thrall of the grim reaper himself. I wanted to believe it was a higher message, that my mother and father held me within their grasp and protected me from travelling to heaven or hell.

If that was so, then even they knew my time wasn't finished.

And so I relived the day I had dressed in my military garb, attaching the captain's bars to my shoulder, the first day I ever had done so. I relived the feelings of trepidation and happiness. I saw it all as though it were yesterday, heard the details right down to the click of the magazine in my Beretta, the echo of my boots on the hard concrete floor of the hanger bay.

And then, when I had seen the event in its entirety, when I had felt sufficiently confident that this honour was truly mine, when I could finally relax at having done something completely right in my life, I felt the draw of my soul back to its mortal ties.

I fought against it, I pleaded to the god's to reconsider and let me remain in the happy space of time I now occupied.

And, in answer, I opened my eyes.

Second Time Around

Consciousness came to me in waves as sight returned, the fuzziness of my vision giving way to clarity as the smoothness of the concrete walls and white-panelled ceiling came into focus, then the sound of the soft hum of the recessed lights above. Next came the sensation of touch with the hardness of the bed and cold of the moisture through the walls. Lastly came a feeling I knew only too well from being injured as a soldier: that of pain as I moved on the bed and felt a strong twinge within my guts and spine.

My hand instinctively went to my wound, feeling bandages wrapped in layers over my midsection. Somewhat in disbelief over my conscious nature, my palm rested on my belly and pushed to test the spot of entry.

My own anguished yelp surprised me as my hand jolted from the spot and the other made a fist, my knuckles implanting between my teeth to stifle the sound.

"Well that was stupid," a sudden voice within the

shadows of the other side of the room startled me, my body jumping in response, my outward cry more apparent. I cringed as I felt a wetness begin through the cotton wrappings.

The man came out of the darkness slowly, clean-shaven and resolute. "Now you've done it—probably ripped the stitches." He came over slowly, reaching toward my bandage as he leaned over the bed.

I tried to move away but by now the pain was becoming unbearable. Instead I lay still, willing the tears in my eyes not to fall. The man tucked my shirt out of the way and pulled at one of the wrappings, looking just under it, and hissed, "Yep, clean out. I'll have to call the doc."

Quickly he went to a panel on the wall, opening it and pulling out a receiver. He paused, then confirmed, "She's awake. Get the doc over here." He hung up immediately and returned to his chair. While I was writhing in pain I could feel his glare searing into me.

Mere minutes passed before the door opened, another man entering. He headed for me, mimicking the guard's hissing in disapproval. He hunched slightly over the bed, the item affixed firmly to the wall on one side, waist-level to the man.

"How the hell did you manage this?" he asked as he unceremoniously rolled up my shirt and started cutting away the wrappings.

I clenched my teeth, the agony compounding as the gauze brushed the open wound.

"Dammit, I'm going to have to sew it again." He opened each of my eyelids wide with his thumbs, observing my pupils, feeling my head for fever and wrist for pulse.

As he saw me cringe, he paused long enough to chastise me. "You're too weak, I can't give you anything for the pain so you'll just have to bear it," he pulled his implements from his bag. "If you pass out, so be it. But I won't have you die under my care again, I already spent long enough bringing you back last time." I saw him take up his needle and thread, poking at the area.

My eyes grew large at the revelation as the needle popped through my skin. "What do you mean, last time?" I asked through choked whispers.

"I mean when they brought you in." He quickly pushed and pulled the needle through, suturing the wound closed once more. "I didn't ask what happened, it isn't my place to, but by the time you got on my table you were barely there. Once I started repairing your insides, you flat-lined, and with nothing else to do you stayed that way for several minutes until I could stop the bleeding and repair the damage. Then I brought you back. Had a damned hard time of it too."

"I was dead?" My voice was haggard, sobs threatening to escape as the last stitches were put in and he tied off the line.

I couldn't have died—I am too young, too strong.
It was just a dream, I know it was...

"Are you having a problem hearing?" He seemed to genuinely want to know. "You came, you died, you were resurrected." He took out more gauze to pack the wound, taping it in place.

"Why?" The tears rolled down my cheeks without permission. "Why would you bring me back?"

The doctor took off his blood-covered gloves and folded one into the other to dispose of later. He shrugged and glanced over at the guard. "I was just following orders."

He stood and turned to the seated man. "She needs to stay still for a few days until the tissue starts to bind. Can you manage that?"

My gruff babysitter grumbled an answer, likely unamused with his current posting. "How about I strap her down? Then she can't move," he said sarcastically.

The doctor looked back at me, assessing the situation. I closed my eyes, knowing what his answer would be before he spoke it.

"Fine," he said, "just do it gently. I don't want to be called back before the next time." He closed his bag and left.

I was starting to lose consciousness, the smell of the antiseptic used and dull roar of pain becoming too much.

"The next time?" I slurred, fighting to stay awake for the answer. I was afraid, fearful of my permanent demise and what they would do with what remained.

The guard came over, pulling restraints from

somewhere, putting the soft fuzz-lined loops around my wrists and ankles. He grinned. "Wouldn't you love to know?"

I stared at his evil smirk only a minute before my eyes rolled back into my head.

Waiting

When I awoke again, I tried to move naturally, prevented wholly by the restraints on my wrists and ankles, several straps holding down my stomach and chest as well. I struggled but was warned by a new voice not to try it. Looking sideways, I saw a new caretaker there, a stocky, dusty-haired, ugly man, smoking and unconcerned by my plight. He motioned to a table by the door.

"Food is over there if you're hungry."

I craned my neck, assessing the pain in my body but finding I felt almost hale, albeit sore where my wounds on my stomach and back healed still. I looked and saw a few trays with empty packages, only a couple bites of a sandwich remaining on the one.

"How am I supposed to reach it?" I asked, my voice stronger than I would have thought, daggers shooting from my eyes as I glared at him. Another part was forcing me to be more standoffish than I would like.

"Sounds like your problem," the man responded. He brought the cigarette to his lips and blew the smoke in my direction.

With nowhere else to look I stared straight up at the panelled ceiling, my eyes finally free of tears but knowing if I could shed them I would. I was obviously a prisoner here and while my injuries were being tended it appeared comfort was not a prime concern. My stomach rumbled quietly and I realized that without knowing how long I had been unconscious, I had no idea when the last time was that I had eaten.

Lost in thought and with not much to look at, I started dozing throughout the day. The guard was quiet when not lighting another cigarette from his pouch or receiving and eating the meals. He began to take a thrill in being my daytime caretaker since he was there dawn till dusk and those were the only hours food was delivered to us. He began taunting me with it, staging his chair so I could see him easily in the light.

He would open my drink, sucking out the majority of the contents before bringing the last of it to my lips. He often dropped the cup after I had a sip or two. I began drinking large gulps, the act backfiring when he would tip the cup forward and I would choke on the onslaught. He would chew my sandwiches methodically, making a point of dropping a few pieces then slowly tossing them into the garbage on the trays.

He tortured me as such until, after a few days, I laboured against the restraints, trying to reach him in a futile attempt. He thought he had broken me completely. He started suggesting things I could do to earn that bite of meat or mushy vegetable or pudding.

After four days, marked only by the daily appearance of my guard, I was starving and started seriously considering it.

It was on the fifth day I decided anything would be better than starving to death. I now wish I could have gone back and reevaluated.

A doctor arrived again that day, removing one of my wrist restraints to feel my pulse. He took a long look over me, turning my head from side to side. "You've lost weight. Your eyes and cheeks are looking hollow." He furrowed his brow and frowned. "Has she not been eating, Claude?" he asked the man with the cigarette.

Claude. I now knew the name of the first enemy I would kill when I escaped.

"I offered every time but she didn't want anything," Claude answered, a sadistic grin spreading when the doctor looked away.

"You have to eat or you won't heal," the doctor chastised. "Luckily I figured this would take a little while. I ordered my lunch here."

The grin disappeared from Claude's face.

The doctor continued with his exam, treating my stomach wound and removing all the restraints so he could look at my back where the arrow had punched through and small sharp anchors had bit deep. Claude objected, but by this time I was so malnourished I couldn't have escaped if I had wanted to. The doctor rolled me onto my side as I grunted, re-dressing my wounds and nodding in approval. I was starting to heal, albeit slowly.

The door latch moved then and a tray full of food was passed in. Apparently the doctor was considered high enough to get the good food: fresh fruit and vegetables, soup and a hearty baguette with fixings. I eyed the tray longingly as he picked up an apple and took a bite, taking a break from my exam.

Seeing the way I was eyeing the food he glanced at Claude suspiciously. "She wouldn't take any of her food?" he asked again.

Claude knew he had been caught but had no choice but to continue the lie. He shook his head.

"Rejected it every time."

The doctor picked up the loaded baguette and took a bite. Dressing and toppings oozed out, falling to the plate in a satisfying heap. "This is very good, very good, indeed. Claude, why don't you go to the kitchen and get one for yourself. Tell them I sent you so you get the good stuff."

Claude hesitated after smiling at the thought. "But...I'm supposed to stay here to guard her at all times."

"I think we will be fine," the doctor laughed. "She's too weak to even move. I'll stay here until you get back. Take a nice long lunch. I need to do a thorough exam anyway."

Claude hesitated for a minute until the doctor took

another bite of his sandwich enticingly. The guard mumbled in confirmation as he rushed out of the room, closing the door behind him.

The doctor finished swallowing, then picked up the soup and approached the bed. "I suspect the grumbling from your stomach and hungry look in your eyes means you have been denied food," he rested the soup next to my head. I shut my eyes tight, not wanting the torture to continue so close to me.

"Here," the doctor said somewhat tenderly, slipping his hand under my head to raise it slightly. He brought the broth-filled spoon to my lips. Still wary of his generous nature, I opened my mouth slowly, feeling the warm spoon deliver the broth over my tongue. I closed my eyes, a tear finally escaping as the moisture seeped into my tissues.

"He was starving you," he said matter-of-factly. "He shouldn't have done it and I am sorry for that. You must be in considerable pain from your injuries without hunger as well."

I took another few gulps of the liquid, the warmth slipping down my parched throat and into my empty stomach. "Why are you being so nice?" I croaked quietly, my first words in days.

The doctor went to the table to put the soup down and grabbed a banana and the glass of water. "I'm doing my job. As a doctor, I took an oath to do no harm. As one of his, my orders are to get you better."

"You work for the man with the cigar," I tried to lift

my hand for the fruit, but my muscles were too weak.

The doctor laughed aloud at my comment, sitting down again and breaking a small piece of the banana off, feeding it to me. "Do they still call him that?" he continued without an answer. "Rochester. His name is Rochester."

I looked up at him, slowly chewing my food, drinking when he brought the glass to my lips, and thought about what he said.

Somehow, it was strange knowing the name of the man we had been fighting for years, a man who had tormented the world and killed numerous soldiers from my team, so many children from the school. A man who I had been injured by personally many times before. Stranger still was that this man who was being so nice to me right now was on a mission to keep me alive and well.

For him.

I did not talk after that but merely ate and drank what the doctor allowed me, conscious of the fact that my empty gullet could not take a full meal. I had no idea what the criminal mastermind Rochester had planned, but I knew at this point I was at his mercy.

I would not be able to escape and trying to starve myself now would be fruitless—the doctor would do whatever he had to do to keep me alive. Until I could find out more, my best chance at survival was to gain back my strength.

Claude did not return that day or any other. A new day-guard, a woman this time, took over instead, one who understood the importance of orders. She was diligent, feeding me every meal, encouraging me to eat my fill. As I got stronger, and with the doctor's blessing, she removed the restraints. With a hand on her hip holster, she watched me roll off the bed and stumble around the room, my hand heavy against the walls for support.

The doctor returned every few days after that, making sure his orders were being followed, confirming that my wounds were finally on the mend. After a week I was strong enough to wander without aid. A few days after that my guard started seeing me as a threat. I had tried talking to her, tried being polite and casually chatting to lighten the mood and make her comfortable with me. But she was a soldier and would have none of it.

Then I tried to grab her gun.

It was almost two weeks after the doctor had made his discovery with Claude, my measurement of the passage of time estimated again by the appearance of the guard every day. I was feeling much better and could freely move, though I was still cautious with my actions, careful not to reopen my healing wound. I had been asleep on the hard bed when our lunches came. The guard accepted them, then indulged in some playful banter with the man on the other side.

When I awoke, I noticed my chance and silently

slid off the bed. Creeping around the room, out of sight of the outside guard, I approached mine. Slowly, I reached out, my hand only an inch from the holster. My fingers twitched as I reached the clasp, looping under the cover when the leather creaked slightly from underuse.

My eyes grew large as my guard's head whipped around in my direction, one hand jumping to the holster, the other snapping forward to crack her heel into my chin. Pain exploded from my lower jaw as I fell backwards, my balance still somewhat compromised. I hit the ground hard, the wind knocked from my chest. The guard turned, straddling my legs as she stared down at me, a look of amusement across her face.

"Well, we're feeling better, aren't we?" she asked. I shook my head, trying to clear the stars in front of my eyes, my mouth sore and swollen already.

She nodded to the outside guard, letting him know everything was all right. Grabbing my arms, she dragged me to the bed. I was still disoriented and fighting was not in my interest. She picked me up and settled me on the metal slab, immediately attaching the restraints.

As my head finally cleared, I turned and spat out the blood from my mouth, frowning. I had misjudged my guard, something I had never once done on a mission. Luckily, it hadn't been Claude—I shuddered to think what he would have done with me helpless and compromised on the ground.

But then, they did have orders to keep me alive, at least for now.

The Trial

It seemed like an eternity before anyone came for me again, the doctor or otherwise. The hours began to drift into each other and I lost track of time, whether it had been a few days, a week, or more.

My guard was on patrol outside my cell now, keeping me restrained except for a few hours each day during which she would watch me, hawk-like, as I stalked my small chambers like a pacing tiger always glaring at my prey across the room.

Then one day the locks of the door could be heard, the unmistakable squealing of the metal on metal I had grown accustomed to when my guard entered and exited each day. I grew excited at the prospect of yet another visitor, but my guard quickly pulled out her gun and pointed it at me. She had been quick to let me know after my last attempt that they had been told to keep me alive—they had never been told they couldn't shoot a body part to immobilize me.

So instead I flattened myself against the wall and behaved, wanting to avoid unnecessary pain.

I was such a fool.

Two men marched in, dressed in scrubs, and nodded to the guard. She eased her stance and put her gun away, a slow, wide grin emerging.

They approached me warily. The handsome one reached me first, slowly placing his hands on my arm, righting his grip as the other reached forward also.

I snapped.

Within seconds, a strangled growling noise came from my lips, my limbs all resorting to the fighting mode that was once as automatic to me as breathing air. My arms flailed, trying to remember the defensive martial arts patterns I had used not so long ago, and the first man went down. The other man tried to keep hold, his grip stronger, and I struggled to keep ahead of his actions.

Then I heard the click of the gun.

I looked toward my guard, my eyes wild, teeth gritting, and saw the weapon pointed at me. The safety was off. I breathed heavily, that animalistic mode of survival still coursing through my veins as reality popped back. My muscles started to relax and I stepped back against the wall, my eyes still stuck on those of my guard.

A needle jabbed the base of my neck. It hissed as it released its fluid into me. It was the handsome one, a small bruise forming over his eye but otherwise fine. He pulled out the needle, tucking it into his pocket, and grabbed my arm.

I struggled again but the liquid was fast-acting. By the time we walked to the door, my legs gave out. Steps outside the room, my head lolled.

Everything went black.

I opened my eyes to a brighter light than I had ever experienced. I blinked, then squinted, turning my head to get away from it. That only gave new insight into the dangerous game I was in. To the side, I could see nothing. The light was so concentrated that everything else lay in darkness.

Then I smelled the smoke.

My body tensed as the bright light moved back, the other lights in the room brought up enough for me to see my surroundings. My wrists were shackled above my head, my body horizontal, lying flat and tethered to a table. The man with the cigar, Rochester, sat just beyond it. He nodded in approval as I awoke.

I tested the restraints, wrenching hard with my hands and feet but it was no use, my limbs were connected to the table with strong steel links.

Rochester took the ash-tipped cigar from his mouth. "So you do think she is able for this test, doctor? It will not be accurate unless it is as though she was captured unharmed."

The doctor came around the corner. "Yes, her wounds are still healing, but they will not affect her performance and I can pinpoint if they do."

Rochester nodded. "Excellent. Prepare the tank

then," he called out to someone behind him and I began to see shadows in the background working. Apparently this room was much bigger than I had anticipated, emphasized by the echoes of his calls.

A tank?

I was now fully awake and alert. "What are you doing with me?" I asked quickly, only part of me really wanting to know.

He smiled, putting the cigar in his mouth, and leaned back casually in his chair. "It always amazed me, when I saw your group, that you were so determined. After all, you are but a small group of children and young adults." He blew out his smoke in a large billow, watching the white tendrils swirl and disintegrate into grey nothingness. "I never understood how they were able to indoctrinate you so thoroughly that you would put everything on the line, including your lives...for what? For the school? For StPatrick?"

I startled a little when he said the headmaster's name, the one who had recruited us, our commander-in-chief at our small vigilante faction. Rochester knew the operation better than I would have thought.

The man chuckled, observing my reaction. "Yes, I know his name. We were..." he paused to consider what term to use, "—old friends, shall we say. Besides, it is best to know the name of one's enemy." He took a deep drag on his cigar, the end glowing red then becoming ash.

"Was it worth it?" he asked.

I licked my lips with what little moisture was in my mouth. "It was for us. For justice."

He laughed then. "What do a pack of children know about justice?" he asked. "Who is to say in this world who is evil and who is good? How would you even know if you were fighting on the right side?"

I was silent. Rochester had a point and that alone chilled me to the bone.

"Either way, after time and time again of seeing the same of your soldiers who I knew had been injured, ones who had been sliced and shot and crushed, I began to develop a theory. Would you like to hear it?"

In the background, I heard a large bang as a heavy object was moved into place and a whooshing noise began, much like a running river or an industrial-size fan.

Taking my silence for an affirmative, Rochester continued, "I suspected there was something special about your group, some reason you were picked beyond the other students. I thought it was talent, but at the young ages Patrick took children on, anyone could be taught." His eyes held a silent thrill, the sides of his mouth curling upwards in enjoyment. "Then it hit me... *blood*."

That chill I had a moment ago turned to complete ice.

"There is a very good possibility that you soldiers have something in your genetics, a type of survival gene. If I could test it, could isolate it, I could possibly inject it into my own." He paused and nodded as someone called to him from behind.

"You were really the trigger, you know. We had hit you with a vehicle once and your arm and leg were mangled. From the speed and position you ricocheted, there must have been other damage done as well. But when I looked out the window, you got up and limped away. It got me to thinking."

My eyes grew large as I recalled that day. I had been fairly new to the team, only sixteen years of age. I remembered the pain of my injuries, and recalled thinking I could lay there to be captured or go back to the helicopter and escape. Being the victim was not an option.

He was correct about my condition. When finally our helicopter was received back at the complex, my captain had made sure the doctors tended to me immediately, my arm swelling alarmingly and skin pale. I was in the infirmary for a few weeks—a lifetime to a new soldier—my calf and forearm bones snapped, two ribs broken, and internal bleeding that needed time to heal.

"And now we are going to start testing my theory," Rochester slapped his thigh and stood so one of his men could remove his chair. "It is apt that this all started with you, so it may as well continue and end there."

I wanted to speak, to ask what they had planned, to object as the men came up to me and began removing the restraints to drag me off the table and away. Rochester watched me intently as I struggled against my captors, observed as I lashed out and jabbed my elbow into the ribs of one man when he took hold of me.

Rochester chuckled but insisted, "Remember, I need her unharmed. Carry her if you have to."

Another three men came forward, taking me by the arms and legs as they held tight, lifting me into the air and hefting me into the vast space. I struggled, but it was pointless. They were strong and I suspected we were almost to our destination.

A minute later, the men stopped their shuffling and I was laid onto a steel platform on top of a large box, held down once more.

Rochester came and leaned over, examining the experiment. "I don't want her restrained with steel for this. I want it as realistic as possible."

I clenched my teeth, angry now both at my ignorance and Rochester's insistence that I stay just naïve enough to feed my own growing hatred.

"She is strong, sir. One person won't be enough. Her legs being free may be a problem." The husky-voiced man motioned to my lower half, which was still being held down by a few others.

Rochester looked at the speaker, a bulky darker-skinned man with rippling muscles, his lips and nose bulbous. "If one fails, another will take his place. I do not want her strangled, either. That will compromise the goal."

At the word "strangled" I struggled to keep my composure. Now I understood. Rochester had made sure I had no escape. Even if I broke free and snapped all of these men's necks, there were always others.

Still, my muscles tensed.

"I could sit on her legs, not my full weight, just enough to restrain her," the muscular man said calmly. He glanced at me and our eyes met, his unreadable gaze hidden behind jet-black orbs before turning back to his master.

Rochester nodded, tapping the collecting ash from his cigar. "That would be acceptable."

The muscled man turned back to me and, using his thickly corded arms, hoisted himself on top of the box. Stepping into place, he lowered himself so he straddled my legs. He reached up, grabbing my wrists from those assisting, holding them together in one massive hand, placing them over my head. He put the other hand on my chest to hold me down. It was heavy and I could feel the strength in both. The other men let go of me and stepped back.

Bewildered that I still had no idea of the ultimate purpose, my anger gave way to despair. I watched as Rochester nodded to someone at the end of the box. A switch was flipped, a mechanical whirring noise began. Slowly, the table began to descend. I struggled, but the man was big and heavy and had me held in a way that was to my disadvantage.

I felt moisture beneath me.

Since I was a child, I had never liked the water—it was too fast and something about being covered with a life-giving liquid that could just as easily be deadly frightened me. I had learned to swim quite proficiently as part of my training at the school, but I always paused before entering any body of water, no matter how small, my heart clenching in my chest.

Here, the water did not hesitate. It was against my back, coming through what must have been small holes in the platform. Then it was up to my ears, soaking the light shift I now wore, up to my hairline as I tilted my head back to raise my mouth above the tide. I knew I had to take a deep breath, I knew I could survive at least a minute if only I could calm down.

The warm water washed over my forehead. It touched my lips. Too late, I took a breath, and the water was over me entirely.

To the muscular man's credit, he never smiled, never changed his pressure on me. If anything, he shifted slightly so I felt I had more control, but in reality this was my intended fate.

He means to drown me.

The water continued for a few inches and when I had stayed still, counting silently to thirty seconds, the burning of my chest began, the sensation of holding one's breath for far too long. Still I tried to stay alive and began to test my manly bonds, hoping he would give up before I did.

Instead he persisted and I started to panic.

Unwillingly, my muscles went into flight mode, clenching and unclenching, my legs trying to move back and forth. Soon I was forced to breathe out and with that came the onslaught of water into my mouth as I began my muffled screams under the clear liquid, my eyes shut tight, my head thrashing back and forth.

I was losing.

Had I possessed more consciousness at the time, I might have worried what this result would mean. Instead, I let a primal animal nature take over, hoping by some miracle to overtake the man.

Blackness danced over my vision as I opened my eyes one last time and I felt my arms and legs weaken. My mouth opened involuntarily, letting in the last of the water, and the darkness overtook me once more.

A deep gasp was my first motion as I reawakened, followed by gagging as my lungs forced out the liquid I had consumed in my trial. I sat up with difficulty, turning sideways and throwing up all the bile and water that had built up, retching up more and more until my stomach was aching with emptiness, my lungs burning from the new air. My limbs were sore, stiffened in some of my joints from immobility. Someone approached, putting their hand on my chest to soothe me back down onto the floor. I couldn't argue, I was now exhausted and didn't have the energy to fight.

I was examined. By the doctor, I presume. A man's

voice said aloud that I had survived my death excellently, basically fine aside from extreme muscle fatigue, a few bruises around my wrists and hips, and signs of asphyxiation around my eyes. Had I had the energy to speak, I would have told him my throat, both inside and out, felt raw as hell as well.

My head rolled sideways and I opened my eyes briefly as boots came into view. Rochester bent down to eye level, a new cigar lit and already exuding smoke. "You are doing very well," he smiled. "I cannot wait for the next one."

The next one? I thought.

I lost consciousness.

This continued, for how long I couldn't say. Sometimes it felt like only hours between what they liked to call my trials, other times it felt like days. Of course, it depended on the injuries afterwards. They always let me heal completely before the next trial, a scientific measure to keep the results pure.

Considering how many trials there were, you would think I would have blocked some out, that their details would start commingling. But no, I remembered each one distinctly, the details of each so vivid. And why not? Each marked both my death and rebirth. Morbidly, I began to look forward to what trial would take place, what event would have me meet my demise that day.

More importantly, I looked forward to what trial would be successful and leave me dead.

The Continuance

My next trial was a bloodletting, a small slice in a major artery on the throat to see what effect the loss of the life-giving liquid would have on my system while again I was held down. It was disheartening, seeing my own blood pool and soak into the white shift I wore. Meanwhile an audience stood by and waited for the doctor's confirmation of my death and the resurrection they hoped would occur after. At least, I thought they hoped for a resurrection.

The same doctor attended me throughout, and while the manner of my deaths seemed to shock him, I could tell he was a seasoned veteran. Still, his hands were gentle, his techniques well practiced. And while I could hate him for the job he performed, his proclamations of my passing and reports of my re-life and healing measured and calm, I could only respect his loyalty and obedience, even if it was to a murderer. I even thought once that he would make an excellent soldier for the cause if not for where his loyalties lie.

I hated myself a little for that thought.

It took me a long time to die this time, much longer than I would have thought. I had hoped at some point I would pass out, saving me the inconvenience of time wasted and new memories of my death made. Instead, I stayed conscious, my eyes glazing over as I felt the coldness consume me and my limbs become evermore limp. My brain was strangely conscious, however, and even after my lips became deprived enough of speech, my mind screamed at the people to help me.

It was one of the longest trials I would endure.

It was after that time that I too began to wonder what it was that kept me alive, or rather, what made me reanimate. I doubted the theory of genetics since I had seen my own parents killed. Obviously something else tied me to the mortal plane.

Next was the strangling, quick but somehow doubly discomforting knowing that another's hands were actually touching my skin at the time of death.

A strangulation with bare hands was murder.

It was the muscular man who did it, carefully instructed to constrict my airways but not crush my neck. He nodded with a harshly detached expression, his face neutral as he once again straddled me on the table. Again I was restrained to reduce the chances of my interfering with the desired results.

He clamped his wide hands around my neck, his hand width large enough he probably could have used just one. He placed them carefully and waited for the nod from Rochester. Receiving it, he squeezed ever so slightly.

It was enough. Immediately my throat tightened, my airway constricted. I gasped, my hands flexing involuntarily, my wrists and ankles fighting against the bonds.

It didn't take long and the entire time we stared into each other's eyes, the muscular man and I. He was impassive right to the end. I tried to be strong but still a tear escaped just before I lost my fight.

Another fight, another life.

What a waste.

While I remember every detail of each death, the order escapes me after that strangulation. The next times were more impersonal and could occur by accidental means: a construction accident throws a pipe through a passerby, a swimming trip turns tragic, the sorrows of the world force a young person to take matters into their own hands.

I remember a bludgeoning—my skull beat with a large copper pipe, making a sickening cracking noise. There was a common beating, performed by Rochester's all-too-eager minions, bare fists and polished boots taking the place of a weapon. There were even poisons: by radiation, by spoiled food, by sour gas. Those were messy and disgusting in all regards.

Then the test of burning alive, unnerving

considering people were watching me writhe, my skin cracking and peeling as it roasted. Of all the initial trials, I hated that one the most, pain scorching me from the outside in, my only saving grace the suffocation of my lungs from the fumes of the accelerant I had been doused in beforehand.

The most memorable, however, was the last of the regular trials in this sequence. Because it was the closest I had come to real death, it stuck out the most in my mind. I was so close to letting go and finally having my eternal rest.

This time I was sure I would die.

I certainly hoped so.

It began like all the others. I had been given time to heal, time to eat and rest and get back my strength, the bruises and wounds disappearing. Then three guards showed up to my tiny dank cell, shackling and dragging me to the big empty room I inevitably died in every time. I had learned that the room was adaptable to the situation—it was wide and deep and could handle as many men as Rochester felt he needed. It could also handle any and all equipment required.

This time, the room was empty except for a simple chair. That in itself made my blood run cold. I turned to the men as they unshackled me and pushed me through the door. "Is this some kind of joke?"

They never answered, staring at me warily as they backed out and shut the door, locking it behind them.

I waited. Minutes passed slowly and eventually I sat down in the chair but I was uneasy about this change in routine.

I should be dead by now.

The feeling that I was late for death was unnerving.

Finally, the doors opened and I shot up from my seat. Rochester and a few of his minions approached, long spear-like devices in hand. I watched as the door, my only escape, shut.

"My apologies, we were...detained," Rochester's voice was unhappy and I suspected something on his end had gone horribly wrong. "Shall we begin?"

He went to the chair, draping his furry jacket on the back and sitting down casually as the men fanned out around the room, constantly moving.

"Why no table, no restraints?" I asked, eyeing the men.

Rochester smiled. "You noticed that did you? Are you that eager for the firm hand of a man's touch, the hard bonds of steel against your skin?" He eased back in his chair, his curiosity piqued by my interest. "This being the last of the simple trials I felt it would be prudent to do it with some dignity on your part. Feel free to fight against the men, but know that for every one that falls, another is ready to take his place."

I tried to keep my back to Rochester as I moved around, holding the men within my sight. I knew by now the villain preferred others to do his dirty work and he would provide no interference.

"And you? Aren't you afraid I will take you out?" I hissed, a false confidence in my voice—I knew the vile man would never allow it.

The man laughed. "I have my own assurances that you will bring me no harm. I am merely an observer in this."

A few of the men tried to catch me on the side by surprise. "What is this trial?"

"You will find out soon," Rochester's voice oozed with malcontent.

With that, one of the men dashed forward, thrusting the spear at me. I deflected it with a foot against the shaft as another man came forward from the opposite side. Unfortunately, his weapon struck true.

I felt a burst of pain from my side as a myriad of electric tendrils hit, and stinging spread from the point of contact. My breathing seized, my major body functions halting as the energy ripped through my organs. When the man stepped back, I stumbled into the area the weapon had just been, shaking my head to deflect the haze.

"Modified cattle prods, really. Of course, we enhanced them so they would be closer to a high-powered taser, but you get the idea." Rochester's voice was dripping with amusement.

My body quivered with the after-effects of just one shock. I put my hand against the area that had just felt the wrath of the prods—my shirt was hot, singed. I suspected my skin was the same.

"So you're going to electrocute me to death," I caught my breath, my head down as I tried to regroup.

Rochester said nothing, but I knew, behind the hand holding his smoldering cigar to his lips, he was smiling.

The men dodged forward, the prods jutting out. I deflected one before another struck my skin. I cried out as it hit my shoulder, the pain immobilizing my arm even after the prod had been removed. I was beginning to see how this would go—they could easily have gone for more vulnerable parts that would take me down faster.

This was meant to take more than a few minutes.

The next shot was to my thigh, and while the pain seemed less, whether due to my getting used to it or the fat it landed on, my muscles in the area jumped after, making moving difficult.

I limped in circles, trying to keep track of my attackers, attempting to evade their spears. They always struck true, a second hitting me where the first failed.

My body was slowly charred by the weapons, my muscles responding more sluggish each time, my senses dulling. The time between the attacks was stretched out and I knew they were directed by Rochester with a flick of a finger, a motion of a wrist.

With my breathing now labored, standing becoming more difficult, the final motion must have been made. A long prod to the back made me scream. The well-positioned electric attack ballooned from the small tip of the spear into my spinal column. It radiated up to my brain and down through my nerves, right to my toes and fingers.

I fell to my knees, my entire body spasming and shaking. Without hesitation, a second prod came forward directly over my heart. The current ripped through my veins, my arms thrusting out at my sides, my fingers splaying as the prod from my back came around to join the one on my chest.

My joints cracked with the strain of extension and I could do nothing but make a strangled sound as the electricity surged. Seeing I was not going down yet, I saw Rochester nod and the third prod thrust out, placed beside the others, a burst of electricity ripping through me.

My voice turned to a howl of agony as I fell involuntarily to my back.

I was not dead yet, but I was close. I could feel it, a tunnel of silence descending over my ears, my body limp and unresponsive to my efforts. The only movement was the jumping of my muscles, animated by the surges slithering throughout.

A boot touched my cheek—my head fell to the side, my eyes open but glazed over. My body parts were still sizzling and I suspected they would do so after I was gone. As the buzzing in my ears subsided, a horrible noise reached them, a sound between a moan and a gasp for breaths that I realized came from me.

A few taps and light kicks from the three men proved the work almost done. I could not move.

I heard the scraping of a chair as I saw Rochester's boots move, then his body as he came down to my level on the floor. Kneeling carefully a bit away as not to be affected by the residual electricity of the prods, he leaned down. "Almost done, are you not? Good thing, too, the amount of burns across your body," he looked over the flesh I could now smell cooking. He leaned forward so his lips were close to my ear as he whispered, "If this really is the last time, I want to see the life go out of your eyes."

Go to hell.

I wanted to scream. I wanted to reach out with my anxiety-chewed fingernails and claw at his temple, scrape out his eyeballs from the sockets. But all I could do was lay there.

It made my end unfulfilled.

As he sat up again, I felt the prods come down, although where exactly I could not say, my flesh was raw and had no feeling on my skin at this point. I felt the current in my muscles, my joints and bones and veins. I felt it radiate into my jaw and ears, creating a droning noise that blocked out my own quiet moans. Finally, I felt it behind my eyes and in my brain, sizzling the last of my consciousness.

Just before I gave in, my eyes grew large. Behind Rochester, the doctor appeared, sympathetic smile on his lips and a knowing look on his face. The man hefted his black case, which held his medical devices, and tugged at his white coat, nodding once to me. I shuddered with a last blow of the current, my eyes remaining open but my body giving in.

All went black and I knew no more.

An Attempt

My experience in reanimating from death could best be described as waking after a long night of drinking. First, there is the audio haze. Much like a trombone belting low tunes at the end of a tunnel filled with water, all noises, both mechanical and human, are muted and warped. An attempt at listening harder only ends with a massive headache and the noises seeming farther away. Inevitably, one has to wait until the water effect subsides and the audio becomes loud and obnoxious white noise of another kind.

Next, you strive to open your eyes, to see where you are, and what you are laying on that is so very uncomfortable. Any surface you are laying on as you resurrect feels hard and unyielding, a response to your back's extended stiffening. Unfortunately, your sight too is extremely sensitive and any and all light, no matter how dim, seems both painfully bright and annoyingly unnecessary. Again, all that is to be done is to wait out the effects.

After this, it becomes harder to define what steps

occur in order. It becomes painstakingly obvious that every muscle, every bone, every sinew, every follicle is aching and protesting the slightest movement, even involuntary. At the same time, as the noises are becoming more recognizable, a horrible sound reaches the ears, a soft but agonizing keening that is promptly recognized as coming from your own mouth. It is your own body's recognition that you are transitioning from one realm to another.

It hurts like hell.

Your veins open at once, coaxing the life-giving liquid that delivers nutrients the organs so badly needed. The heart pumps hard and deep with the effort and you could swear it was about to thump right through the ribs, the beating is so intense. The lungs re-inflate, taking infinity and longer and yet only seconds to take in the oxygen they so crave.

While this process seems to take an eternity, it is an illusion. To the observer, it is merely seconds to minutes, and the timing of non-reality into re-life in itself throws one's senses for a loop. Having undergone it so many times while in Rochester's hell, I thought I would be used to it, but this time was, in fact, different.

This time, they hadn't thought I would come back.

My body began to shiver violently as both consciousness of mind and body came forth. A somewhat unsteady voice ordered restraints and warm blankets. A strong set of hands held my shoulder, tilting me sideways as my mouth opened and sputum threatened to come out.

Instead, I coughed and retched, producing nothing.

The man held my head between burned skin and asked if I could hear him. I opened my eyes and stared at him, hearing the words but not comprehending the meaning behind them. He shone a light into my eyes while speaking to me and then set my head down gently, shaking his own as he turned to walk away.

My own vision remained concentrated on the white ceiling panels above, my eyes glazed over and unrecognizing.

I stayed that way for quite a while.

I am unsure if they tried to keep me alive at that point. As the timeframe eluded me, I could not tell if it was days or merely hours before I started to come back to myself.

Ever so slowly, I did. And, I was changed.

When my guards realized my mental state had shifted, they sent for a doctor again, a different one this time. Maybe he was a psychologist. I hardly cared. He tried to get my attention by snapping his fingers and clapping. The loud noises startled me and immediately my brain flipped into survival mode. A growl escaped from my lips unknowingly and I rolled off the bed painfully onto bare feet and legs. Before the man could call for help he was already dead on the floor, his red-rimmed eyes wide open, head twisted at an odd and deadly angle.

A broken neck would do that to a person.

My guard was unsure what to do and merely backed out of the room while I stumbled about, raw emotion fighting through disparate pain in my skin and muscles. I remember parts of the event as though someone would recall a bad accident, bits and pieces connecting to make a whole.

Rochester was delighted.

He refused to have me sedated, instead wanting to test how far these raw talents could take me. He sent in a few of his lesser guards, all of them ending up in a heap of skin and bones on the floor. He then decided to go further, sending in his men with martial-arts training and pure power behind them. Mostly, I won.

Sometimes I lost.

These times I would be the one to wind up on the floor, a head injury, lumps, bruises, and cuts littering my skull. But the men had been given explicit instructions not to kill me.

I was now Rochester's play thing.

It was after one of these challenges that my true test came. I could remember vaguely I had just fought against the muscular man, my body laying on the cold concrete in the fetal position as I nursed my aching head. Usually a good thump or, as I had experienced this time, a smash against the corner of the table, was enough to take me down. So I lay there, my frayed hair collecting the pooling blood from my wound when a loud and foreign noise reached my ringing ears.

It was an alarm, and it frightened me.

Both hands instantly went to my ears as I tried to block out the klaxon, my feet kicking against the legs of my table where I had slept. All I remember is fighting against the sound.

The door opened then, and I was vaguely aware of someone coming in, the door closing quickly. I was still keening and fought to regain some control.

Then the hands came down on my shoulders. A terrifying noise ripped from my throat as I again went into survival mode. Jumping up, I reached out my bloodied digits, aiming for the neck of my next contender before hearing a name spoken aloud.

Both the name and voice were familiar to me and I froze as the man said it again. I shook my head to clear the liquid that was now running over my eye, my own blood from my head wound. I gritted my teeth and grabbed the man around his wrists, forcing him against a wall and knowing I could snap the bones and kick in his knee in one swift move.

The man didn't fight back.

Instead, he opened his eyes wide and attempted to talk to me, something that was still outside of my understanding. It reached me enough that I was forced to look into his face.

Tomlin. The name reached my lips and brain at the same moment and instantly I knew this person was not after me.

Fighting   my   primal   nature,   I   flung   myself

backwards across the room, flattening against the wall and watching the man who in turn was staring back at me, alarmed. He rubbed his wrists absentmindedly, a ring of blood transferred from my hands to his sleeves.

I could tell he was scared for me. I could smell the fear. His own personal defeat was palpable as he tried to reason with me.

Looking back now I am sure he was asking me to calm down, to leave with him peaceably. He held up a sedative that would perhaps make it easier.

I saw him hold up the needle and I went crazy. Tomlin's eyes flashed disbelief as I hurled myself toward him, my hand raised in combat. I landed four good punches to his face and head before the man threw a strong kick to my midsection that sent me stumbling back, crashing against the wall.

He looked down as his wrist watch chimed. I knew his time was up as he shook his head. With a sad expression, he wiped the blood from his mouth, a heavy line still trailing from his nose, looking back at me one last time before he re-opened the door, leaving quickly.

It would be days before I realized what had happened.

I had sabotaged my own rescue.

Never-Ending Hell

Rochester told me he had watched the attempt as it happened on his cameras and was overjoyed. The break-in had been unexpected, but the results more than satisfactory. Only a few guards had been killed and the man with the cigar had ended up with a best-case scenario.

I was his.

My change in status came with an effort of peace. He sent to my room a couple of women to clean me up—a sponge bath, a shampoo and bandages. It ended with two more bodies and a mess all over.

Rochester's intention may have been true but his method was mislaid. So, Rochester tried a new approach. While I slept fitfully on my hard pallet he had me drugged, ensuring my cooperation.

I awoke later in a soft bed, a real bedroom with sheets and quilts, a dressing table across the larger room, an armoire and adjoining bathroom, though the door had been removed. I sat up, confused, and looked around me. Unsure of where I was I got up, my body feeling surprisingly good after knowing I had killed two seemingly innocent women and attacked several men.

I remembered my head wound and reached up, finding my hair soft and smooth beneath gauze that was wrapped around. I pulled off the dressing to find stitches on the top of my head and while the spot felt tender, it was healing. I glanced down as a wisp of fabric brushed my legs. A nightgown now replaced my dingy shift, my skin raw but pink from a well-needed scrubbing.

My hands too were pink, all traces of blood washed away, my broken and bloody nails manicured, trimmed short and the cuticles clean. Holding my fingers up to the light, they were unfamiliar to me.

Then, past my own digits, I noticed the window.

It was barred, and too small for any human to fit through except maybe a small child. Still, I flung myself at it, clutching the bars with both hands and pressing my face against them to suck in the fresh air in deep breaths, the window pane beyond the bars propped open.

I stayed this way for a long while until I heard a rustling behind me. Lowering my hands, I turned slowly, noting it was not a guard who had entered with my food but a young woman close to my own age. Her crystal-blue eyes were nervous, darting around the room, trying not to focus on me. Her hands shook as she lowered the tray of food to the table. She folded her hands in front of her at first then took a few steps sideways and sat on a chair nearby. She avoided eye contact at all costs.

I looked at the tray from across the room and realized I was famished. Stepping forward slowly I made another discovery I had not previously noted— the pain in my limbs was gone. I wondered how long I had been out for. I glanced down at my arms, seeing the flesh scarred in a few places but otherwise free from the burn wounds it had previously gained from the electric rods of my last trial. Last I remembered, my flesh had still bared witness to the atrocity, my skin tender and raw.

I saw the woman observing me then, and I took a few steps forward. She flinched. I wondered if I was really that terrifying. Slowly, my feet took me to the table and I sat hard on the chair with a grumbling belly. Picking up the bowl of soup, I raised it to my lips and began to slurp it down, dispensing with pleasantries of silverware. I was hungry.

No, I was starving.

The woman continued to sit, watching me as I did the same with her. She was pretty, this young woman, her auburn hair swept into a small gathering at the nape of her neck. It was shining in the sunlight and I longed to stroke an errant lock that had fallen, the woman tucking it behind her ear.

Her features were graceful and thin, her eyelashes

long, her cheekbones high and skin fair. A collection of light freckles dotted her face, dancing across her nose and cheeks under her eyes where she now blushed, probably unused to such attention.

The woman looked away then, her gaze landing on my fingers, which trembled from the clarity of sanity that was returning. The food had helped somewhat, replacing nourishment to my empty stomach and parched anatomy. But now with a return of my faculties came an influx of memories, a remembrance of what I was, of *who* I was.

I wished I could forget.

I tried.

The woman stood when I finished my meal. Even then, she remained until I saw the moonlight through the window and settled down to sleep. I heard her footsteps retreating and the door close shortly after my head hit the pillow.

She was already there, waiting beside my bed the next morning.

I was unsure what to make of her still. Her timeframe of being my silent companion ensured a sort of surveillance, but there was more to her watchful eye. She stayed close to me although she was also careful to be out of reach. I was confused by her presence, knowing her duty to me lay in the commands from Rochester. Still, she was kind and considerate to me, genuine in her efforts to ease my suffering. She rapidly became what I knew a psychologist would call my crutch.

No other option, I doubled my efforts to forget all I knew of my past life.

Again days passed and with no other visitors I followed a primal schedule. I ate when food arrived, slept when I felt like it. Sometimes that meant I stayed up for hours, enjoying the warm sun on my skin through the barred window, my companion watching me warily. Other times I sat alone in the dark night of my room, staring up at the bold white moon against the blackness of space.

After some time my inner consciousness began to surface. It came in brief hints, a stab of remorse as I remembered the feeling of bones grinding between my fingers, the memory of the slickness of blood on my hands after a kill. There were no faces.

I don't know if I had ever bothered to look.

My companion became more relaxed in my presence as she learned my habits. She learned to make a motherly shushing sound to calm me when loud noises startled me. She encouraged me to eat when food was provided and more than just what I needed to survive as was my wont, my body having become skinny, my small muscles looking corded beneath sunken skin. She tolerated my tendencies of little modesty, providing shelter of cloth held up when I was prompted to change shifts, encouraging discretion when I needed to use the bathroom.

She too had her routine and I noted it, the way she ate, when she took her brief breaks. And I noticed finally that she wore no uniform, that she carried no gun, possessed no knife.

I began to notice the change in seasons by her dress, first light-colored wispy sundresses, followed by light sweaters. It was when her woolen turtlenecks, jeans and boots were replaced by her airy sweaters and short pants once more that I realized I had been held captive throughout an entire winter. Then I noticed the unlocked bolts on the door and it hit me hard—I was no longer a prisoner.

I had become completely complacent to my role. I had missed that my companion very often did not even close the door upon entering.

I realized I could be free.

But did I want to be?

The thought was not welcome anymore, perhaps I was indeed too far gone. My first time I took a step toward the door the thought of leaving hit me so hard I doubled over with anxiety. My reaction was so strong that my companion jumped to her feet, hesitating as she reached out for me then thought better of it, calling for help.

The guards came quickly, too quickly for them to have been far, and the sharp stab of a needle against my neck came again, a feeling I had become far too comfortable with.

When I awoke in the dead of night, he was there.

I knew by the expensive cigar lit between his lips, the smell of sandalwood and mint wafting toward me.

He leaned in as I stirred, only a few inches from my eyes as I turned my face toward him. I did not move again, did not attempt to attack him. I stayed still, assuming I was restrained but not testing the situation to see if it was true.

My complacency pleased him.

He began talking, asking me questions. My gaze wandered through his babbling and only his hand against my cheek, forcing my gaze back to him seemed to hone my attention.

"I really did break you, did I not?" he asked, almost sadly. He put his cigar back in his mouth, clamping his lips around its shaft.

Rochester shifted his weight then, standing and looking down on me with pity. He moved to the entrance and waved his arm with a flourish. "This door will be open all the time now. You are free to come and go as you please." He didn't have to say the rest—to see what I would do.

The man left me then, leaving the door open as promised.

I stared at the doorway all night, contemplating what this meant for me.

Still it went unused by me for days. I eyed it warily, as the possible object of my demise.

It was close to six sunrises later that my companion, wearing an airy pink sundress on her small frame once again, stood just outside the door, smiling softly and motioning to the hallway. I watched her gestures, which she repeated every few minutes until I finally swung my legs off the bed. It was another couple minutes before I stood. It was nearly half a day later before my journey found me at the doorway, watching my feet as though they stood before an invisible field.

Forgetting herself, my companion chuckled lightly and reached out to take my hand and pull me through.

My body went rigid, my muscles taut with the instinctive response of snapping for the kill. But when I noted her shocked expression, something in me diminished.

I opened my mouth to speak, wanting to apologize, but extended time with no real language had taken away the faculty. I closed my lips together and nodded instead.

I didn't attempt to leave the room after that, afraid of what I might do if I lost control. To her credit, my companion took my resolve with pity and worked even harder to enrich my life. She began to read to me and let me listen to music—quiet orchestral pieces of times long past.

I lost track of time.

It was days, perhaps a week, before Rochester came for me again. He stopped inside the door, watching me listen to my companion read. I watched her lips move, her fingers turn the pages, with my own unexpected hunger.

Such luxuries as holding books had been taken away from me long ago for fear I would turn them into weapons.

As she finished the chapter and closed the book, he removed the cigar from his lips. "She tells me you have been very well behaved," he started, entering in a few large steps. Both of us women glanced up.

"I think that calls for a reward."

My companion hesitated, averting her eyes as she waited for the man, her master, to continue.

"You will come with me," he stated, then shrugged toward my companion. "You too, you seem to have a...calming effect on her."

The woman stood slowly, resting the book inside the drawer of the desk that she immediately locked. She came over, threading her arm through my own, her hand resting above my wrist. "Come now, it will be all right."

Rochester grunted as he placed the cigar back in his mouth, his expression over my serene state somewhat muddled.

The man turned, his long fur coat swishing with the movement, and started out the door.

I knew I didn't have a choice, but still I hesitated at the door and waited until I felt the pull on my arm from my companion before continuing.

The Room

Stepping over the threshold, I followed the man through the complex, my companion steady beside me. Rochester made sure we were always moving, and that he was more than an arm's distance away. Still, he never showed fear. I doubted he had ever experienced such an emotion. He reeked of arrogant confidence in his actions.

A short while later, Rochester opened a door and entered, not bothering to motion for us to follow anymore. I noticed my companion's hesitant glance in my direction before she too entered the room, pulling me by the hand to follow.

The room was mostly dark, previous skylights blacked out and hazy pot lights in the ceiling creating an ominous glow. Rochester wiped the back of his hand across his brow and removed the fur from his shoulders. Casually, he strode to a contraption by the door and threw his long jacket over it, turning again to address me.

"Well?" he began, opening his arms and gesturing

palms up to the expanse of the room. "What do you think?"

My gaze travelled from him slowly to the various devices in the space. The room was large, that was apparent, despite the darkness. Along every wall rested another piece of equipment kept clean with draped sheets, bars and weights anchored securely. Looking down, I followed a heavy white line in the floor, walking part of the way to find it was a large circle, perhaps twelve feet wide.

"It is a combat circle," Rochester said, his face one of pure enjoyment as I took in the sights. He didn't seem to care that I had not made a comment yet. "A dohyo. I believe you have seen it before."

He was right. The dohyo was a common feature of vigilante training, the idea brought from Asian practices.

"Since you have been so good and no more guards have been killed or injured in some time, I felt a celebration was in order," Rochester responded to my silence, his interest in my reaction growing as I now looked at the equipment that was uncovered, my fingers trailing over the metal and plastic.

"You and your companion can come here any time you like, for as long as you like." He grinned then, tapping the ashes of his cigar carefully away from the edge of the circle. "And perhaps, eventually, you will feel comfortable enough to take on some human competition…."

I turned then to look at him, my eyes piercing as I silently asked the question. If he was talking about human competition then this must be....

"My apologies," he nodded slightly in our direction, "it is so dark in here you must not even be aware of what this is. Allow me." Taking a half dozen large steps toward the door, Rochester threw a switch.

Blinding light hit my retinas, the soft hum of the bulbs encroaching my sensitive hearing like a gong being struck. My hands flew up to my ears, my head bowing low as I sought to keep out the new sensations. Within seconds I felt a hand descend on my shoulder, intending to be supportive.

My feral half took possession.

I spun around and jumped out of reach, my hands whipping down from my ears. My limbs creaked with the unfamiliar actions of defense as I lifted my arms in a martial-arts stance I once knew so well. Crouching low, I centered myself, my teeth grinding, eyes wide.

My companion looked terrified, holding the hand that had been on my shoulder as though I had injured it.

Looking over her expression, my thoughts backpedaled, apologies written in my eyes. I straightened, lowering my arms and standing tall once more. I nodded to her twice, an acknowledgment that what I had done was wrong.

Behind me, a slow clapping began.

Trust and Competition

The hours passed rapidly into days, the days into weeks. With permission to enter my special room anytime my companion and I made a habit of going early in the morning and staying late. Often we would skip lunch, eating the cold food that afternoon when we returned to my seemingly permanent habitat.

At first, I had been uncertain as to what purpose the special room served. But as my companion and I lifted heavy sheets off the equipment, it became clear. The first piece we revealed was a running machine, most practical for gaining back some of the strength I lacked in my legs. The second, a weight machine for use with arms. Day by day, every piece was uncovered, until finally we took off the last sheet and my mouth ran dry.

Before me was something I remembered, deep within my brain, from years gone by. Allowing myself to feel and regain the thoughts for once, I closed my eyes briefly. There in the confines of my memory was a girl approaching such a contraption, her fingers trailing over the hard surface of one of the arms. Slowly, she raised an arm, tapping the first horizontal plank that extended from the tall totem. Immediately, the arm swung around and hit the girl in the face, the hard flat bat smacking her cheek.

Jolting out of the memory, I jumped back, my hand to the phantom injury on my cheek. I paled as I observed this piece, so like the one from my memory but infinitely more dangerous, small sharp spikes lining each of the horizontally rotating arms of the training device. My companion stepped forward to offer comfort but stopped short, aware of the actions her solace had caused not long ago.

The device stood unused for a better part of a month, the red surface a blemish upon the efforts I made within the confines of the space.

Then came the day that my first competitor entered the room.

Dressed in black pants and a loose tank top, the well-built man nodded solemnly to my companion and I, before sidling carefully around the room. He was a guard, I guessed by his stature, his exuded confidence suggesting an experienced one. He examined the equipment, stopping before the red device.

Quietly, I let go of the bars I had been doing chin-ups on and padded barefoot a few steps to the side, gaining a better vantage point. As I watched him, slowly he reached out and pressed a fingertip to the steel points on the arm. I craned my neck to observe what he was doing and unconsciously began walking toward him.

Just as his finger reached the shiny point he yelped in pain and jumped backwards, nursing his hand. His back to me, I stepped even closer, now within an arm's length of both the man and the dangerous equipment. I watched as his head raised, suddenly aware of my proximity, and turned toward me. Holding his finger tight with the other hand I saw that where he had touched the spike had caused a laceration through the flesh to the bone of his digit. Blood flowed freely as did the pained expression on his face.

I cannot explain the rationalization of my motives that came next. But it is safe to say the trigger was the blood.

When my eyes set on the deep gouge that was the man's finger, on the white bone and poppy-red blood that trickled through the man's other fingers to drip on the blue mat below, it was as though a match had been set aflame. Staring at him intently, I saw the man watching me, observing my inaction, and saw him make the decision that I was no threat. He turned back to the device, his blood drops trailing his few steps.

I saw his intention only too well, his leg raising in a first step to attempt to break the totem-looking base in half. He breathed in, reserving his strength for the mighty blow, and with that last deep breath began to move forward.

Seconds later, the man was flying through the air,

landing hard on the blue mat ten feet away. His finger was bleeding more heavily now that his other hand lay limply aside. His unconscious body lay at an unnatural angle, his face covered in small punctures and his own poppy-colored vital fluids.

I was crouched low over a bent leg, one hand on the mat below for balance, the other outstretched. I was hardly aware that the spinning arm that was coming to a halt above my head was the reason for the man's current demise, even less conscious that I had been the cause. Standing to avoid the arm, I breathed in slowly, catching my breath as my heart thudded in my chest. I looked up at the small studs in the arm, the smooth red polish, and felt the corners of my mouth curve upwards.

Not hesitating any longer, I arched, leaning backwards, my sleeved arm tapping the device's arm into rotation. It spun wildly and fast, the momentum pulling the other arms below into motion, all of which I avoided neatly as I danced in circles around the device, ducking and blocking as needed.

As the arms sped up to my occasional block with my forearm or side I deftly re-learned that which had been my first nature so long ago. I was grinning for the first time since my capture now, the usefulness of my previous athleticism seeming to be coveted at the moment.

I was not aware that, while I was engaging the red beast, my companion had called in a medic for the man on the ground. Once the door was open, the sound of the wheeling machine and my own grunts had attracted passersby and eventually Rochester himself.

Sweating profusely and breathing heavily from the steps, ducks, jumps, and parries, I never heard the small crowd of people enter one by one, not even hearing when one came up behind me. As I completed another strategic pattern of avoidance, a hand grabbed me by the upper arm.

Spinning around, I saw Rochester's form just before I realized I had misjudged the action, not avoiding the swinging arm in time. The heavy piece came across, smashing into the side of my head just as the man's cigar fell from his mouth. He tugged my arm to prevent further injury as I stumbled from the blow, my head a dozen points of pain from the spikes, an unbelievable wetness spreading down my face.

Darkness descended slowly, first sound becoming a hollow tunnel, my vision a blur. Still the man held my arm as I opened my mouth to speak but my dry tongue flapped soundlessly from months of disuse.

I started blinking rapidly to clear the red haze that was falling over my eyes. My knees buckled and Rochester drew up his second arm, his hands holding me up by the shoulders on either side. He was frowning now.

"Wouldn't it be ironic if this was the way it happened?" he asked no one in particular. The tunnel I was now listening through made it difficult but not impossible to hear. I was no longer aware if anyone else was in the room, my vision was closing on Rochester's form.

In response, I blinked twice then collapsed, letting the man take on my full weight. I felt his arms readjust to behind my knees and back as my body was picked up. My injured head lolled toward his chest, one last burst of pain, then nothing.

Ironies of the Truest Form

When I opened my eyes, I felt like a gourd, emptied of my contents. I felt nothing below my neck, and briefly had the notion that perhaps my body was missing, that I was merely a head.

Immobile, my head was turned sideways, my gaze looking at nothing in particular when the faint muffled beeping reached my ears. It took me a few minutes to realize it was the sound of my heartbeat, dangerously slow but quickening slightly.

My companion came into view, her face coming closer to mine as she looked into my recognizing eyes and choked out a sob, smiling tenderly.

"You're alive...I wasn't sure...." She bit her lip as she regained control of her emotions. Taking a deep breath, she continued, "Mr Rochester had the doctor come and stop the bleeding before you.... He's never done that before. I mean, he has had the doctor keep you alive in the past, but never bring you back with such drastic measures...." She looked down at her fingers, white from holding on tightly to each other.

"I'm glad." she smiled at me again.

He had me brought back? I wondered.

I turned my head, my movement stiff and restricted. Reaching up to feel my face, I found gauze covering most of the side and a large tender lump on top. I tried to pull off the dressing but my fingers were shaky and weak.

Gently, my companion took my hands in hers and removed them from the area, shaking her head. "Leave them be, you were injured badly and it took many stitches. I'm so happy we have a competent doctor on staff. He knew what to do right away once Mr Rochester gave the order."

Again, curiosity struck me.

Why did he save me?

Soundlessly my eyes met the woman's, my eyebrows furrowing.

Reading my unsaid question in my expression, my companion leaned in close, whispering, "You are around his daughter's age, I believe. Similar look to you, with your longer brown hair and fairer complexion...." She hesitated, glancing toward the door to make sure no one was there before continuing, "She died last week."

Rustling came from outside the room as the doctor entered, the same one that had attended me at the beginning, his medical bag slung on one arm. He balanced a tray with clean bandages and ointments in his other hand.

"How is she doing today?" he asked jovially, putting both items down on the nightstand. He turned to look at me as my companion rose and nodded her hello to the man. "Oh, awake, I see." He smiled. "Good. Let me look over you." He motioned for some space as the woman shuffled sideways toward the foot of the bed.

Sitting on the side of the mattress, the doctor removed the pads from my skin that were connected to the monitor, and took out his stethoscope, listening to my heart. After checking a few spots, he lowered the ear pieces. "Are you able to sit up?"

I bent my arms, using my elbows for support. Shakily, my upper body rose.

"Can you come around and help support her?" he asked of my companion, who hurried to do his bidding. Carefully pushing on my back, she got me to a seating position. Elevated, I groaned in protest as my ribcage tweaked.

The doctor's head jerked up at the sound. He pulled lightly on my companion's arm so she was sitting more behind me than anything, using her body as a permanent support. He showed me his empty hands, before touching my side under my arm. "You will need to tell me where it hurts," he was quiet as his fingers crept around the bones there. Finally they touched the spot of contention.

This time I cried out louder, my body spasming in response as he pushed lightly. He sighed and nodded. "I was afraid of that. A broken rib. Do you remember when you got it? From what?"

I thought for a moment but the past was still a haze, the exact details a blur. I shook my head slowly.

The doctor met my eyes, looking me over more carefully then. "Why aren't you answering me?"

My companion shifted uncomfortably. "Doctor, she hasn't spoken since I was assigned to her. Since...well, it's been months."

Months...

"That's troubling." The man sighed slowly and nodded. "It's an issue we will need to address eventually. But for now, I need to bind your ribs. If this one is broken as a result of the equipment I saw, then I suspect others are splintered as well. We need to make sure they don't move or they will cause internal injuries."

I glanced down, shifting my body in the process, pulling at the break once more. Instinctively, the doctor's hand jumped to my arm, forcing me still.

"I mean it, I need to stabilize this or the splinters could shift." His expression was dour as he removed his fingers, lowering his head to mine to force me to look into his eyes as he mumbled, "I highly doubt a bone fragment through your heart would allow for your re-animation again."

My sight became more focused as I processed what he said, his words giving me the possible escape from the never-ending hell that was my life. But as I took in the sadness the doctor extended, reading his intention, seeing his true efforts to save my life, another purpose with goodness hidden beyond my mental reach, I gave in to his silent plea, nodding.

He stood, gathering some supplies out of his bag and spoke to my companion. "I'll need you to remove her shirt. I'll have to put the bandage around her chest several times tightly." He then looked at me. "Do you think you can stand? It will be painful, but more effective."

I watched his face change, now filled with sympathy. I glanced at my companion, who nodded in support. Lowering my head in reply, I followed her lead as she shifted off the bed and came around to rotate me so my feet were on the floor, my arms in hers. In a process that was as slow as it was excruciating, my companion got me on my feet and standing almost straight. The doctor lent a hand in holding my arms while she worked at undoing the stays on my top and removing it from my shoulders.

With that gone, I could now see more damage that I had inflicted on myself with my stint of exercise. Both my arms were wrapped in gauze, small pinpricks of blood showing here and there through the white bandage. Looking down I saw bruises blossoming across my ribs, spreading generously across my sun-deprived skin.

Becoming modest in my half-naked state, I reached up to cover my breasts with my arms, only half succeeding since binding my ribs meant the Doctor had to wrap a tight bandage around my torso.

Gently, the bandage was applied and pinned into place. I took a few breaths, warned by the doctor against large ones until the bones began to knit together. "One week of rest," he told me, to which my companion nodded. She lifted my shirt to be put on once more.

"Wait," the doctor said then, my companion hesitating with the fabric bunched up in one hand, the other helping to support me upright.

"He asked me to bring this to you, in case you are well enough to see him," he pulled a brown wrapped package from behind his bag. He passed it to my companion, helping to seat me on the side of the bed.

"I am going to go report to Rochester on your health. As long as you rest sufficiently I see no reason why you shouldn't see him and be able to take short walks." He turned to my companion. "I have ordered a hearty, nutritious lunch for her. Don't let her eat too fast or she will be sick."

The woman agreed quickly and they shared a look of accomplishment, their lingering gaze sparking at each other before he half-bowed to her and left my room. I wondered if they were lovers.

With the doctor gone, my companion turned back to the bed. "Should we see what Mr Rochester sent you?" she asked, smiling, not waiting for the answer. At her optimistic attitude, I wondered again what her purpose here was, whether it was greed, an order, or blackmail which kept her in Rochester's service. I had long ago decided it was not outright slavery—she was far too content in her role for that. Still, she was too kind of a soul for caretaking of a prisoner to be a willing career.

Unless she doesn't know...

Carefully, she pulled at the paper, unwrapping the gift one layer at a time until she reached the goods. Inside was a soft green fabric, folded carefully.

Taking the garment by the shoulders, my companion stepped back from the bed, the light fabric slithering out of the paper. It was a floor-length dress, small silver embroideries covering the bust and shoulders. The arms were long, and I recognized it as one of the fashions I had seen in Paris on my travels, one that must be reaching North America now.

Assuming I was on that continent still.

The style of the dress was old, based on a trend gone by hundreds of years previous, a historical pattern made new by recent fashions outliving their creative outbursts.

I didn't want any part of any gift from the man who sought my death—his presents always seemed to end badly for me. But despite my efforts to reject the outfit, my companion was insistent.

With some effort, we were able to get the dress over my head, the gauze on my arms catching on the fabric. It took a while, but eventually I was able to lean upright on the foot post of the bed, my companion stepping back carefully as she took in my appearance. A smile slowly grew on her tender lips as she backed up again.

"I was saving this for when you asked at some point, but that dress is so beautiful. I think you should see it like I do." She walked quickly toward the desk, pulling at the brown board behind it. Tugging it free, she dragged it around, revealing its true nature. On the backside of what I thought had been the backing to the desk was a full-length mirror.

Leaning the item against the wall, my companion came by my side. She rested her hand gently on my arm. "See? It is truly beautiful." Slipping behind me, she carefully gathered my long unkempt locks. "And if we pull your hair off your face...."

She took the two front pieces and placed them skillfully around the rest so my face was free of them. Her eyes beamed with pride at my appearance. Quietly, she let the hair fall again as she reached up, untying a ribbon from her own hair and using that to retie mine in place.

I frowned, taking in my appearance, gauze taped over half my face. I couldn't be happy at such a frivolous thing as the beautiful dress, its fabric hanging off my emaciated form in gathers of green swatch. I couldn't appreciate my companion's efforts to beautify me for the man who wanted me dead, who had arranged it so many times before.

I breathed out, anguish replacing my previously

temporary peace.

I couldn't help feeling as though I had just been dressed up for the slaughter.

Memories

I stared at my reflection in the mirror, wondering at the changes it held. The last time I had really gazed at myself had been in Africa.

I was different then, so changed from what I was now.

I had been travelling along the Nile River, observing the various animals, following a nomadic tribe that had taken me in. We stopped alongside the river to let the herding animals drink. The women banded together, entering the river to our knees to wash our faces and splash our sweat-drenched bodies briefly while the men watched for crocodiles. I hurried, never a fan of the sensation of the large fishes nibbling at my fingers and toes in the shallow water.

Afterwards I sat on a rocky ledge nearby, letting the sun dry my now wet shirt and shorts, my drenched hair crackling in the heat. Pulling a bandana out of my rucksack I leaned over the edge to dip the cloth in the water, willing it to take on the cool water the rock's shadow afforded.

As the ripples calmed, I stared at my reflection. My skin, now a suntanned brown, was healthier than ever. I had lost some of my militia-trained muscle but had gained that which hard work in the fields could develop.

Within the last two months the women had taught me how to weave nets and traps, the men reluctantly allowing me to partake in the hunt, the activities increasing the strength of my biceps. I had been presented my own hunting staff a month ago and trained in a sort of stick fighting, aiding in the strength of my calves.

My cheeks held a gentler curve, my eyes bright against my darkened skin. The hazel color contained brilliant green flecks, the sun off the wavering water reflecting in them. I reached up with a hand, my reflection showing the digits touching the side of my face. Next to the hand a small green gem glistened from a post through the one nostril.

They had given me my first piercing.

My reverie was interrupted by my companions insistent chatter and deepening frown. She had seen me grow still and—if possible—more silent than usual. My gaze went deeper than my reflection allowed.

I shook my head, clearing the thoughts. It did not go unnoticed by me that Africa was my first true memory of my time as a young adult since...my eyebrows furrowed as I struggled to remember when. Giving my companion a firm nod in acknowledgement that I was all right, I took a step toward the mirror.

I reached up, touching the spot on the mirror where my green-gemmed post had once been, removed when I had continued my travels in France and needed to appear less eclectic. The hole where it was since closed but I remembered exactly where it had been.

My hand travelled sideways across my face, touching the gauzed half gingerly. Letting it fall, I knew I wasn't seeing what my companion saw. While my hair was tied back and the dress gentle and pretty, my face was still injured, my arms still thickly padded. I wanted to see myself as I truly was, now more than ever.

I motioned to my companion for a drink and she hesitated—I never requested anything from her. Her wariness turned to enjoyment a moment after as she agreed, squeezing my hand in friendship before leaving to seek out a guard to get some refreshments. As soon as I was sure she was away, I moved both hands up to my forehead, seeking the tape on the edge of the gauze. It took a few moments to find and get my fingernails under, but once I had it I felt the gratifying sting of the adhesive ripping off.

Slowly I removed the bandage, piece by piece. Finally, under the last piece of tape, I felt the satisfying pop as it let go of my flesh. Carefully, I pulled the dressing off, letting it fall to the ground.

I stepped forward again as I stared at my reflection in full.

There before me was a young woman, her cheeks sunken in, her eyes rimmed darkly from lack of sleep. Her ribs showed slightly through the thin cloth and bandage around her torso. Even with her hair pulled back, it appeared limp and lifeless. Her arms, though padded with gauze, were obviously thin, her bones showing prominently on the back of her hands and wrists. And her eyes...the once-brilliant shade of hazel with bright green flecks, had lost their lustre. Now they just sat there within her skull like two pool balls waiting to be struck.

Where the facial gauze had been was simply an odd shade of brown, bruises healing and a dozen puncture spots, smart black stitched x's holding each spot closed.

It took a few minutes for me to process what I was seeing, to understand that the young woman was my own reflection. My gaze returned to my hands, so skinny and thin. The exercise I had been doing had built up muscle once more. Without increasing my diet, however, little fat existed on my limbs. I pulled the dress up so I could see my legs, sinew corded beneath my skin in ripples of muscle.

Someone once told me I had a dancer's legs....

My hands shook slightly as I dropped the dress and touched my chin and nose, the angles more prominent from my loss of weight. They fluttered to my injured cheek and touched a sewn spot close to one eye. I was thankful it had not been any closer.

My companion entered, a drink in each hand, and paused at the doorway. She frowned as she put the drinks on the desk and hurried over, sympathy in her eyes. "I know it looks bad now but you will heal fast, you always do."

That was what I was afraid of.

A Meeting with a Cigar

As I had expected, Rochester's request to meet with me was less a request and more an order. After taking a sip of the drink that had been my rouse to remove my companion from the room, I was hurried by her out the door and into the hallway.

Taking her place at my side, my companion put her arm through mine and led me through the complex. We winded down corridors, stopping periodically so I could rest although I had to admit with my chest wrapped my ribs barely hurt. I fumbled a few times, both from exertion and the long dress, unused to walking now with fabric draped around my ankles.

As we got closer to our destination my companion became distant, her usual bubbly chatter halting. Her hands were sweaty and I knew she was worried. I wondered if she knew something I didn't.

Stopping at a large wooden set of double doors, the guard nodded to us in acknowledgement—he had been expecting us. He gestured to a seat next to the doors. My companion squeezed my hand in goodwill then led me to the chair, which I refused. With her sitting before me, I waited for the guard to do a specific knock then open the door for me. I entered sluggishly, willing my feet not to stumble. I wasn't sure if it was because I wanted to appear stronger than I was or because I wanted to impress him.

Rochester was facing the roaring fireplace, his back to me. His hands were resting, spread on the enormous mantle. In one hand, a stemless glass with a brown clear liquid. The other, a lit cigar.

I was silent as I stopped in the middle of the room, my hands at my sides.

"The doctor tells me you will be all right, after a measure of healing." The man shifted his weight, bringing his cigar to his face. I could hear his indrawn breath and saw the billow of smoke rise above his head as he blew it out.

Like always, I remained quiet.

"Things have been set into motion, things that were beyond my control." He sucked at his shortened cigar again, then threw the tip into the fire. He blew out slowly. "I need to know where you and I stand."

He turned slowly then, his drink still in hand. He brought it up to his lips as he revolved, taking in a mouthful of the acquired liquid and facing me, taking in my image.

He paused. After his eyes drifted over the injured half of my face, he swallowed. "The doctor told me he had you bandaged." He took two large strides and put his drink down on the mahogany desk. Like everything else in the room, it too, was over-scaled.

I stared back at him, silent.

Stepping close to me, he glanced down, looking more intently over the dress, the padding that showed through the arms, the slight bandages on the torso. I was uncomfortably aware that without the bandage around my chest the man, who was a good head in height over me, would now be looking down my cleavage.

After holding my gaze for what seemed an eternity, the man broke away. "I am sure you have heard of my daughter's demise. It does not matter how it happened, only that it did," he said gruffly. "She had been...an unexpected surprise years ago, one that I chose to pursue without the support of her mother."

He stepped back, sitting in a red wing-backed chair that had been turned toward the center of the room. He motioned to the other one that was close to me. I looked at it out of the corner of my eye, but shook my head.

"Her mother did not want to have the baby in the first place, let alone have her raised here." He reached over to pick up his drink, taking another deep drag. He hesitated with the glass an inch from his lips as he swallowed. "So I had no choice but to remedy the situation."

As he drank the rest of the contents in one gulp I considered what he had told me. Knowing what I knew of him, that could only mean he had the girl's mother murdered. Somehow, this act by him no longer surprised me at all.

I instantly felt a stab of sympathy for the now-deceased daughter.

"I had been grooming her to take over, and she was doing quite well, too." He put down his glass on the desk again and leaned forward, his elbows resting on his knees as he glanced at his interlocked hands. "She made one lethal mistake. She decided to get her hands dirty." He looked up at me. "It is a policy I always served religiously. After all, if you do not personally commit the acts, how can you be accused of them?"

I cocked my head slightly as I thought back. When I had been hit by Rochester's car, he had been in the passenger side. When my first death had taken place with the grappling hook, it was his lackey who had taken aim and pulled the trigger. I understood the words he spoke were true. And the power behind them. Essentially, he would always be untouchable—beyond the power of reasonable doubt and the law.

Standing, Rochester came before me. "Tell me." He reached out to take one lock of my hair in between his fingers. "What would you do if your team came back to rescue you again? Would you attack them as before, or would you go with them?" He stroked the softness of the tress before letting it fall back on my shoulder. "Do not lie to me, I will know if you do."

Somehow, I knew he was right. Without ever

having physically committed an act of crime himself, the man's skills lay expertly in observation.

I had always wondered how the man was able to get away from us so quickly and efficiently. Now, after being under his people's care so long, ensnared in his prison, I understood. He was correct. Despite my best efforts, I would not be able to deceive him.

I looked away, unsure how to answer. To be honest, I didn't know what I would do if any of my soldiers were to appear. Silence remained to be the best course.

"I appreciate your honesty," the man whispered, leaning in. I could smell the three or four drinks he had consumed earlier reeking from his breath. I wanted to back away, not sure of this uncharacteristic demeanor, staring at him, watching his actions. I had seen the man drink before, several times in fact, but it was always brief and he was *always* in control.

The man before me was too sloppy in his actions. His eyes were glassy and his posture a bit slumped. It occurred to me briefly that the man was compromised, that if I had not been just off my death bed I might have enough strength to reach up and grab Rochester's head. From there, it was a quick twist and his neck would break, the nightmare would be over. At the very least, I should be able to incapacitate him.

I blinked twice and turned my head as I dismissed the option. Rochester started to chuckle deep in his throat.

"You are right, of course. I am not myself and you

could simply take care of me right now," he said, not unexpectedly. I was sure he had observed my intense stare, the way my hands had twitched, my muscles tightened for the possibility. "But you forget."—he took small steps, coming around to my backside as he lowered his deep voice—"I am still the Master here. One wrong move and the others would destroy you."

I could feel his grin as I looked straight ahead, my gaze falling on the fire. "Even in my death they would be mine."

I could feel a drop of sweat move slowly down my spine as Rochester pulled another cigar from his pocket, followed by his cigar cutter. He held out both to get a better look but I knew he was at a disadvantage, the only light thrown from the fireplace. Lowering his hands, he held the pair beside my ear and snipped quickly, my body jumping at the proximity.

I knew he had me.

"You know, my daughter would have inherited everything—the complex, the vehicles and money, my men..." he began as he placed the cigar in his mouth and struck a match to light the end. Puffing a few times to get it started, he tapped the ash off the cigar, letting it fall on my shoulder.

I closed my eyes as my skin sizzled, remembering the fire trial and knowing this small amount of pain was nothing.

"You have been loyal this past while. I know you have the inner control now. You certainly have the strength and command ability. And there is the damned tenacity for staying alive." He came around to my front, cigar smoke gathering around him as he stared into my eyes. His were glassy with both his intoxication and excitement. "What would you say to an opportunity?"

I froze in place. Rochester was staring at me, waiting for an answer, watching my body movements for an affirmative or denial. I was silent as the possibilities and consequences of accepting the offer flashed through my brain. Rochester waited for almost a minute before becoming impatient. I was sure the doctor had related that I had not spoken for a long time. Still, he wanted a verbal answer.

"I asked you a question, soldier." My body instinctively stiffened, years of discipline taking over as I stood at attention. I closed my eyes, wishing it wasn't so.

"I have no desire to be your daughter," I whispered.

I could almost hear the man's head snap around in surprise as I spoke my first words in months. My tongue was numb with speaking the sentence. I felt as though it was still flapping, unsure what its purpose was.

"Well, well," the man responded, amused. He sidled up closer to my back and I felt a heavy hand on my bare shoulder where the ash had fallen. His fingertips stung the flesh where small burn marks were sure to be. "You do not have to be my daughter," he said in a hush, close to my ear.

The silence of the room permeated the space. Tension raised between myself and the man who wished me to call him Master in whatever regard. I struggled to catch my breath, raising my chin in defiance, glaring into the flames. What he was suggesting was something altogether different.

"Think on it." Rochester removed his hand, dusting the ashes off and came around to my front. Suddenly he seemed perfectly sober and I wondered if he had been faking his inebriation. Going to his desk he tapped a button which chimed.

The door opened, my companion standing there in readiness. Rochester waved his hand for me to be gone.

I turned, taking a few strangely confident strides toward the door when I heard him speak again. "You really do look beautiful in that dress."

I glanced over my shoulder in his direction as I stopped momentarily.

His voice held a hint of amused sadness with his next words, "Your mother did as well."

Contemplations

My mother. *Rochester had known my mother.*

Sitting on my bed that night, I stared at the moonlight streaming in through my window. It lit a path along the cold stone floor. I knew very little of either of my parents—I was so young when they had died. I knew StPatrick had known them, as he had mentioned them a few times, but how closely I wasn't sure. They were in the same inner circle, I was positive, but whether that meant they were once in the same vigilante faction, again I didn't know.

I absentmindedly ran a hand over my stomach, my fingers trailing the dressing. I glanced down, seeing the bright white bandage wrapped so neatly around my middle. Since it covered me just above my navel to the top of my breasts I had seen little reason to wear a top after stripping the gown from my body.

On my legs I wore a comfortable pair of sweats my companion had brought for me, probably absconded from the staff locker room supplies. At least in this I could be comfortable, a far cry from my drafty prison shift, and holding less dangerous possibilities than the dress.

Looking up, I caught my reflection in the mirror, my face pale white against the dots of dark stitches. Seeing my bound arms, I thought about removing the gauze there as well but I knew I would find much the same. Better I dealt with one horrifying body part at a time.

My mother. No doubt Rochester had brought it up to unnerve me, likely as he thought it would keep me around longer so I could try to coerce the information from him. Still, even knowing it was bait, it was compelling.

Keep me around longer. Had I really thought that?

My brain was playing tricks on me now, the psychological mind games the mastermind had arranged for me finally taking their ultimate toll. My deaths, my torture, the taunting and isolation, my almost-rescue, the kindness of a young woman who offered friendship in the unlikeliest of places. All had chipped away at my mental state bit by bit, building me up and breaking me down in a well-orchestrated play of events.

I knew my sanity was progressively slipping away, first with the attacks on the maids who had been sent to clean me, then with the guard in the training room. Now this, a killer's promise of a future, of a comforting paternal presence or a warm body beside me in bed. I was considering this change in future, all the while knowing deep down that I had none. No matter what I chose, my future was no more.

But what if it could be?

Either way, I was here to stay until my captor decided otherwise. Since the trials had proved no way to kill me yet, that seemed a very, very long time off.

Depression slipped over me like the water from my first trial. I felt like the choice I couldn't dare make was holding me under, the reality washing over me endlessly. I knew I couldn't take the man up on his offer—either one. To become what I had spent half of my life training and working to eliminate was not right. And to sleep with that...

I shuddered to think what rewards a sexual relationship with Rochester might bring but also the penalties to my own soul. I thought of his daughter's mother, and wondered, *what if that had been me?* I wouldn't want a child brought up in this place, either. Not with a father like Rochester.

I'd rather kill myself first...if I knew how.

I decided I would tell him in the morning and suffer the consequences.

The regret I felt was astounding.

Having made the decision, I leaned back against the headboard, pulling the blankets up to my neck. For all I knew, this could be my last night in a comfortable bed and despite my discomfort I meant to take advantage of it.

I was up before my companion entered, attempting to get dressed on my own. She halted at the doorway, seeing the unexpected sight, but smiled as she took it as a positive sign.

"Feeling a bit better, are we?" she asked, coming to help. She pulled the dress over my head, the same I had worn yesterday, and adjusted the fabric around my arms. I put a hand under her elbow, halting her movements, and stared at her, looking into her eyes.

Seeing the expression her smile faded. "What is it? Are you in pain again?"

Her powers of observation were not as keen as her master's.

I lifted two fingers to my lips, pulling them away like a cigarette, unsure of why I didn't speak now that I knew I could. Still, she understood quick enough either way. "All right," she nodded. "We can go see him now but I am not sure if he is even in his office." She reached up to fix my hair and make it presentable. Again I put a hand on her arm to stop her and after looking over her face once more, remembering her kindness, I put my arms around her in a hug.

My companion tensed, only having viewed my physical contact with others end in death or massive injury. When she realized my embrace was meant in friendship, she returned the gesture, the hug lasting for minutes.

It was the clearing of a throat behind her that broke us up. "He wants to see you," the guard averting his eyes from the tender act.

We dropped our arms and I put the palm of my hand against her cheek, kissing the other one. There was a chance I would never see the woman again after today—the one part of my decision I regretted already. Whatever her orders were, she had been a soft respite among a nest of vipers.

And I didn't even know her name.

Lowering my hand, I stepped around the woman, following the guard. It did feel as long to reach Rochester's office as it did the night before, although this time I hesitated at the open door in anticipation. The guard shoved me through the doorway and closed it.

The fireplace had no fire lit. The room seemed cold without it. I wrapped my arms around myself as I watched smoke billow from behind the chair at the desk.

"You have decided already," the man said. It wasn't a question.

I started to nod, but knew it wouldn't be good enough. "I can't." My unused voice was still hoarse.

"Can't, or won't?" Rochester spun around in his chair to face me.

I stared at him. "Both."

He sighed and stood, coming around to approach me. There were no signs of the previous afternoon's binge, unlike the dark circles under my eyes from a restless night of wrestling with my own decision.

The man saw this and nodded. "It is something that you considered it, at least." He put his cigar in his mouth, speaking around it as he crossed his arms. "I thought we had finally broken you, and I believe we almost did." He watched me for a moment before continuing. "I cannot let you stay this way, you understand."

I nodded, understanding his meaning and remembering my somewhat complacent mood after I had started working-out in the room.

"Well," he sighed, an action partially for show. I knew he had made his decision already. "The hospitality I have shown you ends today. My people are not coddled and it is time we put you to use."

My head snapped up as I stared at him. I wasn't sure what he was implying. Had I been more myself, I would have laughed at the idea of the supposed hospitality, not to mention his implication that I had not already served a purpose.

Then the words he had spoken broke through my thoughts. *My people. Does that mean I am truly his now, one way or another?*

"Hold her," he stated. A man came from behind, apparently in the room the whole time, hidden behind a new suit of armor. Confused that I had not noticed this before, I blamed my ignorance of observation on my exhaustion.

Knowing exactly what to do, the same muscular man from so many times before wrapped one arm around my torso, pinning my arms to my sides as he placed the other arm on top tightly. I struggled, not sure what was happening, and I found that feral creature I had sought to suppress surfacing once more. As I writhed, the man squeezed harder, my ribs tweaking in protest. I cried out. Rochester lifted a hand in halt.

"This doesn't need to be hard at all," he lifted a small item from his desk. He looked me over, still struggling slightly despite my aching chest. "Where to do it..." he wondered aloud, looking over my lower dress. He got down on his knee, lifting the fabric up my leg slowly.

I flailed, kicking out my feet, trying to use the man behind me as a springboard. He shook me hard in response and I cried out again.

Rochester grabbed my ankle roughly. "Stop being difficult. It will only hurt a moment." I stopped struggling outwardly as I glared at the man who just last night had offered me his whole world. My muscles were taut in flight instinct.

He considered my flesh, running his fingertips down the length of my thigh as he nodded and tapped my flank just below one of my tribal tattoos. I saw him lift his cigar to his lips, puffing a few times, then watched him lower the cigar to the item he held. Within seconds, the tip was red. My eyes grew large as I realized what it was.

"Only for a moment," Rochester re-emphasized as he brought the small trinket to my thigh, meeting my gaze with his filled with enjoyment.

I screamed as the brand dug into my fat, cooking the skin and membranes below. My body convulsed, my muscles twitching and fighting despite the increasing tightness of the muscular man's hold on me. I broke out into a cold sweat, muscles quivering from pain, my mouth tasting bile as I held back sickness.

Finally Rochester took the brand away, tearing skin as it lifted off. He lowered his head to below where I could see him and I could feel his warm breath as he blew on the mark. I stiffened in response, the area smarting. I could already feel the slow continuation of heat as the burn sensation spread. He let the fabric drop and stood again, returning to sit in his chair behind the desk.

Rochester waved to the man who let go of me abruptly and stepped back against the wall once more. I stumbled in his abandonment, my hand grabbing my side where the lower rib screamed at me.

"Now what?" I gasped, my voice harsh with confidence through its shakiness. I felt the sweat dripping off my brow and shivered as the cold reached the moisture on my face.

"Now we begin our second round," he rested his elbows on the top of his desk with fingers steepled.

I heard a boom, echoing loudly within the confines of Rochester's office, and felt a sting as something ripped through me. Surprised, I looked down. A small patch of red was quickly spreading through the beautiful green fabric on my upper abs.

I raised a shaky hand to the spot, my mouth hanging open as I looked up at Rochester. I heard the man behind me put the safety on the gun once more and put it in its holster.

Rochester looked nonplussed. "I told you," he said firmly, "my people are not coddled."

I started to waver slightly as the warm liquid drenched my backside. Even my hand on the front had become slick. I wondered where exactly I had been hit, to bleed so much.

My knees gave out and I sank to the floor, my free hand firm against the stone, preventing me from falling over completely. I heard Rochester's chair creak as he got up, the heavy footsteps from his boots as he came around. He stood beside me, watching me wobble now on hands and knees.

The twilight began to sparkle before my eyes, the tunnel effect happening in my ears.

It won't be long now.

I recognized the feeling of death once more—by now I could readily diagnose the symptoms of bleeding out.

My arm gave way and I fell flat onto my stomach.

Rochester bent down, grabbing the hair on the back of my head and raising my face to his painfully with a twist of his arm. I could taste the blood that was now in my mouth, trickling out between my lips. "Remember when you wake up," he said maliciously, all compassion in his expression gone, "you now call *me* master."

Unwelcome Safety

The cold of the room I awoke in didn't surprise me. Nor did the dampness as I went through my stages of reanimation. I was back in the dungeon section of the complex, a room the combination of sterile medical facility and filthy holding cell. Unlike last time, no guard or doctor came to check on my status. Despite what Rochester had said, I wondered if I had really extended past my usefulness.

I tried to sit up, my arms and legs free of restraints, and found only pain in the action. I glanced down to see I was wearing the plain white shift once more, a fresh bandage on my torso but also a new patch of blood from where I had been shot.

I wonder if Rochester kept the bullet. My morbidity shocked me.

After several tries, I managed to sit up, my stomach grumbling. I half-stumbled, half-fell off the table, my shaking hands catching me from tumbling all the way. Walking hand-over-hand against the cold concrete walls, I made my way to the door, pounding feebly.

A moment later the small slot opened.

"What?" a man asked angrily.

"Food?" I asked carefully. My voice was small, mouse-like in its volume, weak likely from loss of blood. I had figured there was no harm in inquiring.

I was wrong.

I heard the latch on the door immediately, a heavy metal bolt if I remembered correctly from before. I stepped carefully backwards. The door was thrown open, the man entering with determined heavy steps. Another guard grinned, standing in the doorway, his thumbs looped in his belt.

The first guard reached out, back handing me hard across the face. My head hit the table as I went down and I felt a small flow of warm liquid trailing through my hairline. Raising my hand to my head, I looked up, stunned at the man as he took off his gun belt, passing it to the other guard.

"You want food, eh?" he asked as he fumbled with his pants belt and zipper with one hand. He went to his knees before me and used the other hand to raise my shift. I started panicking as I shuffled backwards, a renewed energy to my weak limbs. My legs kicked out as my hands shook, attempting to keep the fabric down. I tried to twist onto my stomach, to crawl away, but both my wound and ribs tweaked painfully.

I cried out for help as my knees were exposed. The fabric was pushed above my upper legs. The man's pants were down, his genitals exposed. He looked over me hungrily. Then my skirt was raised above my hips, my undergarment pulled out of the way and the man advanced.

"Wait!" the other guard called out, looking nervous now. His hand was around the holster tightly, white knuckles. As my molester turned to look at him the second guard shrugged in my direction. "She belongs to him."

I looked down as the man on me did as well, seeing a hideous bright red spot on my thigh, the brand blackening as it healed. The distinctive image of vines climbing around a pair of stag antlers could be seen, the same representation that was sewn so expertly onto the arm of the guard's upper sleeve. *Rochester's insignia.*

My assaulter hung his head in defeat, pulling up his pants and straightening them, still panting in arousal. He knelt back on his heels, hands on his knees, then looked up at me with a sly smirk. "You may belong to him, but everything else with you is our jurisdiction." He made a fist and punched me hard in the side of the head, a fresh flow of blood coming from the injury.

I lay there dazed and listened as he put his hand around my neck, raising it so I would be forced to look at him. He squeezed, cutting off my air just slightly. Reaching up, I placed my hand over his, trying to get him to release me as I gulped.

"You'll eat when we say you eat," he hit me hard again.

I passed out long before the beating was over.

Forgotten Time

I woke up to the sound of my own moans.

I opened my left eye, the other swollen shut. I was laying on the floor in the fetal position, my body cold and stiff. The lights were still on in the room so I hoped I hadn't been out for long, or at least if it had been, I hoped the guards had changed out. I was confident the brand had saved me from a devastating rape, but I still had no desire to be at the receiving end of that particular guard's discipline again.

Shakily I pulled myself up, using the legs of the steel table. My back arched uncomfortably, my shoulder hanging limply from its socket.

That guard was experienced in beatings—he knew what he was doing.

I glanced down at my arm, reaching up with the good hand. Feeling along the joints, I could feel what I had been dreading—the limb was dislocated. Luckily I had been through it before, such injuries a regular hazard of my job. Unfortunately to fix one's own shoulder was extremely painful and very difficult. I leaned my hips against the table, wondering if I would be able to do it in my current state, how injured I really was.

Using the shiny metal surface as a sort of mirror, I leaned down over the table-like bed and observed my head wounds.

My right eye was indeed swollen shut, but some quick prodding and careful opening of the lids convinced me no ocular damage beyond bruising had occurred.

Sadly, it was another area I had experience in.

One hazel cornea stared back at me, its gaze dull and almost lifeless. Both lips were split and swollen, my gums bleeding. Backing up, I assessed the rest of my body. Deep bruising tinted my leg and stomach. I suspected my neck was black and blue as that was tender as well. All in all the guard had still had his fun, just in a different way.

At least I was alive.
Alive to do what?

My daily routine was established after that. After a fitful sleep I would peel myself off the floor, a more comfortable solution than the narrow metal table that served as a bed.

Sometime during what I assumed was morning a meal would be passed through the small opening in the door, usually something unappetizing like lumpy overcooked oatmeal, some stale raisins thrown on top. I would choke down the food, only because I knew the next meal, always of similar menu, would not come until late that evening. Then my tedium would begin. Nothing to do, nothing to look at in particular.

Only me.

An inspection of my room provided only this: four white walls approximately fourteen feet apart, fairly clean, no cracks or divisions in tile that I could see. One heavy metal door with a small glass viewing window and an even smaller slot for the meals. At one end of the room was a toilet, the other end was the metal table-bed held up on four sturdy metal legs bolted to the floor. The lights above were recessed into the ceiling, no possibility of using them to my advantage.

There were no windows, no linens, no other comforts.

I had no visitors, as I might have expected. No doctor came to inspect my injuries. I was left to my own devices and field-medic training from the school.

I became hopeful each day as I heard the slot in the door open that a doctor was being announced, but none arrived. I began the ritual of testing the sore spots around my head, ribs, and stomach, poking them gingerly for pain. I watched the burn around the brand for what I knew to be signs of infection, lancing a rapidly swelling spot with a forgotten pin from my bandaged torso. It was both a horribly painful and awfully relaxing feeling as the pressure from the spot drained. I used gauze from my arm to wipe away the results.

Three days after I woke up, I set my own arm, catching it awkwardly between two spots on the table legs to keep it still while I turned my body. The cracking pop I felt and heard after a half hour of effort was both satisfying and excruciating. My shoulder became bruised and swollen, having been disconnected for so long.

Evidence of my foolishness—a well-deserved punishment.

The days and nights ran into each other easily, the distinction between each only when the lights were turned off in what I assumed was the evening. Sometimes I wondered though if the guards weren't playing with me, flipping the switches at random times.

They are doing it on purpose. They want me upset.

Or the days are getting shorter. How many hours are in a day? Five? Eight?

I was growing weary, illogical, and paranoid.

I tried to keep my mind sharp by focusing on those things around me. I kept my ear to the slot in the metal door while listening to the sounds in the hallway, but the voices were muffled and unrecognizable. Occasionally, a fellow prisoner would scream or yell, but I couldn't be sure who it was coming from or what had caused it, whether it was self- or guard-induced.

My other half would smile. *It sounds like torture—*

what a pretty tone it makes.

I wondered about the other prisoners, wondered if they were like me. I wondered if they were legitimate criminals, perhaps just tangled in Rochester's plans, or other soldiers, or if they were all innocents.

None of us are innocent—we all get what is coming to us.

Figuring working on my body was a good waste of time, I began to exercise as I felt my injuries heal. I did pushups, sit-ups, squats throughout the day, filling time with the physical training I had once felt unnecessary as a young soldier. I would stretch, the movement feeling good after a night on the floor. I tried to keep my fingers nimble, taking strands from my shift that frayed over time and braiding them together.

Eventually I had to stop as my garment grew too short.

Yes, we must keep our modesty, here of all places.

I thought about keeping track of the days, but had no way of leaving a mark on the wall. Once I considered using my own blood from my wounds. Somehow I could not bring myself to do it. I had seen far too much of my blood to use it in play. Besides, I rationalized that without knowing how long I had been held before, it was pointless.

Instead, I tried to measure by the healing of my wounds. But without knowing how fast I really healed, or if I was even recovering well at all, the measure became trivial.

My punctures closed bit by bit. I was forced to remove the stitches myself when their binding within my healed flesh became painful. Regretfully, I had to use a breakfast bowl dipped in toilet water to douse the stitches, making them pliable before I could start the grueling task. Thankfully, by that point, my mind had begun to wander. It was easy to picture myself doing something else as the threads were removed from the dozen spots or more on each of my arms and face.

I'll make you a deal—if you don't cry, I'll recite a poem.

After being lanced the brand healed cleanly enough, doused as well with toilet water daily. My ribs stopped hurting and I removed the bandage, keeping it and the gauze from my arms rolled tight during the day behind where the door opened. At night when the lights went out I would pull them out and use my dingy collection as a small pillow.

Smells worse than the straw pillows in Africa—more comfortable though.

That was my routine, these irrational thoughts, habitual actions. They continued day, after day, after day, after day.

I tried other methods of breaking the tedium. Once I attempted to keep my second meal bowl, for a purpose then unknown. That did not end well, the guards correcting my insolence with brute force.

At some point at the end of each day, or what I

thought was the end, I would stretch out on the floor next to the table. With my small gauze pillow I would relish in the softness of the used items and pull my legs up under my shortened shift for warmth. There I would wait for the minutes or hours for the lights to be turned off. I would stare at the white walls and try to recite memories or poems or anything that required an active mind.

Eventually I would fall into an endlessly light sleep, the screams and unintelligible rants of the others my nighttime lullaby.

Remembered

It was some time later that Rochester chose to remember me. At the time, I didn't know the scenario was his, but afterwards it fell into place like a well-orchestrated symphony and I his violin, string stretched taut and ready to be plucked.

He was testing me.

I had woken up like usual, stretching out my limbs. I sat on the metal table awaiting the familiar screech of the slot door for my mid-morning meal. I felt like I had been staring at the slot for hours when heavy footsteps sounded outside.

I frowned as I slowly got down from the table, my bare feet padding silently on the freezing floor.

The klaxon sounded, the same one I had heard so very long ago, the lights flashing intermittently in a visual alarm. I covered my ears, travelling close to the door, pressing my ear to the slot. Outside my room there were shouts and running. Doors began to slam open and I counted them as I had so many times before during routine checks.

One, two, three, I barely breathed as the footsteps continued running up and down the hall.

Four, five.

Screams of the other prisoners sounded as their doors were opened and they escaped.

Six, seven, eight, nine.

Gunshots and the thuds of heavy bodies could be heard followed by yells for reinforcements.

Ten, eleven.

The sounds stopped and I pressed myself harder against the slot, hoping I was blocking out the noise inadvertently. I held my breath and counted the seconds but after a minute of no activity I became concerned. Standing upright, I lowered my hands off the door, backing up slowly. I jumped when my back hit the wall, but pressed against it firmly then, my fingers splaying against the cool surface.

I waited, but no one came.

My thoughts became irrational, my breathing fast as I fought down a panic attack.

Perhaps the guards were all dead.

I stood still as the sentence replayed in my head.

What if they were all dead? What if the intruders had already left?

I raised a clawed hand to my throat as I gulped in air, my body starting to crumple from the possible reality.

With no one on the outside, no one would unlock

my door.

I would literally starve to death in this fourteen-by-fourteen foot box.

I would die.

My hands went to my unkempt hair, my fingers sinking into the nests of knots, threatening to pull out chunks as anxiety took over.

Then the lock turned.

Slowly, and ever so quietly, the handle turned downwards. The door clasp popped, the heavy metal moving toward me as the door opened.

A woman sidestepped inside, carefully closing the door almost all the way. I looked her over, my body still pressed flat against the adjacent wall. Her hair was neat, tied in a braid at the back. Her grey-black outfit was tight, gun holster shiny. Her boots were slightly scuffed. She nodded to me. "Come with me now and we'll be able to escape."

I considered her as she glanced over her shoulder through the small opening, checking our exit. "We need to go. More guards will be sent soon." She looked at me and stepped forward. "Take my hand." She extended her arm and fingertips in aid.

I took two steps toward her, reaching out as well and then halted when I saw her fingers. Pulling my hand back I paused and shook my head. "I can't," I whispered shakily. I slunk back against the wall, closing my eyes.

The young woman lowered her hand. "You know

it's likely we won't be able to try this again." She reached out, one last effort to help.

I melted against the wall, letting my legs fold below me as I sank to the floor. "I know."

The woman shook her head sadly then squeezed between the opening, closing the door behind her. Silence pervaded the space between the klaxons, the only other sound my heavy breathing.

A minute later, my lock snapped into place, the klaxon ending abruptly.

My body regressed into a state of shock. My hands shook, then my arms, the palsy-like vibration overtaking my muscles.

I burst into tears.

A Visit

The next day I heard the slot open, but no food was passed in. "Come to the door backwards, put your hands behind your back near the slot," a voice came forth gruffly.

I was sitting on the floor in the same place as the previous night, one knee drawn up, my arm resting on it. I didn't know how long I had cried after the young woman had left, but the action had purged my soul it seemed—I was hollow once more, my thoughts clearer. I looked toward the door slowly.

"Come on, girl, I haven't got all day," the man said. I glanced away, looking at another spot of the room.

I don't want to.

"Do it now or I will send in my men to do it for you," he threatened quickly.

Sighing, I got up slowly and turned, shuffling backwards with my hands behind me. My fingertips brushed the metal and two rough hands grabbed my wrists, pulling them through the small opening at an awkward angle. I winced as my skin scraped along the top of the slot.

Cold cuffs were placed around my wrists, anchored tightly and pushed back through the slot. I tested the bonds once, finding them more than secure. I walked out of the way of the swinging door, turning to find out why I now had the special jewelry.

Come in quickly, or there will be a draft.

When the door opened, the guard stepped through, investigating the room. He looked around quickly, presumably for weapons. I cringed as he looked behind the door, his expression smug as he picked up the wad of gauze and bandages and confiscated them. He glared at me. I had no doubt I would pay for the deception later.

Easier to ask for forgiveness than permission, they say.

Still glaring, he called out, "All clear."

Rochester appeared in the doorway, his massive fur cloak seeming to encompass the entranceway in its entirety. He stepped over the small threshold and the guard nodded to him, making his exit. Quickly, he closed the door behind him.

Upon hearing the click, I pulled at the restraints on my wrists. "Concerned about me attacking?" My eyes darted around the space, taking in the man, my thoughts fragmented.

He is too big--this room isn't big enough for us both.

"Found your voice, I see." Rochester smiled. He

took a slow stride around the room, examining a part of his complex I doubted he visited often. "Well," he began, looking at the tiny ventilation duct above the doorway and tucking away his unlit cigar, "one never knows, and frankly you are unpredictable enough to be viewed as a threat."

But I'm such a nice person.

I tried to laugh but the noise caught in my throat, coming out like a coughing fit. "How so?" With the man's continued presence I found I could focus more, my brain finally responding with at least part of the alertness I knew I had to possess if I wanted to survive.

But did I?

You might not want to, but we do.

"You refused to go with her," he answered, ignoring my question. Rochester stood again by the doorway. He folded his arms across his chest.

"Yes," I acknowledged.

"Why?" he asked without missing a beat. He watched me intently.

I answered back, holding his dark gaze, "The ring."

It was not what the man was expecting. He blinked, his eyebrows furrowing. "Excuse me?"

I shifted my shoulders, the inability to move making them sore. The one that had been dislocated especially hated the position. It had never been quite right since I had fixed it, unquestionably sore and stiff, the muscle knotted in a way I could not repair.

I saw the man's surprise at my response and walked

over to the metal table, leaning against it. I was tired and these questions were not helping any. Keeping my concentration was taking too much effort. My head ached. "I was ready to go with her, until I saw her finger." At the man's puzzled look, I continued, "She was wearing a ring. We were never allowed jewelry...it was a hazard."

Rochester shook his head in disbelief. "That was all?" He chuckled despite his defeat.

I stood still, my intent concentration on the man's pock-marked chubby cheeks kept my flitting thoughts at bay. "Something felt off."

The man considered me. "Your mind is still quite sharp. I would have thought a month in this small cell would have had the opposite effect."

I startled and licked my lips, suddenly gone dry. "A month?" I asked quietly.

The man fingered the cigar in his pocket, ignoring my question. He approached me slowly, looking me over. He reached down, his hand laying over my thigh and beginning to press. "Tell me, did the brand heal cleanly?" he asked, knowing the answer. He was taunting me, testing my reactions.

I twisted my wrists, painfully ripping their sweat-drenched surface through the hoops of the cuffs. Gritting my teeth, I grunted as I brought both fists up, hitting the man on either side of his head. He cried out, disoriented momentarily. He stumbled backwards as I advanced, unrelenting. I punched him in the nose and took a deep breath before bringing my leg up, kicking it out with all my force. It landed just above his knee.

Rochester yelled out in pain. He dropped to the floor. I reached out for his cloak. In one movement I ripped it off him and threw it across the room. I grabbed the base of his coat sleeve, tearing it off. Using the momentum I rolled over his back, landing deftly on the other side. The action wretched the man's arm painfully backwards, a satisfying snap coming from the upper bone. I flicked the sleeve forward, around the front of his neck. Bringing my heel down on the base of his spine, I twisted the fabric, pulling it tight.

The man's skin color changed, gagging noises becoming clear. I almost wished I could watch him, observe the light leave his eyes as he had watched me so many times. He was writhing, his hands clutching the noose as it cut off his air. I placed my foot between his shoulder blades, twisting my hands so I had a better hold on the fabric.

I paused, growling out my reply. "Clean enough." I leaned over, seeing his bulging eye watching me from his turned head. "You did say you don't like coddling." With a yell I tugged at the fabric and heaved down my weight at the same time.

His heavy body went rigid a moment before going slack, his head flopping from the broken neck.

I blinked, coming back to myself. It had been a delusion, the murder a hallucination of my increasingly unstable mind.

"Thank you," I whispered, answering finally. In the end, the brand had saved me from rape by the guards at least.

In front of me, Rochester's lips curled into a grin. He had seen in my expression the gist of what I had daydreamed. "You *are* ready to be useful then."

He called out for the guard, the door opening quickly. "Bring her to the observation room," Rochester said firmly, then hesitated. He raised a finger. "Unmolested."

The guard nodded once, grabbing me by the upper arm to lead me out of the room. At the door, my shackled hands shot out awkwardly, catching the doorframe. "Before I go," I asked, looking down as I expected the worst, "—my mother...."

I heard the large man shift, his heavy furs swishing against the corner of the steel table. "She was an affection once, long ago. For a time we were inseparable, her and I."

She was his whore.

My shoulders hunched as I heard the words I had most dreaded, that my mother could have been at some point what I spent years fighting.

As I shuffled away, I could hear the man, my new master, his roaring laughter filling the hall.

Untrained Sympathy

The guard led me to a different level, pausing at the door to plug in a code and press his palm to a panel. He held my arm as the door slid open mechanically. We stepped inside and paused as the door closed behind us.

The observation room was set up like my fine room from before, only sparsely appointed. The walls were a bright white plastic, the floor white poured concrete. There was a basic bed, coarse linens on it, made neatly. A heavy steel table and chair rested nearby. A clean toilet and sink sat against the wall across the room, surrounded by frosted glass which provided some privacy. The space was big, much larger than my fringe room, three times what I had been afforded in the past.

Home.

The guard, a young man and obviously new to Rochester's cause, watched me turn around slowly. I looked over the room, saw the high ceilings and breathed a little easier. Along one side up above, a series of windows lined the wall. I suspected this was where the observation occurred.

I only noticed my cuffs had been removed when my hands dropped to my sides. I looked over my shoulder as the guard came around from behind me. He stood still, a soft frown on his mouth, his eyes wide with sympathy. I looked over the handsome man, barely out of boyhood and noted his untamed good nature. He reached out his hand to place on my shoulder in goodwill.

He was too nice for the job. He needed to harden if he wanted to survive as a guard.

I smiled back slowly, my own hand resting on his for but a second before I grabbed his wrist and twisted my body, flinging his form over my own. Landing hard on his back, I heard the air whacked out of his chest as I spun around to straddle him, my fingers punching into his throat.

His eyes widened and watered as he gasped for air.

"You're welcome," I said quietly.

Having made my point, I got off him, taking a few steps away. The young man held his throat, still trying to catch his breath as he rolled and got up to his knees and then feet. With a horrified glance in my direction, he fled the room, hitting the button hard for the door to close.

I walked the perimeter of the room slowly, rubbing feeling back into my arms. My wrists were sore from pulling against the cuffs, my bare feet cold.

I noticed one similarity here as with my last cell.

Again there was nothing to keep my mind or body occupied.

For a while, I sat at the table, staring up at the observation glass. I wondered what would happen now that I was out of my cell, wondered what I would be used for. My stomach grumbled as I realized Rochester's visit had been before my usual morning breakfast. I rubbed the spot, now wondering if I should be wishing for something to eat, or....

Hours later I was sitting on the floor against the wall when the door opened. It was the handsome guard. He stepped in, waiting for the door to close behind him.

He carried a tray that he put down on the table. I got up, both curious and hungry. As I approached him he put a warning hand over his Beretta, the safety already off.

I sat down on the chair slowly. "How is your throat?" I wished I could be one of those evil prisoners for him and grin maliciously but while I made the comment to hit the point home to him that guards should be just that, I genuinely worried that I had hurt him.

It was for your own good.

The man narrowed his eyes slightly and cleared his throat. I could see a small isolated purple bruise beginning over his Adams apple. "Eat," he ordered.

He lifted the top off the tray, revealing an apple, some bread with jam on it, a hot bowl of something on the side. The smells bombarded me, my eyes watering in gratitude. It seemed forever since I had eaten decently. I looked up at the guard, not sure what to say.

I could tell the man wanted to comfort me. After all, no one should ever be in the position to appreciate such a meager meal. But there were his orders that stood in his way, his obedience to Rochester preventing humanity from taking permanent hold on him.

As I stared at the man, I noticed movement in the windows above, a few people entering and chatting good-natured with each other before sitting. The smile that had been threatening to grow on my lips erased. Seeing my eyes look past him, the guard glanced over my shoulder. "It's starting. I suppose they want good seats." More spectators arrived, shaking each other's hands.

I glanced back at him, then stared at my plate, my appetite suddenly gone. "Starting what?"

You know what.

He shifted, his hand now resting on the grip of his gun, the other on his belt. He looked uncomfortable.

My mouth went dry as I drew in a breath. "When?" I asked quietly, that one word containing such a heavy question I almost loathed to hear the answer.

More trials.

The man shifted his steps again and turned to walk away.

I jumped up from my chair, the heavy metal scraping along the floor as it moved slightly. "Wait!" I called out, extending a hand.

The man spun around, drawing his gun in a second, his movement completely fluid. The gun poised at my face, I saw again that the safety was off, his finger on the trigger.

Maybe he isn't as green as I thought.

"Don't," he seemed to growl, though the slight shakiness implied his regret at having to pull out his weapon at all.

I lowered my hand slowly. "Please. When?" I could hear the pleading in my own voice.

The gun barrel wavered slightly as he considered. "Now." his eyes changed to sadness as he lowered his gun, placing it back in its holster and turning to hurry out of the room. As the door closed, I looked up at the people staring back at me.

I held their gazes for a few seconds before the lights turned off then changed to a blue hue. I glanced around the room, not sure what was happening.

The people looked excited.

Choices

"You should have eaten when you had the chance," Rochester's matter-of-fact voice came over the intercom.

I looked up at the windows, seeing smoke rise from behind the people pressed up to the glass. While I could not see him, I knew he likely had the best vantage point of all.

"Now, you need to make a choice," Rochester began his speech, "you see, you were never so close to staying dead as when you accidentally almost took your own life. It actually took a fair amount of work on the doctor's part to get you going again."

I looked away, balling my fists. *He should have left me lifeless.*

My other half disagreed. *No, not until the job is done and every one of them is bloodless and dead.*

"So," he continued, "you can choose pills, poison, asphyxiation, or a weapon."

I was trying to process what Rochester was saying. If I understood right, he was asking me to commit suicide...in front of an audience. The order was astounding. "What do you mean, asphyxiation?" I asked carefully, presuming he could hear me. My head was beginning to pound. I rubbed it absentmindedly.

Rochester laughed. "Your movements just answered your own question." I saw him appear, leaning forward from one of the upper chairs. "Have you noticed the noise of the fan?" he asked. "It is working in reverse right now, sucking the air out bit by bit. Surely by now you are noticing the effects."

He paused as our eyes met. I broke the stare first.

Son of a bitch.

I could hear a faint whirring noise. I glanced around again, seeing now the vents in two areas of the ceiling, the image swaying in my view as I realized I was wobbling side to side. My hand caught the back of the chair as I attempted to stay upright.

"You will not have long to decide. I would suggest you do it soon. If you choose any of the other three options, I will certainly have the appropriate items delivered to you. If not...." He chuckled. "I see you are having a hard time staying on your feet. You should make your decision or it appears it will be made for you."

Does it really matter how it is done? Death is inevitable either way.

I tried to grab the back of the chair with my other hand. My left tingled, useless now. I tripped as my legs became numb, falling to the floor. My breathing was raspy, my eardrums beating in reply to my over-worked heart. Scenarios started to play out in my head, the rational part of my brain welcoming the end finally. The other part begged for clemency.

Death should be delivered in battle, a worthier cause than this. My other half was rising on its haunches, daring me to live.

I was past hoping for that.

I was becoming irrational, my mind seeking a way out, an easier way. Deep down I knew there was none. None of the options ended with me happily away from this place. None of them even offered life.

"This is your last chance. I suspect you will be unconscious in a minute," Rochester said firmly.

I tried to speak, my voice coming out in raspy noises. "Pills…" I tried to call out, weaving back and forth. "Pills!" I screamed as loudly as my dry, closing windpipe would allow.

At least then I could control the manner of my death. At least then it would be *my* choice instead of murder and humiliation.

Immediately the whirring changed, louder as a whoosh of air was infused into the room. I felt the oxygen wash over me and let myself fall the rest of the way to the ground, taking a moment to rest. My limbs seemed exhausted from the effort of staying on my body. I gulped in the air like a drink after a drought. A lock sounded, the door opening. Two sets of hands picked me up by the upper arms, placing me upright in the chair.

I opened my eyes and straightened my head. Second by second I was feeling stronger, the oxygen infusing my molecules with a needed essence. The handsome guard lifted my hand, placing the toast in it. "Eat."

Knowing my fate once more, I lifted the toast to my lips, taking a small bite. It was good, the jelly a burst of flavor after my month-long stint of lumpy oatmeal and gruel. I savored the taste, regretting my slow bites when my young guard lifted the tray to take it away.

The other guard opened the door for him, motioning for someone else to enter—it was the doctor, the same one who tended me time and again. He stepped into the room, his eyes resting on me in shock. He glanced at the guard, who nodded in acknowledgement.

With shaky hands, the doctor popped open his medical bag. He reached inside and removed a vial containing white pills. He stared at the vial in his hands, no doubt reconsidering his choice. Despite the fact that the man worked for what our team had always considered one of the most devious and deadly minds, I could see the doctor's good nature. Deep down, he was a responsible man and a good doctor.

The guard took the vial, bringing it to the table. Placing it in front of me, he pushed a glass of water close.

I looked up at the doctor, his hand still out as

though he were willing the pills back.

"Swallow them," the guard encouraged, his arms crossed. Somehow, I was glad it wasn't the young handsome guard.

Glancing up at the observation window, I saw the morbid fascination of the people as they watched our movements, rapt like children against a department store window. I noticed for the first time that they were dressed nicely…they weren't guards, then. I wanted to question if they were investors in Rochester's ventures, or just rich citizens with a penchant for watching the plights of others?

A loud rap on the table brought me back to my present situation. The guard slammed my cup against the surface of the table to get my attention.

I stared at the glass. The water had spilled a little in a wet ring around it. Shakily raising my hand to it, I wrapped my fingers around the cool surface and pulled it toward me.

My other hand touched the small vial as though it were hot lava. I retracted my fingers.

Don't be a coward, you wanted this.

The doctor cleared his throat and shuffled closer. "If you take a bit of water first they will go down—"

"No help." The guard stepped sideways, putting a hand out to stop him. "He said no one is to help. You are only here to confirm the death."

The doctor opened his mouth as though to object but nodded instead after a moment. I wondered what blackmail Rochester had on him to make him abandon his morals. I remembered vaguely learning about some oath doctors took, something about not harming patients.

If he was one of ours he wouldn't break his oath on fear of death.

I took a deep breath and opened the vial, wishing I knew what was inside. At least if I knew what type of drug I was taking, I might have an idea of what symptoms I could expect.

I poured the contents onto the table carefully, each little bright white pill the same as the next. "How many?" I asked, trying to keep my voice calm.

The guard and doctor looked at each other. Neither knew what to say. Of course, any drug in mass quantities is lethal. What I was really asking was, how fast did they want me to die?

The men looked toward the observation window for guidance, my gaze following theirs.

Rochester leaned forward in his seat, a wide grin on his robust face. "Lady's choice."

I observed the pills, knowing I had to do this right—too little and I would be horribly ill for a long time, I was sure, too many and I could be dead within moments.

That's what you want, isn't it? Release from this life? From him? From me?

My other half was mocking me, irritated by my compliance and consideration for my murdering master above.

Neither scenario would please Rochester, and that was something I feared worse than death. I had learned, this past while, that the man's wrath was often filled with horrible pain and extended misery. But the fact that I was rationalizing my own suicide upon orders from a man I hated did scare me. On the other hand, at least my life had purpose once more, even if that purpose was to die.

The guard was getting impatient, the doctor nervous as I reached slowly for a pill with one hand, the glass with the other. I remembered many of the current drugs were taken under the tongue. I put down the glass. Then I considered the objective.

Rochester wanted me to take my own life and I had no desire to be on a psychedelic trip for hours before that. Gathering my inner strength, I grabbed four pills, popped them in my mouth and took a gulp of water, washing the items down.

I stood up then, wrapping my arms around me as I considered my actions. I shivered, not due to the effects of the drugs but because I knew I had just taken four unknown pills that were likely hallucinogenic and would ultimately cause me to overdose. I also knew that I had to make this try count—if I wasn't out cold within the next ten minutes I would need to try to remember to take more pills.

This could be my chance to end it all. Perhaps this time I will stay dead.

Minutes later, I could feel the drugs rush through my system as my eyes grew wide. I looked up at the guard and doctor, wondering how they got so tall only to find myself sitting on the floor. I looked around the room, the bed and table warping in size from top to bottom, the sheets coming alive in a spiral of cotton snakes.

I backed away from the bed monsters, bumping into the chair. I tried to move it out of my way but it had gained one hundred or more pounds, my efforts fruitless. I blinked slowly at the light reflecting off the metal angles of the furniture. Continuing on I bumped into the table that was shrinking by the minute. I rubbed my eyes.

This isn't real. It can't be.

Something tiny and white caught my eye on the table then. Beads, dozens of beads. I leaned over the table as far as I could, squinting to see the microscopic gems. I looked up at the man in uniform again, saying something even I couldn't understand. He put his fingers to his ear then smiled at me.

"Candy," he said, so slowly and deeply I could barely put the syllables together. I stepped back, his smile expanding to curl up off his face. He reached down, popping one of the gems into his mouth and swallowed.

Jealousy erupted in me as I yelled at the man, grabbing as many of the candies as possible, hoarding them. I rambled again as I took a handful, popping them into my own mouth and swallowing them whole as I climbed the nearest metal mountain to keep possession of my treasure. The man in the white coat jumped forward to stop me a second too late, held back by the other man.

I started to laugh out loud, my hands expanding and shrinking at an alarming rate, my arms growing too heavy for my body. I fell, pain striking my leg in a burst. I looked down at my legs which had also grown huge.

My one limb was red, a stick of white coming from it. I laughed as I grabbed it, but the red attacked me, covering my hand like tiny ants. Shouting, I slapped my hand, the impossibly small red beings jumping off my skin onto my face. I screamed, trying to use my fingernails to rip the creatures off before they could go any further.

I was still screaming as one creature grew larger and larger and advanced up my body. It bit me once and I saw black.

Failure

I felt him watching me.

"Did it work?" I asked in a whisper, my throat raw.

"It was a valiant try," Rochester answered in his deep voice, shifting on the metal chair. "One more thing to cross off the list."

My mouth was dry, my body shivering against the concrete floor where I lay. My limbs were heavy as I lifted them. I could taste metal in my mouth and found the source on my tongue, its surface jagged and swollen from my own tooth marks. I tried to sit up and gagged. Still, I dragged my heavy body upright against the bed.

"There is always tomorrow," the man stood to leave.

Now half propped up, I saw blood on my hands and leg. I lifted my fingers, the thick burgundy coagulation flaking off in places.

"You climbed on top of the chair, balancing perfectly on the back. Then, without warning, you jumped off." Rochester took his fur cloak off the back of the chair. "It was quite amusing."

My overwhelming disappointment at my failure at death was offset by my other half.

Should we bleed you out and see how amusing it is?

The threat was empty—I was too weak to carry it out anyway.

I was sickened to find my lower leg jutting out at an odd angle, one of the bones broken and punched through the skin. The image made me queasy. "Will the doctor be attending to this?"

Rochester shrugged on his cloak. "I do not see how that is necessary. Not if we try again soon. Not tomorrow, of course, that was a joke. But I do not see much harm in allowing another chance within the week, do you?"

Another try at death, another suicide on my soul. And probably another failure to come, then another....

"No, I suppose not."

This will never end, I will be damned to this eternal abyss of pain forever.

I took deep breaths through the anxiety that was mounting.

The formality of Rochester's visit was interesting and yet unproductive. While it enlightened me to how I had broken my leg it provided no aid other than to let me know roughly when my next attempt would be. There had been no sense in arguing. Still, it was a little disheartening, to think that the injuries I would sustain between attempts would remain.

Hot food was delivered to me minutes later. I tried

to stand, avoiding pressure on my broken leg. I was determined to go to the bathroom but with my mangled appendage I couldn't make it on foot. I dragged myself to the table, turning my heavy chair around with difficulty and pulled myself onto it, eating the little I could keep down. When I was done I slipped the heavy tray out from under the place setting, taking it with me as I inched my way off the chair to the floor. Scooting to the bed I decided to deal with whatever came in the best way I could manage. I took the sheet off the end of the bed, using my fingers and teeth to pick at small loose threads in the fabric and tearing it into strips.

The door opened abruptly, the guard running in when I began banging the tray against the corner of the bed. He stopped short, watching my activity. I was unsure at first how I was going to use the tray to my advantage but ever so slowly the tray bent.

Winding a strip of linen around my bare leg over the injury, I twisted the cloth on itself twice and created a tourniquet. Sufficiently tight, I held the fabric in one hand while with the other I applied pressure with the heel of my hand.

Gritting my teeth in pain, I felt the bone shift. I screamed out in agony as it slipped back inside its cover of muscle and flesh. With shaking hands, I removed the tourniquet and put the tray, now an awkward squared-off U shape, around my leg to keep the bones straight. I wound the rest of the fabric around it and tied it off to keep it in place.

I was not convinced that it would set right at all, but at least the pain would be somewhat more manageable. With any luck, without the bone exposed I could avoid a massive painful infection as well.

You desire death and yet you aspire to avoid pain?

The guard stood with his jaw hanging open as I completed my mission, watching me lean back against the wall when I had finished. I only rested a moment— I had to try out my system to see if it would hold. I looked in the direction of the bathroom. I had pressing matters to take care of.

Using the wall for leverage, I stood, careful not to twist my injured leg. Once up, I put pressure on my foot. I cried out as pain shot up my limb, but at least the makeshift cast held. I stumbled to the bathroom slowly, using the toilet and then setting out to clean off my hands and exposed leg of the blood from my gruesome experience. The guard was waiting by the door, watching to see what would happen. I thought of asking if that were part of his orders and thought better of it, remembering what happened in my other cell when I asked questions.

Don't be stupid, neither noise nor silence is rewarded or punished here.

The days ahead were mindless, nothing to do but sit and do short laps around the room and try to heal. The guards were better, at least, than the others—they replaced my ruined sheet without question and stayed neutral in their treatment of me, giving me neither kindness nor malice.

Then one morning the guards carried in an oblong container of steaming hot water, a towel, and a fresh shift. They placed the container on the ground, the cloth items on the chair near it.

The young guard, who I recognized now as a regular, approached me uneasily. "I am supposed to ask if you need assistance. You need to bathe and dress to get presentable."

I considered the tub. It would be interesting getting in and out myself, but not impossible.

But to have the handsome man help me in would be a pleasure too....

I turned my gaze away in embarrassment for my other half's thoughts.

"I can manage." Mostly, I wanted to enjoy the luxury on my own with no spectators, especially the male guards who often watched me with a look of distasteful hunger.

When the water cooled slightly I awkwardly shuffled onto the edge of the container, swinging my left foot, the up damaged limb, into the wet heat.

I sat in the tub with my leg brought up against me in the water, my right leg draped on the edge, still bandaged. Lathering with the ball of soap left inside the tub, I washed my hair thoroughly of the dried blood that had been there since before I had been relocated. When I was finished, I hobbled out, the water thoroughly filthy, and dried my hair with the towel, water dripping onto the floor.

Scrubbing clean and dry with the cloth I was almost shocked to see the true color of my skin, stark white from being kept indoors without the sun for so long.

Discarding the bloodstained towel on the chair, I slipped the shift over my head. It was not quite as shapeless as the one before, and thankfully more modest, extending to just below my knees. I ran my fingers through my damp hair, taking the knots out where I could.

Dressing us up for our adoring psychopathic fans...you are pathetic....

Thoroughly scrubbed, dried, and dressed, I sat on the bed and waited for the audience to arrive for my next death.

Breathless

"You know this option usually does not take long, but you also know that we are trying to keep it realistic, so we will be altering this test slightly." Rochester's voice sounded as confident as ever as I stood, watching the people in the observation room.

There was nothing I could say, so I simply stared at the man and waited.

I had chosen asphyxiation this time, only because I felt almost human in my new shift and clean skin. It seemed a shame to ruin either with the messiness of blood from the slice in an artery or vomit and liquids from a poisoning. That, and I knew I would have to do it at some point—might as well get it over with. It was a purely rational answer.

Rational? Rational would be stealing something from a guard and using it to fashion a weapon and escape this hell.

Nearly ten minutes passed before my guards arrived, rolling a monstrosity into the room through the thin door. I was not entirely sure what I was looking at, but it resembled possibly the chassis of a car. I watched the men park the machine, then turn on the engine so it revved to life, the four leaving quickly.

"Suicide by car fumes is quite popular," Rochester piped up once more. "It will take a bit longer than it would in a garage, since the room is so big, but it was necessary to ensure the investors had a clear view." He leaned back in his chair so I could no longer see him. Only the smokey tendrils remained, drifting aimlessly above the other spectators.

I coughed as emissions began to build up in the room. Most of the haze rose up in front of the observation deck, obscuring the people's view.

It became hard to breathe. The exhaust made the air deadly right away. No desire to be injured further, I opted to sit where I eventually would end up.

I barely remembered the smell or feeling of doom as the fumes filled the bottom half of the room as well. I simply went to sleep. When I woke up later my lungs still stung from the toxins.

It was the easiest and most peaceful way I had ever died. I wish it had worked.

I knew it wouldn't.

When Rochester came to visit me next, he indicated his disappointment. "Those people are investing an awful lot of time and effort to be here for these tests. They expect a little flair."

Screw you.

Briefly, I was in accordance with my other half.

"So my deaths are not entertaining enough for them?" I choked on a laugh. "What do they want exactly? I'm not sure how much more fun I can make this." My voice grew loud and angry.

Don't waste our energy. Those people are privileged—they have never seen the true plight of man before. They are here for the entertainment value purely.

I knew what my counterpart said was right, but still I stared at Rochester, glaring with hatred.

The man shrugged. "They have started betting money on which test will do the job permanently. They are leaning toward the last one we have planned." At my shocked expression, he continued, "Healthy competition is good for their spirits, and the continued financial support of my endeavours."

Rochester let me pick the order of my demise. It was some small comfort, although not all of the details were ever disclosed. Either way, I knew I had another five tests. Next would be the weapon, then the poison. Since we had not had success thus far, my recovery to life seeming to come faster each time, extra tests had been added for good measure.

Last would be the hanging.

I agreed with the investors—there seemed little chance I would be able to come back from a broken neck and spinal column.

Rochester seemed unnerved by the prospect of my

permanent demise. I wasn't sure if that was because of some emotional attachment to me, or because he just liked watching me die. When the tests had been added I concluded the answer was the latter.

When it came to these last tests, Rochester had agreed to some extra conditions. After all, it was supposed to be as though I was choosing.

I was not surprised when the guards brought in another bathtub. Long and narrow, it was white with gold claw feet. I had to admit, it was beautiful. Rochester had good taste in the finer things in life, if nothing else.

The men grumbled as four of them heaved, lifting the tub off the wheeled trolley. They groaned and complained quietly as they brought bucket after bucket of scalding water and filled the tub. Finally full, the guards left, leaving behind the young one.

He must have been ordered to stay and observe, as the others had in the past. As he pulled the razor blades out from his pocket and put them on the far edge of the tub he glanced into my eyes miserably. I wondered if him staying to watch me die was his initiation into some higher order within the organization.

He was pale. He looked ill as he turned to stand by the door. I couldn't blame him. I myself felt like being sick. After all, I had not killed myself by slashing my own veins before. I hoped it would be quick and final.

No, it's not time yet—we must come back to finish

the job.

Again that disparity of the will to live versus the truth that I would die today existed.

I hoped, mostly for my guard's sake, that it would be a quick death. Knowing Rochester and his investor's penchant for flair, I knew it could not be.

Reaching out, I trailed my fingertips along the cool smooth rim of the tub, feeling the hot water gradually warm it. I looked down at myself. I had requested a new shift and would wear it throughout, no desire to be naked in front of the group of observers. Although the cloth was white and would be nearly see-through when wet, it would preserve a little of my modesty, something I did not see as an acceptable additional loss.

He has already taken almost everything else from me, it is enough.

Sticking out from the shift was my makeshift cast, the bent tray sticking out on either end. I sighed, knowing what would happen if the metal tray soaked in the heat of the water. I glanced up at the audience that was beginning to take interest in my actions, then reached down, trying to untie the knots on the strips. I had no desire to add severe burns to an already constantly aching appendage.

The knots had tightened in the weeks I had worn the cast. I sawed through the bindings with the first razor-blade, the tray falling to the floor with a loud clatter. I saw the spectators' eyes widen, faces turning my way. The people above were intrigued. I could almost imagine their mindless chitchat as they watched me work.

Discussing money and politics and the weather, I'm sure. No concern for our death.

The blade was effective, cutting through the fabric like butter. At least I knew that part would be easy when the time came.

As the last of the bindings fell down around my ankle, I saw a man and woman in the observation area cover their mouths with their hands. I looked down at my swollen red leg, the wound discolored with a tinge of green. I had an infection under my skin, although exactly where, I had no idea.

Placing the blade back down on the rim of the tub, I put my hands on the edge for stability as I climbed in. I bit my lip hard enough to draw blood as the hot water hit my wound, the sting going deep to my bone that was still partially exposed between the spreading gash in my flesh.

Breathe....pain is merely a reflex of the mind. It tells us to be careful—it tells us we are alive.

I lowered myself and watched the water slosh over the edge, appreciative that at least I could relax in the warmth before I would ultimately go cold. I closed my eyes, breathing deeply.

Minutes later I was aware of the many sets of eyes watching me, waiting. I opened my eyelids, looking up at the eight or so people, stopping when my sight met Rochester's. He barely nodded but it was enough of a movement that I understood.

It was time.

Remembering what the man had related about the investors wanting a show, I first made myself ready. Knowing that if I survived it was unlikely I would get another bath anytime soon, I lifted my left leg out of the water slowly, using the blade at just the right angle to shave off the fine layer of hair there. I was careful not to cut myself—they would get their blood soon enough.

The job didn't take long, my hairless limb lowered under the water's surface before I knew it. I raised my right leg and shaved carefully around the gash that now marred it. I lowered my throbbing leg back into the water and stared at the second blade, unused and sharp.

I didn't realize how long I was watching that tiny piece of metal until my guard cleared his throat uneasily. He must have been prompted by Rochester's voice in his earpiece.

I took a deep breath and struggled to calm the anxiety mounting in me. Once again, my hands were shaking, a common step in each of my alleged suicides. I was always nervous, anxious for the death to be over. Part of it was the impending disappointment I knew I would feel when it didn't work and I breathed again.

I told you, it isn't time yet.

I held my hands under the water to warm them, hearing a gulp coming from my own throat as I lifted one and grasped the sharp blade between three fingers.

I shifted in the tub uncomfortably—I had chosen it because I liked the idea of a clean death for once, none of my body fluids scattering on the floor or walls. Here, it could be contained.

Soon enough it will be their blood that will need to be contained.

I glanced once at the observation window, at the many eager pairs of eyes following the metal within my grasp.

Raising my right arm, I exposed the newly cleaned wrist. Bringing the blade to it, I applied a slight amount of pressure, feeling a prickle as the skin was cut. A fine line of red swelled against the metal, running in a small thread down my arm. I hesitated, no longer wanting this to be dramatic, no longer wanting to please the investors or Rochester.

I just wanted it to be over.

Again I met the man's eyes above, those of my proclaimed master, my gaze hardening. He shook his head slowly, reading my thoughts in that one single glimpse, warning me not to do what I silently threatened.

Do it, do it now.

I clenched my teeth and pushed hard with the blade, drawing it quickly down my lower arm.

I threw back my head, my eyelids slamming shut as pain blossomed through my wrist, my fingers becoming numb. I could feel my heartbeat above the point of the carving, echoing the hard drumming of my heart in my chest.

The blood flowed as though a river meeting an ocean, tinting the water pink immediately. I slumped in the water slightly, my arm growing tired and knowing that I was going to run out of time. I passed the blade from my left to right hand, pressing my numb fingertips around the item willing them to hold firm. I was uncertain if I would be able to do the deed twice.

I knew once I had the sharp tip to my left wrist that I had been in error—my right hand was too drained to be of help. Shifting in the tub, I pinned my right arm beside me under the water, the blade facing up, my fingers held around it. Without hesitation I brought my left wrist on it, hitting whatever spots I could. I felt the blade prick and slice a number of times, unsure if it would be enough.

A noise near the door caught my attention. The doctor rushed in, fumbling with his medical bag to remove his stethoscope and place it around his neck. "Damn training exercises, sorry I'm late," he mumbled just loud enough for myself and the guard to hear. His eyes met my dazed pale expression and he stopped short. He caught his breath, stifling a sound. "God." His expression changed to one of sadness and awe.

I blinked slowly, the water seeming colder now, the liquid sucking all warmth from my body as it chilled itself. My grip on the sides of the tub slipped, my body sinking further in. I craned my head back so my mouth remained out of the water but the life was pumping out of me. Consciousness was fleeing, practical thought escaping.

My blood was no longer clotting and I didn't have the strength to stay afloat.

"She'll fall beneath the water and drown." a faint voice said. I tried to identify the speaker and recognized it as the doctor.

"It won't be a true death by bloodletting," he finished, waiting.

I stared at the ceiling, blinking slowly again. My thoughts were so delayed. Everything felt like it was taking an eternity. I heard a muffled voice as my ears drifted beneath the water line. My head continued downwards, my eyes closing as the red liquid rushed over them. I tried not to breathe under water. My hair drifted above my head in wispy tendrils.

My lungs urged me in silent nudges for air, I filled my mouth with the metal-tainted aqua.

The blackness of death approached like a grim reaper, hobbling against his scythe, quiet and threatening. I welcomed it with open arms.

Deep within me, my other half argued, fighting against the impending tide.

Strong arms gripped under my armpits and pulled, dragging my torso above the water in one large tug. My head lolled forward, the water draining from my mouth. I let it dribble out, no strength left to cough.

I opened my eyes one last time, focusing on the doctor's kind face as he removed one of his hands from under me. He moved my head backwards, leaning it against the edge of the tub, smoothing the hair off my face. *This might add the drama the investors are looking for*. It was a gesture of unexpected gentleness in a cold sterile room of despair.

He gave me a reassuring smile then moved his fingers to my neck, measuring my pulse. "Not long now," he said to the observation window above.

I liked to think he was saying it for my benefit.

Drifting Away

Another day, another set of scars.

I stared at the lines on my wrists, jagged and irrationally made in the end. I wished that I had made more effort to think through the process, to at least have made the marks symmetrical. I was not a vain person, but if I had learned one thing about myself it was that the scars from my deaths always remained. The slices were closed now, healing to a bubbled pink. At some point they would hopefully become faintly white. That is, if I lived long enough.

It had been almost two weeks since I had cut myself. Since then, a sense of peace settled over me. Against my other half's judgement, I gave in to my master's mission completely. With the acceptance of my recurring fate, my life—if one could call my meagre existence a life—was easier.

My healing had been interrupted momentarily by the poisoning trial, an unpleasant event of consuming rat poison. I had become very, very sick. Surprisingly, the most injury I had gained from it, aside from my temporary death, was extremely sore stomach muscles from heaving over the toilet.

Of course, exercise could come in worse forms.

Rochester was not happy about the results from that test. I suppose he had expected something different, more dramatic, like what had occurred with the blades. Perhaps he had anxiously awaited foam coming from my mouth, my body dancing across the floor as seizures overtook me. But in the end, it was quick. I ate, I got sick, I collapsed in my own vomit, dead.

With the last scheduled trial, the hanging, approaching, he decided to leave nothing to chance. The man had his guards bring in the rope, attaching it firmly to the ceiling beam. They put it out of my way in case I had thoughts of trying it myself before the appointed date. I wouldn't get the luxury of killing myself prematurely.

What a bizarre thought.

They tested the height, ensuring it would be correct, the stretch of it so I wouldn't jump off the table and merely break my legs. Then they rose it, adjusting for my slight weight and size. They brought in a pair of boots for me, making sure my feet would fit them. A guard told me they were going to be fitted with weights—enough to make sure that my neck would snap with the distance and weight combined.

One day before the event, they brought in a maid around my size, gagging her and placing her head within the noose to make sure it would fit all the criteria, making me watch. Her eyes had teared up and she struggled to get out with muffled pleas, but the guards had ensured escape was fruitless.

Like I said, Rochester was leaving nothing to chance.

The guards left me alone after that to contemplate the act I was to commit later that week. Mostly I looked over my many new cuts and scars and my mangled leg. I hoped this would be the last injury I was to sustain. I hoped it would be my final trial, that the rope, weighted boots, and gravity proved true and led me to my eternal rest. Somehow, it didn't seem fair that my twenty-year-old body, possibly twenty-one now, should have so much evidence of so much violence.

I heard a clang as the young guard brought in my tray of food, setting it on the table. He had been strange toward me since that first day he had watched me die.

I got off the bed, limping on my bad leg toward the table. I hadn't bothered to re-bandage my wound after the bath long ago. There didn't seem much point to it. The wound opening had more or less healed, a bulbous lump under the skin where the tip of the bone still pressed, the flesh still flaming hot, red lines snaking their way across the skin. It was the angle it had healed at that was more of the inconvenience: I now walked with the one leg making my hip a good inch and a half shorter than the other.

With any luck, my discomfort is almost over.

I took the top off the tray, seeing a sugary pastry there along with my usual hearty 'last meal' customarily given to me the night before a trial. My eyes widened at the luxury.

"The doctor said it was for good luck." The guard shrugged, leaving the room.

I should have known.

I enjoyed my meal, or as much as one could enjoy a stew with limp vegetables and some kind of meat drowning in a thickened gravy-like broth. The full meal was not provided out of compassion, it was merely a way to ensure I had strength for the next days ahead. I downed it with a cup of water and a slice of bread, freshly baked. It was a welcome change to the usual dry toast and gruel twice a day.

I thought about saving the pastry for later, perhaps a midnight snack, but the thought of the treat was too inviting. In the end, I decided on one bite, just enough to satisfy my curiosity but not enough to make me ill. France had been the last time I had eaten such sweetness and I doubted my body could handle it anymore.

I lifted the pastry gently, the flaky sugar-coated surface breaking off in parts and falling to the plate. The dessert was almost to my lips when I looked down, noticing the note. Underneath the pastry, written on a small honey-smeared piece of napkin were the words "Eat all."

I recognized parts of the handwriting as the

doctor's, seen a few times as he would write a note in his book that he carried with him containing all his patient's ailments. Debating whether or not to trust in the suspicious message, I considered the alternative.

I looked up the wall at the wavering shadow of the noose, dangling five feet above my head. The rope was my fate, my chance to end this miserable existence, if my soul would only give in to the perpetual death licking at my heels.

Screw death. We won't die for good until they do.

I shook my head, silently telling my other half that dying was inevitable.

I don't mind dying—as long as they do it first.

Opening my mouth, I took a large bite of the item.

It was flavorful and so very sweet. I continued chewing and swallowing, and wondered if I would make it through the entire dessert as my stomach knotted. Popping the last bite into my mouth, I grabbed the glass, draining the water and swallowing.

I waited, sure something would happen. Instead, it grew late, my stomach cramping from the pastry's sweetness.

Once, I had been so bored that I had counted the seconds in Mississippi's until the time had reached thirty minutes and the ventilation fan noise began. A series of counting in succession had proved the pattern. It was my only way to gauge time here, but I appreciated the consistency that I could live out my existence in the room by. I could tell by the intervals that three hours had passed when I finally decided to get up from the chair.

I moved to stand and my hand slammed down on the table to stabilize me. My legs were like jelly, my arms not much help. I took a step forward with a foot that felt like a lead brick and fell down, rolling as I went.

Landing on my side hard, I tried to groan but my tongue lolled numbly. I could at least swallow and my eyes were open, scanning the room slowly, willing help to enter.

The bastard poisoned us.

A commotion outside my door caught my attention through scattered thoughts. My head flopped to the side, too heavy to hold up anymore. A bang reverberated through the metal door as something hit it. Again it sounded, and again. One last time saw the door burst open, a body falling into the open doorway, the death-stricken eyes wide in surprise. The young guard, probably trying to protect me, just doing his job.

Or trying something else—he was the one to deliver the plate.

Intruders entered, dressed in grey-black clothes head to toe, ski-mask type fabric covering most of their faces. They looked around, the tall one pointing actions to the others who went back to the door to guard. The tallest one, towering a head above the others, studied the room, staring at the noose above with narrowed eyes filled with fury before his gaze rested on me.

His expression changed and although the only thing exposed was his eyes, I saw the worry there etched in them. He rushed over to kneel on one knee, looking over my body. He reached down to grasp my wrist gently as he examined the healing slashes, seeing the awkward way my leg lay, the flesh still odd-colored over the once-torn gash. He nodded and blinked tears from his eyes.

Removing his mask, the intruder, a young man, put a hand through his short hair, slicking it back. He shook his head at me. "Don't worry, we'll take care of you." His voice was familiar, but when he moved to put a hand under my back and legs to pick me up, I panicked.

My eyes grew wide with fear, my thoughts slow and jumbled from the drugs I had been fed. Logically, I knew staying would bring only tragedy. But leaving, it seemed unfathomable. It was my place to stay, to see through with the hanging, to reach my never-ending death.

Loud words could be heard by the door as the doctor stumbled in, tripping over the body of the guard. He startled at the sight, beginning to bend down to check for a pulse when one of the other intruders stopped him with a hand to his arm and a shake of the head.

Shaken, the doctor turned toward us. Seeing I was in distress he too came over and knelt by my side, his voice frantic. "He's coming with reinforcements. If he catches us...."

"He won't," the familiar young man responded, "not if we leave now."

Why can't I remember his name?

My head lolled as the men picked me up, the tall one supporting my slight frame easily. The doctor draped a blanket over me, tucking it in. If nothing else, it helped to preserve my modesty as the white shift moved precariously as I was lifted. He instructed the young man that I needed to be kept warm. I glared at the doctor as my eyes rested on him.

"Don't blame me," the doctor pleaded, "drugging you was the easiest way to ensure this would work." He looked up at the noose still dangling. "I couldn't let them do that to you. Not again."

I jumped at the loud bang as the bullet shot through his forehead, his eyes growing wide momentarily before the light left them, his soul gone before his body hit the ground. A quick trickle of blood escaped and ran down his face. It took my slowed brain a moment to realize the shot had come from outside the doorway.

"Take cover!" the man holding me yelled, putting me down and reaching out to shove his weight against the heavy metal table. I watched as the muscles in his arms corded and strained through his shirt and the table shifted. Another of the intruders, the hump on her vest divulging her gender as female joined him, pushing with arms outstretched.

The table crashed sideways to the ground, providing perfect cover from the bullets now littering the air around us. The unmasked man pulled at my blanket, bringing me closer to him and out of harm's way. He pulled a device from his backside, speaking into it quickly and listening for a response. The other intruder listened to him as he spoke to her in code, then ran to convey the message to the others, now hiding behind the bed which they had also pushed over for cover.

The man took my face in his hand, his thumb and index fingers around my chin as he turned my face toward his. "We're leaving," he said softly. "You need to trust me."

The strange thing was, I did.

Flying

The roof blew out seconds after that in a bright array of explosions and cascading sparks from the debris and electrical in the ceiling. A helicopter high above dropped a rope ladder into the room we occupied. The man had donned his mask again while I was distracted by the bright light of day and attached a harness around me and my blanket, hovering over me to protect me from any of the ceiling's falling structure.

He yelled at the others to get on the ladder, the three acknowledging and throwing themselves onto it, climbing up like monkeys. Taking out his gun, the man stood, laying down a round of bullets and shooting a canister into the fray. Gas billowed from it, my eyes tearing as he hoisted my body and clipped my harness to his and then to the rope. He put one foot onto the ladder, his hand gripping a rung while the other arm wrapped around me tightly.

We began to rise, flying through the air as we finally cleared the building. The ladder was slowly pulled up hand over hand by the other intruders. As we got closer to the helicopter, I blinked slowly, for a moment relishing in the feeling of fresh air against my face as the blanket shifted down, my tangled locks whipping around wildly. The sensation was short-lived as it was replaced by my thoughts.

We might be free, we might be saved!
Or I could be damned.

I was terrified. The consequences of being caught by Rochester while in the thrall of escaping were too horrifying to dwell on, but they were there nonetheless. It paralyzed me with fear as I watched my prison become smaller and my rescuer brought me closer to the freedom my other half grasped for.

At the helicopter finally, several hands came down to hoist me aboard as the young man aided in pushing me up. Once inside, I saw him come over the edge as they pulled him in as well. They moved me against one wall for the moment, the intruders removing their masks, revealing a band of teenagers and young adults.

The young man grabbed a medical kit and came over to wipe my face and eyes with a wet cloth, the stinging sensation I had been feeling from the gas subsiding. Handing the med-kit and a bottle of water to the next oldest person, the man left to speak with the pilot. I could overhear his questions. He was concerned about the rest of his team.

I looked at the woman treating me with wide eyes, flinching as she tucked my hair back and spoke in soothing tones. She looked over the injuries she could and sighed when I resisted her help. Shaking her head in defeat she offered me the water instead but I would not drink anything she held out. Despite the good will, I couldn't help but feel this was another test. I refused to fail. I couldn't.

It wasn't worth Rochester's ire.

The ride turned out to be a long one, the team members each taking a seat and strapping themselves in upright as they stretched out for a deserved sleep. They hadn't been able to strap me in due to my protests, but the drug the doctor had doped me with and the drop in adrenaline was taking a toll. I rested sideways on the floor, my head on my rescuers folded-up jacket, laying wrapped in my shift and blanket.

I looked around at each soldier, my eyes resting at last on the young man who had chosen the seat closest. While he looked to be only a few years older than me, he possessed an air of confidence I envied. He was staring at me, his pupils boring into mine. Smiling gently, he unstrapped himself and moved to the floor, shuffling toward me. He sat down after pulling two blankets from a compartment nearby and laying another one over my body.

"The doctor said you needed to stay warm," he responded after the kind gesture, his face falling. "It's too bad, he was a good man." He looked at my face, my eyes still big with anticipation of what was to come.

"They all volunteered, you know," he broke his gaze to look over the dozing individuals. "All of these soldiers wanted to be there, to help rescue you." He paused. "We weren't even sure if you were still alive until the doctor sent a message...."

I wanted to thank him for his efforts, to apologize for any team members he might have lost. His melancholy when he had come back from talking to the pilot made me think there were at least a few. But fear stopped me. I couldn't risk Rochester finding out, the punishment wouldn't be worth it. At the same time, this man and his people had saved me from possibly my successful death, which I had both dreaded and looked forward to.

I wasn't sure if I liked the prospect of living. I had accepted the possibility of death so very long ago, embraced the idea gratefully during my suicide trials.

The man saw my inner turmoil and pursed his lips. I shifted under his observation. He moved, going to fix the bottom half of the blanket as it had slipped off my legs. Seeing the right leg jutting out, he cursed, the words harsh from his lips. "One day," he began, staring at my mangled limb, "one day will you tell me what happened to you?"

I considered for a moment, then nodded. I felt somehow it was the least I could do.

The Walk

We touched down as the sun peeked over the horizon, blocked out by the tall buildings in the skyline. The pilot had guided the helicopter slowly through the enormous hanger entranceway and touched the landing rails to the ground effortlessly, shutting off the rotor blades and turning down the engines. The double-wide door of the aircraft was opened, the pilot nodding to the inhabitants.

The young soldiers yawned and rubbed feeling back into their legs as they stood, arching their sore backs and jumping out with a tired effort. The young man beside me spoke to them with authority, telling them to report back at a certain hour for debriefing.

Some began unclipping the many guns and ammo they stored on them, undoing the fastenings for their bullet-proof vests as they trudged. Other people in the hanger trailed them, collecting the weapons and garments before they hit the ground.

I stayed behind, tired but nervous, watching from my sideways view laying on the floor. I was not sure where my place was here. I sat up with some difficulty, feeling finally back in my tingling limbs, holding the blanket around me tighter. The young man helped me arrange them and reassured me again that everything would be all right, his chocolate brown eyes holding mine without the pity or disgust I would have anticipated.

An older man appeared in the doorway, out of breath, his peppered hair disheveled. He wore a smart grey suit, his tie flung over his shoulder. His blue eyes grew wide on his chiseled fair face as they rested on me. He opened his mouth to speak as he flushed, looking over my appearance, but his deep gasps of air prevented him. My other half wanted me to stand up straight in respect.

He's one of them, their leader.

I didn't move, didn't ask how my other half knew. I felt it too.

A doctor came in the doorway, recognizable by her white coat, a gurney and other medical staff behind her. The younger man next to me shook his head in warning at the newcomers. "You can walk, if you'd like." I met his gaze and saw within it a flurry of images. A young woman, my former self, stood tall and suited up in the same grey-black garb. She was taking precise aim in target practice, fighting with an admirable efficient fluidity. I could feel the man's pride.

I looked away, ashamed at the twig of a thing I was now. Still, somehow he knew I needed to walk out on my own. Extending his hand out to me, he smiled softly.

I took a deep breath and grasped my blanket tight in the front, taking his hand with my other gingerly. Although this test of Rochester's seemed to be highly elaborate, I didn't have much choice but to cooperate. Standing slowly, I wavered slightly but stayed up. The young man helped me off the helicopter, effortlessly raising my legs over his arm as he lifted me like a child and passed me to the ground below. The older man reached out to take me and I recoiled. The doctor, a woman with wide eyes and a fiery spirit my other half responded to, put a hand on the suit's shoulder and shook her head, offering her hand out for stability instead.

I looked down at the creamy skin, the perfectly manicured nails, and lifted my own digits, the fingers bony and white, nail beds uneven and caked with the-gods-only-knew what despite my recent bath. I turned over my hand to find my palm scored with small cuts, below them the healing scars of my bloodletting suicide.

I quickly lowered my wrist, shaking my head as I stepped back and bumped into the tall firm form of my rescuer. His hands came gently to my shoulders, lending their silent support.

We started to walk.

The older man, the doctor, and some of the team members flanked me on all sides as we travelled the halls, set by my agonizingly slow pace. My limp prevented me from going too fast. Doors opened on either side as we strolled out of the darkened hanger bay and hallway, up a large lift, through the main hall. Children in all states of dress cameout to watch the spectacle although I doubt they saw much, their view of me obstructed by my entourage. Still, I was glad I had chosen to walk on my own, though my leg was aching fiercely now, wobbly from the exertion.

There is strength in pain, and pride in persevering, my other half encouraged me.

We reached an elevator at the end, large enough to accommodate most of us. A few of the team members said their good-nights there, to finish sleeping off the mission, I assumed. The door closed, the elevator moving gently. Suddenly exhausted myself, I leaned against the young man inadvertently, drawn to his warmth. He looked down at me with a soft smile on his lips and asked, "Would you like my help?"

I wanted to say no as my other half adamantly denied the aid, but nodded once instead. I was in no condition for a hike such as this and my strength was rapidly declining.

He carefully lifted me as before, one hand under my knees, one behind my back, cradling me. By the time we reached the infirmary, my limbs were shaking, as much from the aftershock as from the continued recession of drugs from my system. I could feel them waning, the surge of tranquilizer-gun numbness giving way to pure exhaustion.

I was put into a warm bed and with the young man nearby, drifted into a thankfully peaceful sleep.

In and out of consciousness for days, I recalled violent outbursts I made, worried glances and syringes being dispensed into the many tubes that fed into my veins. I remember restraints. I remember heated discussions between the doctor and the older man.

I finally emerged with a few wide blinks to a state of more permanent wakefulness. At first I was frightened, only the sound of the heart-rate monitors nearby to keep me company. Within seconds of the beeping becoming rapid, the doctor appeared, looking relieved. She turned to the nearest nurse, making a terse request then gave me her attention once more. I looked around frantically at the tubes sticking out of my arms, the bandages on my wrists and white wrappings over my elevated leg. My fingers were clenched tightly, my knuckles white as I contemplated my escape only to realize there was none. I could see two soldiers standing outside my door, baring the exit.

I heard yelling as an argument erupted outside of the room. The doctor huffed and spun on her heels, going to the door to resolve the issue quickly. Quiet resumed once more. The young man entered with flush cheeks, looking grateful to her. He approached slowly and smiled.

My hands unclenched a bit.

"I don't know how exactly they did all this but you have a lot of scarring internally," the doctor stated carefully, standing back at my side. She spoke directly to me but explained for the benefit of the man. "We put salve on your wrists to try to help the rest of the healing. With any luck some of the marks will disappear. As for your leg," she paused hesitantly, "we ended up having to remove the infected bone and replaced it with an artificial one. We had to reopen the point of infection—it was a mess." She moved to pat my hands that were now grasping the corner of the blanket tightly but she thought better of it. "It's a wonder you didn't die of blood poisoning or the infection itself."

Taking notice of her speech finally, I glanced up at her words.

She doesn't know. She can't.

At the impending silence and intent stares between the young man and I, the doctor cleared her throat. We watched her adjust the drip on one of my IVs and leave the room with a nod and a promise to return.

"They need you to stay off your feet for a week at least, to let the injuries heal and get your strength back," the young man moved quietly and pulled up a chair. "I can stay here with you if you would like." He waited for confirmation.

I lowered my eyes and shook my head.

I grieved my current state, the fact that I was alive and apparently going to stay so, kept invalid for now by the medical devices around me. *And I can't accept that this is another test if you are around me, being so kind. ...*

The young man acknowledged my decision with a smile of disappointment as he got up immediately to leave. He walked toward the door.

But we need him.

"I know you," I half questioned.

The man stopped short. "You know all of us, for the most part." He turned and came back to the bed slowly, standing at the end. He rested his hands on the footboard. "You grew up here, with me, with us."

My gaze drifted off as I tried to remember, tried to force my brain to validate something about my childhood...anything of my life before.

"I'm sure it will come back to you eventually." The man came around hesitantly. "Do you want me to tell you some things, see if it helps?"

I nodded for what seemed like the millionth time since he had rescued me.

Sitting down in a nearby chair, he crossed his arms. "You came here when you were very young…."

He told me we had met when we were both children, getting to know each other better when I had been assigned to the team. He explained what they were, their objectives. Young soldiers, hand-picked from the wide selection of fresh students at the school, trained to a noble cause to ease the suffering of the world outside.

As he spoke, food arrived and the young man arranged it on the wheeled table nearby. He helped me sit up slightly through my painful grunts, trying not to move my leg too much, bringing the meal to me. I warmed up to the man, whose name I had finally remembered—Tomlin. He was easy going with me and I suspected we had been good friends once, the feeling only emphasized by his thorough knowledge of what I had been before.

We talked late into the night, enjoying each other's company even if the conversation was mostly one-sided.

As the first signs of light hit the window pane and spilled into the room, Tomlin stretched in his chair. "I'd better go," he stood. "I have...something I need to go do."

"A mission?" I asked quietly.

He nodded. "Prep for one, yes." He saw my face fall, not wanting him to go. "Hey." He leaned over, placing a hand over mine. "I will be back soon. And when I am, we can talk more."

My eyes lowered to our hands, my white bony digits slight under the healthy pink of his. Even so, my lips turned into the slightest smile, unseen by the man as he left.

The doctor checked on me again several times that day, unwrapping my bindings. She was right, the salve was working on my scars, the many cuts disappearing to a faint white. As she unwound my bindings on my leg I struggled to sit up. Smiling sympathetically, she pressed a button on the bed, raising the back so I could see.

My leg below the knee was flaccid and skinny, the muscle mass all but gone. A large line down the front where they had cut me open was held shut by neat white stitches. Still the skin was discoloured, the mass of the area red and inflamed. She saw my shock. "It will heal fairly cleanly and we can use the salve after to see if it helps the scar," she watched my gaze. Deftly, she wrapped it in new bandages then sat down slowly in the chair next to my bed.

"I did a thorough exam when you came in. You were highly malnourished, extremely low weight for someone of your height and stature. There were...unexplained injuries: head trauma, damage to your lungs and organs and many marks on your face and arms where someone obviously sewed you up." She paused. "In order to treat you properly I am going to need to know what happened."

I looked away. I wasn't ready to divulge the horrors I had lived, the injuries that had been afflicted, many by my own hands.

"You may experience some psychological side-effects also: memory loss, anxiety, difficulty staying in this time and place. It is expected, given the circumstances—" She sighed and stood as her wristband beeped. She glanced at it. "I'm sorry, I have to go see another patient. Will you be all right here alone?"

I looked down at my folded hands and nodded. As she closed the door behind her it occurred to me that— except when my companion had been with me, or when someone had been snuffing out my life, I had been completely alone while in captivity. Still, I wasn't used to it. I didn't think I would ever get used to being without a friendly face, a welcoming home.

I didn't know if I ever wanted to be without it again.

Commitment

The sun seemed to set early that day. I found myself wondering what season it was. Despite the window along one side of the room, the view was of a tall building in the distance, betraying nothing of the time of year. I hoped it was winter. At least then my convalescence wouldn't be wasted when sun and warmth could be enjoyed.

I noticed a pad of paper left on the bedside table and enjoyed ripping the crisp white pages off, slowly folding, crumpling, and tearing them to create my own illusion of snowflakes, snowmen, and angels. I wanted to laugh at my little creations, barely recognizable as anything but balls of paper.

Fairly content since my delivery to the infirmary, kept subdued by the pain-killers sourcing through my veins, my other half rumbled in quiet enjoyment.

"Having fun?" an older man's voice permeated the space. My head snapped up to view the doorway. It was the pepper-haired man. StPatrick, Tomlin had called him. "May I come in?" he asked, his hands in the pockets of his perfectly tailored suit.

I nodded, swiping the pieces of paper off my lap and onto the floor beside me.

The fifty-something-year-old man was impeccably dressed as he walked casually into the room. His tie was perfect, the knot centered along his neckline, his buttons straight, his black shoes polished to a shiny glow. He stopped beside the bed and leaned down, grasping one of the angels. "Solstice on the mind?" He straightened with the item between his fingers.

I looked up into his eyes. "Happier times," I said, barely above a whisper. I had decided being silent would not benefit myself or the others around me. At least, to some degree.

The man licked his lips and nodded, understanding. He took the seat beside me. "It is unfortunate I have to tell you it is still the summer, then. But we will have snow before you know it." He had an odd accent, like he had once been elsewhere, perhaps Europe, but had now been assimilated so thoroughly into this society that it was but a fleeting memory. Eerily, it sounded similar to the accent Rochester had.

He took a deep breath. "Do you know who I am?" he asked softly but with an air of pronounced authority.

I nodded. "StPatrick."

He bobbed his head and leaned over, resting his elbows on his knees as he folded his fingers together. "I wanted to see you, now that you are coherent."

Tomlin had told me the man ran the school as well

as the training for the teams we belonged to—or, rather, that I used to belong to. With his stories dancing around in my head, I thought perhaps I was beginning to remember. "Why?"

"To see if you were all right. To offer my help if needed. And..." he hesitated and sighed uncomfortably, something that seemed out of character for him, "to ask some questions."

I knew what he would ask. I knew he had to. But I didn't want to talk now, or ever, about what had occurred in the prison-like complex. I also knew it was part of the healing process, if indeed this rescue was for real and not a figment of my imagination or a ploy of Rochester's. "I know." I looked away.

Relieved that I would comply, the man sat up straight in his chair and removed a device from his pocket. He tapped the screen a few times, lighting up the display. "It will record the conversation, if that is all right with you," he responded to my look. "Any details you provide may be helpful. We are hopeful to prevent this from ever happening again."

I chewed on my lip lightly. "Tomlin wanted to hear."

Immediately, StPatrick shook his head. "I will not allow it." The abruptness of his statement startled me.

"I know that you two were once good friends, and I am eager to see that relationship renewed," he. said, halting briefly. "But Tomlin is a good man, light-hearted. He would not be able to stand hearing what I suspect you are going to tell me."

I drew in a deep breath and met his eyes. He was the same as Rochester, I was sure of it. Not in the malicious, evil, conniving sort of way, but in that he too could read the expressions and silent actions within one's mind. He knew I was agreeing, albeit hesitantly.

"What do you remember?" he began.

I started with the days I had spent in my nice room, my companion by my side. I did not include all the details but only those which came to mind at the time: her description, her kindness, my care. I did not tell him about Rochester, or about the meeting in his office.

Absentmindedly, I told him about the room that had been opened for us, the equipment it contained. My mind was replaying the events as though a movie on fast forward and I told him the events as they occurred.

"My companion told me the doctor had worked hard to bring me back from death that time," I shuddered, reliving my experience with the red beast in the exercise room that I had misjudged and which had ultimately caused my death yet again.

His interest piqued. StPatrick leaned forward quickly, the shiny expensive shoe he had been resting on his knee banging on the floor as it fell. He frowned. "He said you had died?" his voice came out rushed.

My lips closed as I realized what I had just told him. I thought back to the conversation with my companion and nodded silently.

Instead of looking shocked, the man was merely

contemplative. "Was that the first time?" he asked, his thoughts seeming to drift off.

Tell him all of it, my other half warned.

When I didn't answer, he met my eyes. I knew he would be able to tell if I lied to him. We held each other's gaze for a while until I broke the hold. He continued to stare.

A soft rap came at the door, artificial light filtering in from the outside as it opened.

StPatrick stood and motioned to a teenage girl who entered with a tray of food, enough helpings for two. She set down the tray, looking admiringly at me for a moment and dipped her head in a sort of bow, backing out and closing the door once more.

"Do you remember, when you were part of the team, that we would debrief you after every mission?" my old commander asked, shaking his head at the girl's display and walking over to the window, looking out at the scene below.

I remembered coming home exhausted, yet fulfilled. I would often be smeared with blood, sometimes my own, and rub a towel across my face before going into a small room to retell what occurred. "A little." I reached for a glass of water.

StPatrick came back to my bedside. "I would like to believe that on the day you were captured, you had returned to us to rejoin. I do not see any other reason you would come back." He held up a hand as I opened my mouth to speak. "But, if that is true, then you were one of ours again which means your abduction made you a prisoner of war as far as I am concerned." His face softened. "Now that you are back, well...." He sat down slowly. "Consider this your debriefing."

The man's reasoning was sound. I remembered I had in fact returned to do just that, help out where I could. I knew full well that meant re-joining the cause. I straightened a little in my bed, wincing at the tug on my leg. "Yes, sir." Even if I had wanted to argue, there was no point—to do his job effectively, the commander-in-chief before me needed to know what he was sending his teams up against.

StPatrick nodded at the words and opened some of the food containers for the both of us. "This time, start at the beginning."

So I did, from the day I left the school, my one true home, to the plains of Africa, the cold hinterland of Switzerland, the posh restaurants of Paris. I told him of the train rides across Europe, the glamorous architecture of Germany and Prussia, the standing stones of the highlands, and the historical menagerie that was England. I mentioned the offhanded news report I had seen of the school under attack and the decision I had made. I told him of the day I had returned, my capture.

I had just finished answering some of StPatrick's questions about that time when the door swung open, Tomlin stepping through. He stood straighter, his hands dropping stiffly to his side when he saw my visitor. "Sir. I apologize. I came to see the patient." He smiled kindly in my direction, heedless of the commander watching him. Seeing the older man reach over and tap the device to stop the recording, my friend's smile disappeared.

"Sir, may I ask what you are doing here?"

His elder pocketed the device and smiled. "Just seeing how she was faring. The doctor was updating me on her condition and I thought I would take a peek in."

Tomlin looked over the plates and glasses, bits of food dried to the edges as they had sat for awhile. "Sir, I have a right to listen if you were debriefing her."

He is good at this, at observations, my other half noted with respect.

StPatrick stood, at his full height a mere few inches shorter than Tomlin. "No, son, you do not—go back to your quarters."

I looked between the men as they sized each other up. Neither budged. I felt my other half raise up, intrigued by the prospect of an even match between the two.

"Actually, sir,"—Tomlin's gaze was cool, his chin raised in defiance— "I do. She had just recommitted herself to my team when the man with the cigar—"

"Rochester," I interrupted by mistake. Both men looked down at me in surprise. "His name...it's Rochester."

Tomlin pursed his lips and looked back up at StPatrick, a new fury in his eyes. "When... Rochester...injured and took her, she was one of mine. So by all rationale she was my team member. She was my responsibility and therefore it is my job to be here as she tells the details."

Sneaky devil—who knew he had deception in him?

StPatrick knew he was lying but instead of calling him out on it he looked down at me. "Is this true?"

He knew it wasn't. I had just retold what had happened that day and no oaths were spoken. Instead, he was giving me the choice, whether to allow the young man to hear or not. If he stayed, I knew this also meant I was back in for sure and would be committing the young man's involvement. I wasn't sure if that was something I wanted yet, but I knew I wanted the option kept open at least.

"It is," my whisper came out tender instead of the strong statement I had intended.

Our commander held out a finger in front of Tomlin's face. "If I let you stay, these events, they never happened beyond these walls. Not until I know what to do with them."

I stared at StPatrick. *He is planning something.*

The young man nodded, relieved that his bluff hadn't been called. He turned to find a chair. "Tomlin," StPatrick grabbed his upper arm, stopping him, "no retaliation, not yet. We do it *when* I say, *how* I say."

Tomlin, always the good Captain, straightened his

back, ready to argue, but backed down against the other man's expression. He gestured for StPatrick to sit and stepped to the opposite wall, pulling a chair over for himself.

"This could take a while." I hoped the men had engagements that would take them away from me.

Tomlin's gaze was cool but prepared for the worst. "We have all the time in the world."

Restraint of Silence

With both men settled, StPatrick drew out the recording device once more, putting it on the nightstand and tapping it active. He nodded in encouragement as I continued where I had left off, describing the conversation I had with the doctor, my guards, the situation I found myself in when I had awoken in the complex.

At StPatrick's insistence, I went into detail about the cell, the room the trials were done in, the trials themselves. After my second death, he reached up to stroke his chin, something that made me wonder what he knew and what he was now thinking.

After the description of each death, Tomlin's face grew increasingly red, the anger mounting behind his eyes. I noticed the muscles in his upper arms bulge as he balled his fists. StPatrick noticed too and shook his head, closing his eyes as he did so.

It wasn't entirely intentional that I left out the details of my meetings with Rochester in his office. My mind simply skipped over the events, perhaps in a method of coping. But StPatrick was too observant—he saw the shiftiness in my eyes.

"Is that all?" he asked about my time in the cell. I had already disclosed about the false rescue, the men folding their arms and smiling in admiration at the fact that I had been able to determine it as such.

I nodded silently.

"Are you sure?" he insisted. I wondered if he was trying to make Tomlin leave the room or to do something foolish. "If there is something else...."

"It doesn't need to be said," I answered through gritted teeth.

The tension was heavy between us. Tomlin hissed. "We should hear it, if there is anything more...."

I closed my eyes, trying to block out the memory of the burning flesh, my own screams as the brand dug into my thigh. "He saved me from a greater threat." I went quickly into the meeting in Rochester's office, the branding, the guards after. I had no desire to relive the feelings of that day, the smells or sounds my body excreted as it was violated in so many ways.

As one hand reached down over the blanket on my thigh under which the brand burned in memory, the other went to my head, a pounding recollection of the gash and pain of my beating.

I flopped back in the bed, mentally exhausted from the re-telling.

"You should let her sleep." The doctor came around the corner, her sensible shoes making barely a squeak on the hardwood. She didn't look impressed, her arms crossed over her breasts.

Tomlin stood with respect for the woman.

"My good doctor, how long have you been standing there?" StPatrick asked coolly as he raised an eyebrow. He moved to straighten his suit jacket, only to drop his hands in apparent remembrance that he had removed it some hours ago.

The doctor did not shy away from his gaze. She stepped around the unused divider in the room—the other bed in the room lay vacant due to my situation. "Long enough to know that if even half the things happened that she said happened, this young woman should be getting as much rest as she possibly can, not reliving her horrors."

"Time could be of the essence, doctor," StPatrick said calmly, "and you should be checking in on your other patients."

"No," the woman dragged out the word as she stepped closer to the man, turning at the last second to come by my bedside. She unwrapped my leg carefully. "What I should be doing is checking in on *this* patient every few hours, ensuring no infection remains, checking her fluid levels. This is something your overly long visit has prevented me from doing until now." She peeled back the gauze from over my stitches, shaking her head. "Damn."

I tried to see, but the angle I was sitting at prevented it. Tomlin stood instead, looking over the bandages at the wound. He sucked in his breath. "That doesn't look good." At the doctor's pointed instruction he wheeled a cart over with medical tools.

The doctor turned away, selecting her instrument carefully. "It's not. I was worried about this—the infection taking over somewhere else." She slowly poked and prodded a few areas, causing me to grab the sides of the mattress in pain. I tried to hold still, clenching my teeth.

"I'm sorry," she apologized, tenderness in her voice. "I can't give you anymore pain killers right now." She went back to work, cleaning the area as best she could. Minutes later she threw the small metal tools in a basin for sanitizing. "That's the best I can do." She considered the limb, touching it with her hands gently to gauge the temperature. "We'll let it breathe for a while, see if that helps."

Putting the trolley by the wall and the basin next to the door for retrieval, the doctor returned with her hands on her hips. "Now, *Mister* StPatrick." She looked down at the headmaster, unamused. "My patient is going to get some rest. Please take Mr Ryder and leave."

I looked at Tomlin. I had never bothered to learn his last name in the past, not that I recalled, at least. When you worked and lived with someone for so long since such a young age it hardly seemed necessary. He gave me a reassuring smile.

Tensions between his superiors increased. They

were glaring at each other, daggers in their expressions as they battled silently for control.

The doctor is strong and spirited. I like her.

She is challenging our commander. She is either stupid or—

I shook my head slightly. Whatever the doctor was, she was no idiot.

"I cannot do that and you know it, Catherine," StPatrick said firmly. "I need to know everything. The sooner you leave, however, the sooner we can finish." At the doctor's dagger-look the older commander glanced my way. "Fine. Then let your patient decide."

I observed the expressions of both, each hopeful in their own way. I closed my eyes for a moment, gathering my thoughts.

I don't want to do this. The doctor is giving me an out.

We have to—our commander demands it.

I can't. I won't.

We will.

I reached up with both hands to rub my face. "Doctor," I began, lowering my hands into my lap. "Please, just let me finish now so I don't ever have to do it again." My look pleaded with her, begged her to let me get the debriefing over with.

She hesitated, then nodded and sighed, her shoulders slumping slightly in defeat. "Fine, but I am staying here. I need to watch that leg to see if the swelling starts to go down and I need to know what went on, anyway, so I can treat you. But if you start showing signs of extreme stress I am pulling the plug on this. Agreed?" She turned toward StPatrick, his mouth beginning to open with an objection when she sat quickly in Tomlin's chair and answered for them both, "Agreed."

The audience of three gave me their attention then, waiting for the finale of my saga. Retelling it made me feel like I had lived an entire lifetime in the complex. I realized I still didn't know how long I had been there— for all I knew it been only a few months, or it could have been years. It certainly felt that long. I reached up to rub the back of my neck as I started, shifting as Tomlin came over to adjust the pillow.

I explained how Rochester had come up the new theory of death, how I had been escorted to the room. The next set of details about each test and the injuries gained by them flowed quickly. I found myself talking faster just to get past each experience. I stopped when I mentioned the door opening, the guard's body falling in and the team entering.

"There's something I don't understand," the doctor said after I had finished and there were a few minutes of silence. "If this Rochester and his doctor were so intent on you healing between each test, why do you have so many unhealed wounds, your leg so badly mistreated?"

My voice wavered with fatigue. "For this last

round, he didn't feel it was important to treat me between. He said there wasn't any point," I whispered.

The three looked from one to the other in silence.

Tomlin asked the next question somewhat shakily, "When did you break your leg?"

I considered the question. It had been during the first trial with the pills, then came the poisoning, the blades, the car engine suffocation—though not specifically in that order. I tried to calculate, four tests, roughly a week between each, almost to the last trial… "Almost four weeks?" I was unsure of my answer, but it was the best guess I could make.

The doctor swore and shook her head. "No wonder the antibiotics weren't working, the infection is probably much further than we thought." She stood, going to look over her handiwork. She stared at my limb, licking her lips in thought before turning to my IV stand. "I'm giving you the maximum dose I dare." Loading a needle from a vial, the doctor jabbed it into the IV, pushing the liquid through. I felt a heat almost immediately through my arm. Looking up, I saw her turn the control on another bag. The drips from the sac increased in speed to the attached tube. "I'm upping your pain meds as well. It's going to be one hell of a night."

I leaned my head back on the pillow and closed my eyes as a medication-induced wave washed over me.

"I thought you said you couldn't give her anymore," Tomlin asked, concerned.

I heard the doctor hesitate. "I can't, but if the infection has gone into her organs and we don't get this under control by tomorrow, there're going to be more consequences than having her die and resurrect," she said firmly.

She does know.

Both sides of me were shocked, amazed that there were three people knowledgeable in the condition I had before it had so unfortunately been made known to me.

"Doctor, what sort of consequences?" I heard StPatrick ask, aware of Tomlin hanging on every word. I lay my head back again, my eyes closing.

The woman rested her hand on my head. I leaned into it in my drug haze, still partially aware. "Permanent impairment, severe necrotizing of the flesh." She took a deep breath. "If I don't see a dramatic improvement by tomorrow, the leg will have to come off."

Decisions

I woke up later in the day, my cold meal beside me. I looked to the side, Tomlin was slumped, snoring uncomfortably in a chair with a small blanket draped over his form. I was damp with sweat, my body itching from the blankets. I fought to remove a few layers, my movement restricted.

Hearing the slight commotion, Tomlin awoke, ripping the blanket off himself and stumbling over to help me. His eyes were rimmed in red, his gaze unfocused but rapidly becoming clearer. I was irritable and asked for some hot food, sending him away. I was in no mood for admirers or pity.

Having passed the man in the hallway, Dr Catherine entered, a reassuring smile on her face. "How are you feeling?" She rested a hand on my cheek. "Your fever has broken, finally. That's a good sign."

"I had a fever?" I asked shakily, my body feeling stiff and sore as though I had run a marathon.

"You did. And hallucinations." She hesitated as she helped to strip the damp blankets off me. "You said some things…I think you were remembering your time there."

I flushed, looking away. "I'm sorry," I mumbled, embarrassed.

"Don't be," the doctor said, looking over my leg once more. "Well, at least it may have been worth it."

"Was it?" I asked, craning my head to see.

She felt at the skin on my leg with practiced fingers, pressing the inflamed flesh. "It was," she said decidedly. "It doesn't look a whole lot better but it's not worse. I will look in on it throughout the day." She pulled up a chair, crossing one leg over the other, her short skirt covered by the white doctor's jacket. "Now, you and I are going to get to know each other. I think you know it would be best for you to tell me each and every injury you got while at the complex and I believe you could use the benefit of some female companionship regardless."

I didn't disagree with either point.

True to her word, Dr Catherine stayed with me the entire day, making sure I ate, arranging a sponge bath from some of the nurses to wipe away the previous night's sweat and the grime from the helicopter ride. She had sent away Tomlin upon his return, letting him know I was fine for now. He hesitated, wanting to be by my side. The doctor didn't give him a choice.

My memories of my time at the school as a child were slowly returning. I had forgotten what a formidable figure the doctor was; head-strong and sure in her desires. She had tended me on and off since I had arrived over fifteen years ago, when she was but an intern, taking care of the littlest of us.

Upon Tomlin's protestations, the doctor pointed to the door and watched him leave. "Either that young man is crazy for you or he feels completely responsible for your abduction." She shook her head. "Perhaps a little of both."

Between the doctor filling me with more drugs than the average human could handle and Tomlin's insistent care, I began to be nursed back to health. My form, so skinny and frail-looking before, began to take on weight. The healed slashes on my wrists faded more, all but disappearing in the light. Even my brand faded slightly, though it would always be there, I knew.

After a week in bed, the doctor finally announced the bone had fused enough for me to start getting up, a difficult but welcome task. Clothes were retrieved for me, pants and a shirt loose enough to allow the doctor access should she need it, but still more coverage than the hospital gown I had been stuck with previously. She gave me a cane, assuring me it would be some time until the artificial bone and my own skeleton would be fused enough for me to walk without aid.

The doctor was honest enough to admit the time for that may never come. For now the fact that I even had a leg to stand on was enough for me.

With the doctor's permission, and tired of meandering through the infirmary a week later, Tomlin suggested a walk outside. Eager to feel fresh air once more, I grinned. It was my first real enjoyment since arriving. He took my cane, placing my arm on his for support.

Stepping onto the front grounds was breathtaking, the sky the perfect shade of blue, the last flowers of the season just fading. We gained an audience along the way, straggling children walking a safe distance behind us. Apparently my capture had been well known, the event meant to be kept quiet, so naturally it was embellished as it travelled from one student to the next.

Tales of magic and a heroic battle circulated. My rescue by the team had been even more publicized, my disappearance into the infirmary adding fuel to the fire, developing into a fairy tale of epic proportions. Now the students wanted visual confirmation. They wanted the stories. They wanted to be able to idolize a legend.

The only problem was, that wasn't me.

My only claim to fame was the unnatural ability to survive through death. This was something the students didn't need to know, but it was still a fact I wondered about daily, the topic avoided by those who knew. The walk outside cleared my head enough to know I had to find some answers, and quickly.

Seeing me so quiet, Tomlin squeezed my hand, our arms joined together in support and companionship. I glanced up at him and smiled. Behind us, young teenage girls swooned, admiration for the pretty picture we posed and hate for me as I had taken the readily desired man, I knew—I'd heard them talking outside my room.

Looking up at Tomlin, I wondered what drew the girls to this choice option for a mate. His hair was kept short in a military cut, natural sun-bleached blond highlights working their way throughout the brown. He was tall, thin, and admirably fit.

On days when he wore his grey-black tight, long-sleeve shirts, one could see the bulges where his muscles were. On days like today, his taut, casual t-shirt made it more obvious, his pectoral muscles and upper arms rippling with small but developed features.

The fact that Tomlin looked just as athletically built in normal clothes reinforced the intimidating façade that the grey-black militia uniform created. It was clear to me the young man looked more than able, but I had no doubt the uniform and weapons added an air of danger.

His face was lean and clean-shaven, his eyes a deep chocolate brown, his mouth thin but full. I looked away, blushing a little at staring at him for so long as a confident smile appeared on his lips—lips that were so longing to be kissed. I think I understood now, what they saw in him.

It was after the fourth time of hearing *oooos* and

ahhs while we were on our walk that I decided to set the record straight. It had become common rumor around the school that Tomlin and I were lovers. We weren't, by any means, but we didn't care enough to kill the comments. We were best friends, as we were before my leaving, and knew what we were. At least, I thought we knew.

Grabbing my cane from Tomlin's hands, I spun around carefully, taking a few steps forward to approach the girls. Instead, I felt the blood drain from my face, my hands growing clammy as I looked at the school and realized I was standing on the exact spot I had been captured from so long ago. Shaking, I held my breath as the memories flooded back to me: the school on fire, Tomlin and the others emerging covered in soot and burns, the vile men approaching....

I doubled over, crying out, and felt the harpoon skewer my midsection once more, felt the sharp pegs dig into my back. I dropped the cane and fell to my knees, clutching my stomach. I could hear Tomlin rush to me, call to the girls to get help. They turned and ran off, yelling out, their shoes throwing rocks in their wake.

Tomlin gripped me by the shoulders, speaking softly, reassuring me again and again that the memory was not happening. I heard him apologizing for bringing me out, begging me to hear him. Finally I felt him hold me upright on my knees, his fingers digging into my shoulders as they held me tight, pressing his lips to mine.

It was a homecoming, compassion and love commingling in one simple action, as blood and gore and pain replayed in my brain, tingling in all my senses.

It seemed forever that we were together, my hands dragging up Tomlin's back as I leaned into him. I melted into his kiss, the warmth bringing me out of my horrific reverie slowly. Both of us on our knees now, we pressed closer, the embrace becoming more intense as my arms wrapped around his neck, his own hands splaying hard against my back, crushing my chest to his.

When my shaking subsided he sat back on his heels, breaking the connection. I took deep breaths upon his instruction, no words to describe either event I had just experienced. He reached out, stroking the tears off my cheeks affectionately. Quick shouting brought me back to myself as StPatrick ran from the school, clearing a path through the rapidly collecting audience. He skidded to a stop. He had seen, I knew he had.

"Tomlin, bring her inside." The older man's suit was immaculate despite his run, only his hair out of place. He looked around at the adoring eyes of the students: it was clear what they had seen. The girls had ideals of romance, the boys imagined their own hero worship and women in their arms, their choice for the picking. Tomlin saw their faces as well and stood slowly, opening his mouth to speak.

"Not here," StPatrick said quickly, ordering the student body to disperse. A striking and imposing figure, he was obeyed without question, the crowd immediately thinning. I tried to get up, using Tomlin as a lean-to but my leg had been twisted in the fall. In the end, he carried me in his arms as before.

StPatrick led us to his office, a vast space lined with wood paneling and bookshelves. It was not unlike Rochester's office, I noted. Sitting me in a wing-backed chair in front of the desk, Tomlin paced the room. "I'm sorry, sir, I didn't think about where we were going. I should have anticipated—"

"—Tomlin, sit down," the older man ordered firmly, now behind his desk in the grand leather chair adorned with brass work. Reluctantly, the younger man slowly sat down in a chair near me, hands rubbing over his face. He was nervous, it was clear his mentor rarely spoke to him in such a tone. StPatrick rested his arms on his desk, "It is time we talked."

"Again?" I asked quietly, referring to the debriefing. I was still shaking but I could feel the color returning to my face, my moment of anxiety fading.

His eyes broke away from Tomlin as the hard look moved to me. "You want to know why Rochester wanted you so badly, why you were able to die again and again and yet still live?"

He knows. He's known all along.

The air crackled with tension as I leaned forward,

letting my cane fall to the ground with a small thud. "Yes."

The man, commander to a ragtag bunch of children now trained to be spies, killers, and experts in the field of espionage, unlocked his desk drawer, pulling out a thick folder. He reached out, throwing it over his desk into my lap.

"You are aware after the war hundreds of years ago the government decided to stop producing and supporting the soldiers in their army." He waited for my nod. "The fighters were left without resources and livelihoods as they were often overqualified for regular jobs. On top of that, their ruthlessness in the field was well-rumored so no one would hire them."

"Upon seeing the disparity between the violent factions going unopposed, the soldiers banded together, creating their own special forces," I interrupted. "We learned this in class long ago. I was always top of the class in history."

Both men were staring at me as I rattled off the textbook explanation. Except for when I had been debriefed, my responses had typically been one and two word answers since my return.

"I remember." The elder nodded soberly, continuing, "What history class neglected to mention is that after several years of barely surviving, the soldiers decided they needed an edge against those who sought to rip apart the nation. So they recruited the top scientists, chemists and geneticists willing to work for the cause, and began to experiment."

I opened the folder, seeing faces, stats, journal entries dated well before any of our time.

"They succeeded, although it held a strange twist."

I stared at him. "Succeeded at what?"

StPatrick glanced at Tomlin and I pulled my eyes away from the contents of the folder to do the same. The young man was staring back at him but was not surprised by what the man was telling me—he already knew all of this, too.

"The genetic will to survive, the ability to heal quickly and fight strong."

"They created an immortal race?" I asked cautiously, flipping through the pages once more.

"In a way." He stood, characteristically going to stand and watch out the window, his back to us. "They found that by injecting themselves with the serum they had invented, it could alter their genetic code, allowing some of them to survive through the kinds of horrors most could only dream of."

"Some, but not all." I touched on the word he had used, seeing why this was such a hidden story. "And...the others?"

He paused then and shook his head. "The success rate was not enough. Those in which the serum did not take would suffer numerous days of blinding pain and sickness before simply succumbing to it. The soldiers lost far more than they gained."

He went to his liquor cabinet, bringing out three

glasses. He held up a bottle, the label worn, inclining his head to Tomlin. The younger man nodded.

"Me too," I said. StPatrick looked at me and he opened his mouth as if to argue. I was still on some medication but I didn't care—this conversation needed a strong libation to get through it.

"Then they discovered something amazing. If two of the adapted people mated, their children too would possess the ability to survive without any application of the serum. It had become a genetic trait, expressed by a dominant allele. Programs were laid out, plans made so that the people with abilities would meet and mate, a new generation of soldiers created."

StPatrick poured a burgundy liquid into the tumblers, bringing them over. "With a more efficient means laid out as time passed, the formula of the serum was lost, all traces destroyed.

"But, like all stages of human evolution, eventually the people wanted to meet their own partners. They wanted to find love and not just breed for the sake of power." He passed the drinks to Tomlin and me, sipping his own. "People who bred outside of the advanced race had a fifty/fifty chance of producing a child with the ability." StPatrick motioned to the younger man. "Tomlin's mother was one such dreamer, meeting his father, a normal human, and starting a family."

I heard the past tense immediately. "Was? Then Tomlin's mother is...."

"Dead." The young man downed the alcohol, putting the glass down hard on the desk. "Our kind do have our limitations. Beheading, for one." He closed his mouth in contemplation.

"The advanced humans can only survive intact. Any removal of a major component—head, heart, lungs—they cease to exist."

I swallowed the contents of my tumbler, feeling the slow burn of the liquid down my gullet. My nerves were better for it.

I thought about Tomlin's mother. If she was an advanced human, then she would have had to meet a brutal end. I wondered how the beheading had happened. I looked over at the young man. "Then you know you're one?" I asked Tomlin based on his earlier comment. "One of our kind?"

The young man shifted uncomfortably, looking down at his hands. "Not exactly. I haven't died so I can't be sure. But my mother was killed, and my father and sisters died long ago. We always figured my ability to stay alive was some indication." I could tell he didn't like the idea of dying at all, whether to validate his theory or not. Having done just that, I couldn't blame him.

"The thing is, the genetic strain only went so far as one generation," StPatrick continued, nodding to the strain family trees that showed the lines of families who had been traced, a symbol on those with the ability. "Two parents with the ability would create children who all had it. If one parent had it and procreated with a normal human, their children would each have a fifty/fifty chance of having the ability. In the children it was the same—two advanced offspring would have all children with the ability, whereas a normal and advanced couple would have only the fifty/fifty chance with their own. Two normal humans could never produce a child with the ability."

I looked at the charts. One after another, abilities were slowly wiped out by the crossbreeding with normal humans, if one could call it that, the ability dropping from the next generation.

I continued flipping, resting finally on a name that matched my own. I looked at the line, a symbol recently drawn in over my name, one on each side of my grandparents, both maternal and paternal. Of the rest of my ancestors there were mostly symbols, an almost pure line of genetic modifications. My parents had none.

Remembering what StPatrick had said about how the abilities passed on, I looked up at him. "I don't understand."

He stared back at me. "We always figured both of your parents had the ability. Both joined the cause at an early age, showing extreme skill in linguistics, agility, military tactics. Almost all with the ability do, for some reason. But the car crash that killed them confirmed they did not."

I rubbed my forehead, taking in what the man was

telling me. "But if they didn't possess it, how—"

"Exactly," StPatrick said loudly, his voice and face excitingly animated for the first time I could remember. "We know they were your biological parents, we had a test done long ago to be sure. I think Rochester knew a bit of this history of the genetic altering. Since he knew of your family he likely thought he had a chance of discovering the secret with you."

My mother. He knew my mother.

I shook my head, the realization becoming too real. "He knew. He spoke of seeing me get up after he had hit me once with his car, knowing no average person could do that. He talked about unlocking the secret behind our ability to survive."

"That solves that, then." The commander nodded. "Your abduction wasn't by chance. He wanted you, specifically. You are the golden goose of this ability. Your parents didn't possess it so by all rights you should not be alive today."

The rest of the visit became a blur as reality struck. Rochester had wanted *me*. He had burned part of the school down, injured and killed so many children, just for a chance to get me.

I felt sick.

Noticing the change in me, Tomlin waved to his commander. "Perhaps we can finish this another time, sir?"

StPatrick looked at my pale face and nodded.

"Agreed. You should go check if the coast is clear, Tomlin. No sense in overwhelming her further." He bent down and handed me the fallen cane as the young man left the room. "As for your relationship with Tomlin, I always suspected you two would wind up together. You are a good match, overcoming the other's weaknesses. Just try to keep the contact in public to a minimum, hmm?"

He straightened his tie and jacket, returning back behind his desk. "And just think, if you two ever started a family together, you could potentially revive the dwindling line of abilities in your own children."

Having died a dozen or more times in my own life, I didn't know if that was necessarily a good thing.

Back to Routine

My recovery seemed slow but considering the amount and severity of my injuries, Dr Catherine assured me I was making record time.

Once dispatched from the infirmary, I had been assigned my old room but with nothing to occupy my time I spent much of it out, wandering the building and grounds, often with Tomlin by my side. I returned to my suite only to sleep and to entwine myself in Tomlin's embrace, his lips and breath hot on my exposed skin as we fondled in the moonlight.

I took to visiting with StPatrick, learning more about the advanced humans, what they—we—were capable of.

I learned they lived normal lifespans after surviving their unnatural deaths. They lived to a maximum of one hundred fifty years, eventually dying of sudden heart attacks or just going to sleep and never waking again when their bodies were worn out enough. They possessed the trait of looking much younger than they were, their rate of aging slowing when they died the first time, operating at full health until the end. And, as I had learned through my own experiences, they often healed at a quicker than usual rate, though not necessarily cleanly.

The scars likely remained for their entire lifetime.

"So are you one too, an advanced human?" I asked once, feeling brassy.

He looked disapproving at the question, as though he were an older women of whom I had just asked her age. Then he broke into a soft smile, unbuttoning the cuffs of his shirt sleeve and pulling it up to reveal a huge scar diagonal across his wrist and lower arm. He lowered his arm to show me.

"I did not move quickly enough and the man's blade cut through my veins like butter," he said, watching the scar catch the light and then covering it again. "I was twenty-eight."

I wanted to ask how old he was now, suspecting that he was more aged than we had anticipated. But in the end, it didn't really matter.

After a month of uselessness and tedium, I complained to Tomlin, whose first reaction was to point out all I had been through. I agreed, but missed having a purpose. When I mentioned that even in trying to die, Rochester had provided me with a sense of fulfillment, Tomlin changed his mind.

A week later, I was stationed in a classroom,

teaching a class about tactical theoretics and ground maneuvers to a group of eager and highly intelligent students, the next generation of soldiers. While I was impressed and pleased by their eagerness to learn, I was missing out—I missed the field.

It hit me poignantly every time Tomlin showed up in his grey-black garb, meeting my eye with serious solidarity. He would always wait in the doorway for me to notice him, always keep a gap between us. While we had decided to attempt a fairly discreet romantic relationship, we never touched when he left for a mission.

It was better not to say goodbye.

Then, when he would appear a day, two days, a week later, relatively unscathed, I would go to him and he would envelope me in his arms, hugging in thankfulness.

This was our lives, repeating over and over. We both settled into our quasi-life together at the school: our rooms separate, our jobs apart, but never far from each other's thoughts. Tomlin became distant as we headed into the second month that I had been back, however. He went to a lot of mission meetings, and even StPatrick became testy. Both were careful not to share what was going on, which made me even more nervous.

Watching the students who were in on the mission look at me warily out of the corners of their eyes, I grew uneasy. Whatever was coming, it was big.

And it involves us.

I went to StPatrick's office later that day, knocking quickly. "Come" he said loudly from within, the sound of shuffling papers heard.

I entered, closing the door behind me. "Sir, I wanted to talk to you—"

"Some other time," the man cut me off, frantically flipping through the papers on his desk. "I have a meeting."

I stepped more into the room, my cane firm in my hand. "Sir, this can't wait."

"It can and it will," he said. "See yourself out." He dismissed me without looking up.

"I want back on the team," I stated firmly.

The man stopped his shuffling, placing the paper in his hand down on the desk and looking up at me. "No."

"I'm ready. I want in on whatever mission they are preparing for." I took another step forward.

"I said no." StPatrick finished fumbling through the paperwork, grabbing a few and tucking them inside his portfolio. Standing up straight, he tugged at his tie, centering it. He gestured to the door with his hand. "If there is nothing more...."

"You know I can do it. You know what I'm capable of," I cut in, blocking the doorway.

"It is because I know what you are capable of that I am saying no." His voice was louder now, stressed. He was involved in whatever the team was getting ready to face.

"I have to be there, why—"

The man picked up a baseball from his desk, one of the few trifle items that occupied the surface. He whipped it across the room. I let go of my cane, catching the ball deftly in front of my face. The wooden cane hit the ground and I wavered on my bad leg, wincing as I stumbled.

"*That* is why," he responded, walking over slowly. He picked up the cane, passing it to me unceremoniously and taking the ball from my hand. "This discussion is over. Get out."

Leaving

A glass smashed against the wall seconds after I hurled it.

"I don't understand, he *knows* I am good at what I do." I threw another one overhand, watching it shatter into a hundred pieces when it hit. "He *knows* I am an excellent shot. Loyal, tactical...." I picked up another glass and hesitated, lowering my hand to my side. I glanced down, grimacing at the cane in my right hand. "Instead he rejects me, all because of this...this stupid...." I threw the aid across the room, wavering slightly, putting most of my weight on my good leg.

"You know what he's thinking," Tomlin responded calmly, getting up from my bed. He casually sauntered over to the wall, picking up my walking cane. We had all hoped I would be able to do without it, but after months of therapy I still faltered when walking. Approaching me, he took the glass from me, setting it down, and held out the stick. "He has to look out for his people."

I used to be one of his people, too.

I looked up at him then turned away, rejecting his help. "He should know I would be fine. Even without the abilities. I'm smart and well trained. Even when Rochester had me, if I hadn't had the ability to survive, I would have at least fought my best." I felt defeated and wasn't sure what about this situation made me the angriest—the fact that I was being denied what now seemed my birthright, or the fact that everyone, including my partner, was moving on without me.

"He has to consider the teams." My lover put the cane down on the bed then came up behind me, placing his hands on my shoulders, squeezing gently. "We like to think of them as soldiers, but so many of them are just well-trained, scared youth. And as much as they go into this with eyes wide open, it is hard not to realize that any of them could come home in a body bag or injured irreversibly. No one knows how long they have until...."

I lowered my head. The reality for me was all too real, having experienced it myself. I was quiet as I thought about the changes my life had taken. "You never told me how long."

Tomlin ran his fingers through my hair, now cut shoulder-length since I had been back. He moved the hair aside, leaning down to nibble on the top of my ear. "How long what?" he asked, his breath hot on my neck. I closed my eyes, reveling in the sensation and leaning back against him, trying not to moan.

I shuddered with ecstasy. "Stop that, you're

distracting me." I moved forward reluctantly, turning toward him and putting a hand against his chest to keep him at a distance. I knew what he was trying to do and my flushed cheeks were evidence that it was working. "No one ever told me how long I was a prisoner."

Tomlin's hands fell off my arms as he made a small strangled sound. I knew that if he had his way we would never discuss the event again. It was too painful for him. He still felt guilty for my abduction. "Why does it matter?" he asked, rubbing his forehead and stepping away.

"Because it's my life!" I insisted. "Because apparently that took from me more than just my physical existence but also my meaning for life as well." I paused. "Because I don't even know how old I am now, with the lapse in time."

A silence gaped as the man considered his answer carefully. "He took you in late July—we rescued you in early August."

"So that's—" I thought slowly.

"Just over a year." he said, bringing his hands to my upper arms once more. He knew I liked their strength where they could easily transfer to an embrace.

I nodded, one part of me complacent to the number, happy it was only that long, the other shocked beyond disbelief. It had felt longer than that, somehow, especially when I had been in isolation.

I looked up as he leaned toward me. Our lips met softly, grazing in sweet tenderness before an eager urgency took over. It was always this way, the sensual tension between us supercharged as though our souls were two halves seeking each other through touch.

Out of breath, we broke apart a moment later, Tomlin's lips grazing my forehead. "I'm leaving," he said in a whisper.

I closed my eyes. "A mission? Where?"

You know where.

"I can't tell you." I felt his muscles quiver as I stroked the back of his neck, still in his hold.

I wanted to cry. I wanted to rip out of his arms and punch him for his stupidity. By his own awkward silence I knew exactly where he was going. Instead I wrapped my arms around him, whispering into his ear, "Take me with you."

"I can't," he said, startled. "StPatrick would know."

I took in a deep breath and shook my head. "He wouldn't have to." I backed up clumsily, rejecting the cane once more when Tomlin grabbed it and held it out to me. Stumbling carefully around the broken glass on the floor, I picked a folded piece of paper up from my small desk. I held it out for him.

Tomlin closed the gap, taking the paper, unfolding and reading it. His eyes grew large as his shocked eyes snapped to mine. "This could be treason."

I snatched the paper back, looking over it. "He's not the freaking president Tomlin. He's just StPatrick. It's merely a somewhat exaggerated request for a meeting with him regarding possible funding for the school, off campus, a little distance away."

The man pressed his lips together tight. "He may be just StPatrick, but in here he is our commander-in-chief, our teacher, our headmaster, for some of us a father figure." He tried to force his voice to a lower volume, "In here he *is our* President."

I tossed the page onto the bed, leaning against the frame. My leg was beginning to ache. "If you go there, if you do this...I'm afraid you won't come back." I reached up, grabbing his arm. "I know Rochester's complex, I know the guards and the servants. I could be whatever you needed: cover fire, a guide. I could help, Tomlin, I really could."

I was sounding desperate now, my voice breaking up. It wasn't that I was being neurotic, it was that I *knew* what Rochester was capable of and knew that since he had thought Tomlin and I were lovers before, he would be targeting him.

"Shhhh." Tomlin put his hand on the back of my head, forcing my face into his neck, wrapping me in his arms once more. My strength gone, I leaned into him, breathing in his scent, feeling his arms clasp me tight as they lifted me onto the bed.

He sat beside me, brushing the hair from my face as he leaned down, kissing me gently. "He was right about one thing," he said carefully, speaking of our commander once more and stealthily changing the direction of the conversation. "You're not up to full health. You know what you would do if you were captain and one of your people came up to you in this condition with the same request."

I wanted to argue but he was right. I would have rejected them, and more unkindly than StPatrick had. But this was different. I didn't know how, but I knew it was.

I felt it right down to the bone in my leg that was no longer there....

Insecurities

I grew increasingly irritable the longer the team stayed away. The first few days I was merely upset and nervous.

Then I got angry.

The students and the other faculty began to give me a wider and wider berth, growing silent and still as I would pass by in the halls, my cane thumping unceremoniously on the carpet. My own students struggled to keep up with my high demands, taking the abuse with good nature and hoping the mood would pass.

"Do it again," I grumbled to one girl as I looked over her tactical visual drawn out on her screen.

She blinked at me, stunned. "But, ma'am, it's exactly what you asked for," she argued, then shut her mouth, standing upright as I looked up at her. "Perhaps if you were clear as to what you were expecting?"

I stood slowly, my hand dodging down to my thigh, its muscles quivering. "Do you know what happens when you are on a mission and someone makes a tactical error?"

The room grew silent as the students watched the interaction. "Yes, ma'am, the mission could fail, people could get hurt," the girl, no more than fifteen, said softly.

"They could get hurt." I nodded, looking down on her. "Or, they could get killed."

I looked over the classroom. Despite my unruly behavior these past five days, I was still somewhat of an icon to many of the students, my return as a damaged soldier a sign of strength and a romantic notion of heroism. They had no idea what had gone on during my imprisonment. They only knew they wanted to be looked at the same way one day. I knew, I heard their hushed whispers in the halls.

The thought made me sick.

My journey from being a prisoner at the complex only to be another here was grating on me.

"Do it again," I said.

"Ma'am?" A student's voice could be heard as a slight knock tapped on the door frame, the door opening.

"What is it?" I snapped, seeing it was one of my other students, newly made a soldier.

The young girl stood straighter. "Headmaster thought you should know. They're back."

My knees all but gave out beneath me, one of the boys coming to my side to offer help. I waved him off, hands on the desk firmly. "All of them?" I struggled to keep my voice even.

She dodged my gaze. "Most, ma'am."

My heart sunk in my chest as I sat. I thanked the girl and glanced at the clock—only a few minutes to the end of the day. "Class dismissed," I said softly, not paying attention to the concerned looks as the students tapped their screens off and passed the tablets forward into a neat pile on my desk.

They knew that Tomlin and I were together now, and beyond that they knew I had been a captain for many years. The disappointment and sadness when soldiers died would always be there. I stared at the pile as the students filed out one by one until I was left alone in the classroom.

I leaned back in my chair and rubbed my face. It would be a while of debriefing and cleaning up any wounds before I would be allowed to see anyone. After my disrespectful display in his office, StPatrick gave explicit instructions that I was not to be anywhere near the operations section of the building.

I knew, I had tried.

Of course, they would also have to assess the dead. A lump formed in my stomach as I thought of the students who may have died.

Were they my own? Ones I taught just this past week?

Then there was Tomlin. It was no secret between us that Tomlin felt like only half a being, unsure of whether he had been passed the abilities or not. While he admitted he did not want to die, the alternative after dying could be worse.

"Still in here?" an older man's voice rang out in the room. I knew it well.

I opened my eyes, surprised to find it was night, the room enveloped in darkness. "I figured it would be a while, so...." I tapped the pile of now-graded tablet assignments.

StPatrick did not bother to turn on the lights. In the streaming moonlight I saw him shove his hands into his trouser pockets. "I am sorry about earlier this week. It was not what I was expecting and I did not handle it well."

I nodded and looked down, knowing the apology didn't mean he had changed his mind.

"I was there, you know, when your father came out of delivery and announced you were a girl." He smiled. "He was so proud. He and your mother did everything to make sure you would have a full and rich life, even though they thought you were normal."

Coming into the room, he offered his hand, which I took, standing. "They wanted you to learn how to defend yourself, just in case. They signed the paperwork shortly before the accident, entrusting you to me during the school year. Your education would have begun in the following year anyway." He helped me take a few steps out from around the desk and looked over my neat hair tucked behind my ears, smart blouse and vest, tighter trousers and polished boots.

"I do not think they expected you to turn into such a wonderful, beautiful young woman." He smiled sadly.

Beautiful.

My face still held on it the scars of my capture, my skin marred by things I often covered up with makeup.

Focusing on him again, I realized the man had actually known my parents very well.

"Considering your talents and who your parents were, I had always hoped you would become my attaché, eventually take over."

I couldn't take it anymore, I had to know. "Is he alive?" I asked quietly.

He nodded. "For now. He is asking for you. I offered to find you."

I picked up my cane, leaning on it heavily as we left the room and went to the infirmary. Dr Catherine stopped me outside. "We're still not sure if he's...." She looked around, seeing several children's faces along the hallway. "It shouldn't be long now."

Entering the room, I saw him there, lying in bed with bunches of padding pushed up against his side, the white cloth almost completely soaked through with blood.

A sob caught in my throat, my cane falling to the ground as I hobbled forward the ten steps to his bedside, burrowing my face in his chest. His hand came up to rest on my head.

"Not gone yet," he said, wheezing. Knowing it was

too late anyway, I lifted his hand with the padding up to view the wound. Something very large had hit him, shredding the flesh and organs beneath on the right side, from just below his armpit deep to his waist. Even as I put the pad back the blood seeped around it.

I nodded. "I meant to tell you to come back in one piece," I said, my eyes wet but the tears not coming forth. I waited for a smart-mouthed response but his breathing was too labored. He smiled instead.

Tomlin passed away some time during the night, his hand in mine. I had fallen asleep slumped over his bedside, and had no clue what had occurred until a hand came down gently on my shoulder. Looking up, Dr Catherine's image swam in my vision. She shook her head. I nodded once in acknowledgement, my head falling back onto the sheets.

New Beginnings

As the morning dawned, I got up from the bed, shrugging off the blanket someone had put over me. I glanced only once at the body that was being left there until we could be sure it would not resurrect, and left.

Using the wall as a support, I went down the hall, painfully maneuvering my way down the massive stairway and stepping out the nearest entrance into the brisk air. Snow lay about in deep piles, typical of mid-December. The children who were staying for the holidays would enjoy all this untainted beauty.

I shuddered—the Winter Solstice was just around the corner.

A large, thick jacket came over my shoulders. I grasped the sides with my frozen hands, unaware of how long I had been outside.

"It is beautiful out here, especially with the frost." StPatrick let out a deep breath that held within it a lifetime of anguish. "It will not be long now before we know. Come inside, you and I will have a glass of something and a warm meal before we go back to wait it out."

"I have no desire to be your daughter." The words seemed altogether too similar to what I had told Rochester as the conversation from the day before swam in my memories, the inadvertent offer by StPatrick. "I had parents, they are dead." I turned my head to look at the man, my breath coming out in puffs of moisture against the cold. "I just want to be useful."

He reached over to put a hand behind my back, drawing me into a hug. Despite what I had said, StPatrick was the closest thing I could remember to having a parent. He put his arms around me, rubbing my back in fatherly support. "I know. And you will be again. I have a feeling your time of being useful here is not over."

Heading inside, we went back to the infirmary. I had rejected the offer of food, my appetite meager as I waited for the revealing of my lover's fate. The doctor was already there with three tumblers of whiskey. She knew it was tradition for those of higher rank to toast the fallen comrades. While I was not necessarily higher, I was included. I had done my time.

We saluted Tomlin and the three others who had not made it, and downed the liquid. StPatrick and I had many more drinks that day, waiting for some affirmation, either negative or positive, of Tomlin's permanent death. I supposed it was also hard on him—Tomlin had come to the school as a young boy and was older than any other student who had ever stayed. He was talented, well-liked by all, a virtually perfect soldier. In a way, he had been like StPatrick's son.

My head was bobbing, my eyes red-rimmed and front lobe pounding from the alcohol when a loud clatter erupted in the room. I jerked awake and sat up, seeing StPatrick was already there to hold down Tomlin as he took in deep rasping breaths, his eyes cracked wide and hands clawing at the man's arms. Dr Catherine rushed in and the younger man relaxed at her tone, becoming more reasonable as he came back to himself. StPatrick looked back at me, our eyes meeting. Both of us knew what it was like, waking from death.

Finally calmed down, Tomlin's eyes darted around the room, resting on me.

Without hesitation, I stumbled forward, throwing my arms around him for the second time in as many days. Burrowing my head in his neck, he spoke soothing words. The dam broke and I burst out crying, only vaguely aware of the look StPatrick and the doctor gave each other above our heads.

A Lesson in Healing

"I don't know how you did it," Tomlin said as he shoved another piece of chicken into his mouth, ravenous after his adventure into death. "It was awful, and confusing, and painful. How did you manage more than once and all alone? I mean, you died how many times?"

I looked away, it wasn't something I liked to discuss or calculate. "A lot. Here, have a drink," I said, passing him the glass. "I learned, most of all, that food, drink, and rest helped to heal me faster."

The man shoveled in more food, considering me. He had been touched by my outpouring of expression upon his awakening and yet, it made him apprehensive and pensive. He swallowed and reached out, stopping my actions as I spooned another scoop of stew into his bowl. "You were right."

"I know I am, here have some more." I passed him the bowl which he glanced down at then placed on the tray to the side. He pulled my hand so I was forced to sit on the edge of the bed.

"No, you were right about the mission." He was serious, his voice lowered.

My curiosity broke free. "What the hell happened, Tomlin? Did they ambush you, did you go through a wrong door?" I asked, pausing when he held up a hand.

He shook his head. "We got in just fine but one of the boys hesitated before killing the guard at the door. It was just long enough for him to trigger the alarm." I closed my eyes and nodded. Fatal human error, then. "But we continued, got pretty far in, too," he drifted off in reverie.

"And?" I was sure now their objectives had not been achieved. Even with some of the team dead, Tomlin would have been a bit happier at the end result.

"He had countermeasures. He had surrounded himself with guards and mercenaries willing to act as bodyguards."

I was right, their goal was Rochester. I raised my eyebrows at him, a nonverbal encouragement to continue.

"And you were right—he was gunning for me. In the two minutes he had us cornered, he talked about how glad he was that I was there, at how he would love to have the opportunity to 'talk' with me as he had you." He looked at our hands, fingers intertwined, and continued, lowering his voice. "He hoped you would come back one day."

That'll be a cold day in hell.

I shuddered and lifted a hand to his cheek, cradling

it in support. He batted it away, his voice a bit broken. "I shouldn't have done it. I shouldn't have let him get to me."

"What did you do, Tomlin?" I asked firmly, removing my hands from his and standing slowly.

He smiled, defeated. "I flipped out, I called out for a countermeasure of our own, our last resort. It worked, and it was our only chance for any of us to get of there alive, but…"

"Now he knows," I said, the chill spreading down my spine. I flopped into a nearby chair, lifting a fist to my mouth.

"He knows," he agreed. "I won't make the mistake twice. But next time we go in there, I want you by my side."

We were both silent, the mood heavy as Dr Catherine entered to check on Tomlin. She asked the regular cursory questions, noting the distance between us. Going to leave, she called to me out the door, "Come on out, I need to speak with you."

Reluctantly, I got up, limping in her direction. She closed the door behind us quietly, turning to me. "You're not using your cane," she said, her arms crossed.

I shook my head. "There's no point."

"And you are moody," she continued, "and pensive, and irritable and you've lost weight."

I shot a look toward Tomlin's door.

"Don't blame this on him, this started before he even left," she snapped. Seeing my raised brows she calmed her voice, glancing down both halls to make sure we would not be overheard. "Do you realize how many students I have had come talk to me about you?"

I tipped my head. "I'm sorry if you had complaints…"

"That's the thing—they weren't complaints," Catherine hissed, her voice still lowered. "They are concerned about you, and so am I. You stopped coming to see me, which makes my follow-up with StPatrick that much harder…" she finished, trying to catch my averted gaze.

The doctor, aside from acting as the infirmary's chief medical staff, was also our resident psychologist. As such, she was uniquely qualified to assess both the team members' physical and mental states and make recommendations to StPatrick therein. "You are quickly becoming a reporting pain in my ass."

I glared at her for the comment, to which she replied immediately, "Either shape up and come see me for a session or I'll put you on report."

"I'm not one of your soldiers, not anymore," I spat out, my shoulders slumping a little at my own words.

She glanced around and whispered, "Not now, but you could be." At my shocked expression she looked around again. Classes had just been let out for lunch, and visitors were starting to arrive for those injured. "Come see me in my office later," she said covertly, patting my shoulder comfortingly before heading over to the gaggle of teens.

I watched her leave, then went back inside, not hearing Tomlin's question at first.

"I said, what did she want?" Tomlin asked, eating once more. He stopped chewing and stared at me, his dark brown eyes piercing.

I looked up at him and forced a slight smile. "She just wanted to know how I thought you were doing," I said, lying.

Looking forward to getting some time alone with the doctor later, I went back to Tomlin's bedside to give him more water. The discussion about Rochester forgotten for the time being, we made idle chatter, leaving me to wonder.

Why had I lied?

Risky Business

I met with Dr Catherine later that afternoon, eager and anxious about her news.

It was a new procedure, vastly untried with humans but successful thus far with test animals. Dr Catherine stressed the risks, but seeing as how I could not be killed by regular means, deemed the chance worth it.

It involved a type of regeneration, not one hundred percent effective yet, but with the procedure and proper therapy it would hopefully enable me to walk without pain and regain much of my independence.

If successful, it also meant I would be able to return to my duties as a soldier.

"Does StPatrick know about it?" I asked, looking up from the preliminary reports she had given me.

She handed me a teacup of a strong English brew and nodded. "I told him about it when you first came in, when we had to replace your bone," she said. "He thought it was too risky."

I glanced back at the documents. I sided with

Catherine. The hazards to the average human were less to me, and with my life going the way it was, I felt the procedure was worth the risk.

"When could we do it?" I inquired, closing the folder and handing it back, taking a sip of my hot drink.

She sighed. "That's the thing, I don't have the equipment here and to bring it in would be too suspicious. A friend at a lab outside of the city is doing the trials. She has agreed to do them on a human as long as we agree to her conditions."

"Which are?" My curiosity was piqued, my commitment almost assured either way.

"She will do the procedure and let you recover for two days at the facility. After that, you would need to return here under my care and instruction for therapy. She can't risk others finding out that she has done the procedure on a human yet."

"Agreed," I said quickly. "And the rest?" I didn't want my chance to slip away.

Dr Catherine put the folder in her locked cabinet. "That if it is a success, she gets to use the records for her results—your name omitted, of course. If it doesn't work—"

"—It never happened." I nodded. It made sense; the doctor's friend would get to test out her procedure without any of the risks to her professional career. I thought about it. "Agreed. There is one problem though," I considered. "How will I leave for two days without StPatrick noticing?"

The doctor sat down, drinking from her cup. "Ah, that's the thing, isn't it?" She lifted her cup again. "In the past, I have been known to invite some of the female faculty to a spa six hours away. It is very secure and secluded, I keep the owner well stocked with rare herbal fragrances I get through my connection to ensure her silence." She smiled, kicking off her shoes and raising her feet to rest on each other at the corner of her desk.

"I thought perhaps if I extended the invitation to you, our newest faculty member, it might open the doors of communication and ease your foul mood." Her shapely legs glowed slightly in the haze of the sun through the window, her short skirt framing her thighs perfectly. I was always taken aback by the woman's classic beauty, her fiery soul offset by the gentleness of her physical features.

I nodded, beginning to smile at the plan, then caught myself. "But if we are only out for two days, won't he notice when I return and can't walk?"

Catherine frowned as well. "There is that." She waved the thought away in dismissal. "But you *will* be walking. We will say you fell at the spa, the area around the hot springs are natural rock and can get slippery after all. You slipped and cracked your leg right on the bone." She nodded twice, the lie firm. "You would have to walk on your leg from the vehicle back inside to the infirmary. I won't lie to you, it will hurt like hell. But at least that would give me an excuse to have it in a bandage, to check on you daily and have you come in for exercises."

The doctor sat up, moving her feet down from the desk and becoming professional once more. "If this is going to work, no one can know the truth. No one," she warned. "All of our necks are on the line here."

I stood, understanding fully what she meant. There were careers being juggled here, all of which dictated our lives. I took a deep breath.

"When do we leave?"

Hidden Travels

"But Winter Solstice, why then of all days?" Tomlin asked, frustrated. He had since healed enough to move around, though he was restricted from missions for another few weeks at least.

He watched me shove a sweater into my overnight pack. "Because," I started for the third time. "I've been over this. The spa the Doctor and I are going to is a popular place usually, but not on family holidays like solstice. This way we can enjoy it without having to worry about being seen too much, if at all." I sighed, hating to lie to the man. "She feels the hot springs and a real massage would do me good and the time away wouldn't hurt either. But we need to do this logically, so that both of us are kept safe."

Tomlin huffed, crossing his arms. "I get that, safety and all, but you just pointed out it is a time for family. I want to spend it with my loved one. I want to spend it with you."

I paused as I tied up my pack, touched by his words. Despite being together for a while now, we had never expressed our love with the actual word. What he had just said was the closest I thought we would ever come to saying it.

But, I was more than ready to go through this procedure, ready to get healed and back to my old life, the one I had before I thought I needed something more. I was excited and nervous and apprehensive and I wanted to express it all to my partner. Instead I shook my head.

"I'm sorry, it's all arranged. The car is on its way now." I picked up the pack, throwing it over my shoulder and sighed again as I grabbed my cane. God willing, my time with it would be short lived. "I hate this thing," I said absentmindedly, not realizing I had spoken until my love came behind me, hugging me tightly.

He moved my hair aside and kissed my neck. "I know you do, but I love it. Cause every day I hear that thing around the hallway corners is another day I know you are here with me, safe."

I turned and looked up at him, tears in my eyes for reasons he hopefully would never know.

I pulled his head down to me for a kiss. "See you in three days."

Hurried Fixes

"I'm very honored ye decided to do this," the scientist and doctor, introduced to me as Dr Vanessa Malley, said, her full Scottish accent dripping liberally through her speech. She led us through her lab. It was mostly dark, the lights turned off for the holiday. At the end of the hall a soft hue beamed through an open doorway.

The woman, looking smart in her suit and lab coat, motioned Dr Catherine and I forward toward the door. "I hoped that my research would be able to serve a higher purpose, help'in' those who make a difference." She stopped and smiled, her face lit up by the light as she opened the door. "Now I will." She stepped through into the room, grinning. "The cause is always a noble goal."

Once the woman was out of earshot, I grabbed Dr Catherine by the arm. My fingers dug into her flesh as I hissed, "I thought this was supposed to be anonymous?"

My doctor chuckled. "For you, maybe. Vanessa has been one of the doctors working with the vigilantes for a long time. She could never make it as a soldier, but she is brilliant—her mind working on projects for the cause is well worth it."

"Course, I never expected my first subject would be you," Dr. Malley continued as she started up the program on the computer that she would be using during the procedure.

I put my bag down on a chair slowly. "I'm sorry, do you know me?" I waited for an answer, receiving a nod instead from Catherine toward the chair that held a hospital gown. I sighed and leaned the cane against the furniture, going to pick up the gown and change where the woman had indicated. It didn't really matter anyway at this point. I stepped behind the bathroom door, keeping it partially open so I could hear.

"The white whale," the Scot said softly. I could hear her typing. "Did ye know there has never been another person documented who has the advanced human modifications when their parents don't? *Never*."

I stepped out from the bathroom, my clothes bunched in my arms, a short blue hospital gown covering my form. "If this procedure goes well, as I am confident it will, I will have given ye a new chance at life." Her voice turned into a whisper, "I will have helped the white whale."

Catherine took the clothes from me, putting a reassuring hand on my shoulder. She was obviously used to the ramblings of her friend. "We need to do a quick exam before we start."

Dr Malley approached me as Catherine helped me up onto the table, rotating me so my legs were on top. The newcomer looked over them, touching the right one and its scars every so often. She then felt over my arms, looking for the best vein for an IV, glancing at the marks that marred my skin now.

"You're a bit battle worn, ay?" she mumbled inquisitively, concentrating. I looked straight ahead in response, not wanting to go into the details.

"Well, ye seem to be a stout candidate," she said then, smiling. "We can get ye an IV line started right away, and have ye on the table within a half hour."

Suddenly a bit anxious, I held tight onto the side of the table. "How exactly will you do this?"

"Ye didn't explain the procedure to her?" the Scot asked Catherine.

My own doctor shrugged. "She didn't want to know the details."

Dr Malley explained quickly how the surgery would go. She would open the leg up, grafting tiny bits of special organic printing plastic onto specific points around the muscle and artificial bone.

First of its kind, the plastic was engineered to adapt, to change form to its surroundings. The muscle-bound ones would become flexible pieces of fibrous muscle, the bone pieces would fuse to both the original and new sections, melding them together. The procedure was only to place the pieces—from there, they would continue to adapt until the process was complete, a month or two in the future. By then the plastic would have hardened, becoming bonelike.

"Isn't there a chance of rejection?" I asked near the end.

The Scottish doctor shook her head. "The plastic we are using has been fused with ye DNA." She looked nervously at Catherine, not sure how I would take that answer.

"When we started talking about this, I had a feeling you would go through with it," Catherine said hastily. "We already had your DNA on file—I sent it to Vanessa so she could get started with the infusion." It was as simple as that, she offered no other justification.

When it was done, my lower leg would be encompassed, under the skin, in a compound of plastic and organic material that would be better than before I had been hurt.

"The procedure will take a bit longer than it will when we finally have the approval for human testin'," Dr Malley explained. "Usually I would have an entire team workin' with me, monitorin' yer status, passin' tools and controlling the computer." She looked a bit put-out by the inconvenience.

Catherine nodded. "I am at your disposal, whatever needs to be done."

Dr Malley pointed to a cupboard labeled 'scrubs' and smiled. "I was hopin' ye would say that. Now, let's get the IV started."

I woke up hours later with a dull headache, a nauseated belly, and a thousand points of fire on my leg. I groaned, reaching down to reassure myself the limb was still intact.

Catherine rushed over and took my hands away from the area, speaking softly. The procedure had been a success and the discomfort was from a stabilizer that was aiding the plastic components to stay in their initial points of contact. Against her advice, I sat up slightly, bracing myself on my elbows to look.

My leg was a myriad of slices and stitches, some as long as a few inches. Connected here and there were long metal straw-like tubes that were vibrating slightly, doing their job to keep the plastic placed.

I choked back sobs as the pain mounted, Dr Vanessa entering in time to give me an injection of a strong pain killer. Her face was impassive, no sympathy written there. Catherine was right about Dr Malley; she knew about my kind and did not bother with the light drugs. I felt the surge of relief through my veins as the women watched. Neither doctor seemed upset at the prospect of taking shifts so someone would be awake at all times to watch the computer work and measure the procedure's success.

It was a long night, filled with consultations of the doctors and the computers monitoring the situation, and random crying out by me as rods shifted and the plastic under my skin grew.

I was happily miserable.

And for once, cloaked beneath a blanket of drugs, my other half was silent.

The only thing that kept me focused was thinking how much better life would be after this. Dr Malley predicted that while I would still have a bit of a limp once healed, it would in no way hinder my ability to walk, run, or climb.

At some point in the early morning, I thought of Tomlin, and other things it would allow me to do. Dr Malley caught me blushing.

"Thinkin' of ye beau?" she asked, smirking.

Embarrassed, I looked away.

"Ye will need to stay away from puttin' pressure on ye knee directly for two or three weeks," she said. "After that it's ride'-em cowboy." She laughed.

Catherine's eyes grew a bit wider at the conversation. She knew Tomlin and I were together, but perhaps because I had never approached her for birth control she didn't seem to think we had been together intimately. Seeing her expression, I wanted to shock her with some of the things I would one day try with my lover, but decided against it.

My two days in recovery passed quickly, the women checking their watches every so often, gauging the time. At some point, Dr Catherine mentioned we couldn't wait any longer and carefully wrapped gauze around my leg, a compression bandage overtop. The pressure on the entry points were torture, but as she pointed out, a sprain or possible break would require more than simple gauze.

Using her arm as a support, I got down from the table, falling almost immediately. Dr Malley came forward with my cane, encouraging its use both to take some strain off my healing limb and to keep up the charade.

I practiced walking around the room, finding the knack to putting just enough pressure on my leg to move but not enough to hinder my stride. I still felt the stabbing pain come every time I moved my appendage, but at least I could walk. I went to the pile of my clothes, untouched, and picked up my shirt.

"The other one," Catherine said in between bites of her quick dinner. "You wouldn't have gone to a spa only to dress in the same thing day after day. She glanced at what I had brought: a nice blouse and a looser pair of dress pants appropriate for the winter weather. She shook her head. There had been no other options for garb but it would be a pain getting dressed, especially since my bandage went from my ankle to my thigh. For the first time, I wondered if Dr Malley had noticed the brand

Dr Catherine put her food down and came over to help me. "We're all women here, it will go faster if I help."

I sighed and nodded, sitting awkwardly in a chair, my leg straight out. Closing my eyes for a moment at the mounting pain, I had to remind myself that I had felt worse before. She helped bring the gown over my head and I opened my eyes, leaning forward to pick up my bra. "Wait," she said, swearing and fell into deep thought.

I looked down at my underthings and realized. I hadn't been able to shower in two days, a far cry from relaxing in hot pools.

"Here," Dr Malley came out of the bathroom, a few damp washcloths in her hand. "I thought a bit and borrowed some of my coworker's natural herbs from her personal stash."

I sniffed the first washcloth as I took it, the floral scent rising. "It's eucalyptus, aloe, and a hint ay lavender," she said calmly at my reaction. "I contacted the spa, askin' whit ingredients they used in their oils, feignin' an allergy."

I had misjudged this woman, whose brilliant mind was hidden behind her ramblings and cold exterior personality.

Hastily, I used the cloths to give myself a quick sponge bath, the doctor aiding with my back and foot that I couldn't reach. That done, I finished getting dressed, Dr Catherine kneeling at my feet to help with my pant legs.

Unlike Dr Malley, I did see a collection of emotions flash through Catherine's eyes, ranging from pity to despair. But there also was a sense of companionship between us, and I thought that despite our age difference I had perhaps made a friend with the woman who tended my body.

I cleared my throat, blinking away grateful tears. "She saw the brand?" I asked quietly, eyeing the Doctor across the room. I bit my lip slightly. While I was not especially vain, the brand was a constant concern of mine, one of my few scars I could not hide the true purpose of. The stag and vines it portrayed were far too pronounced.

Catherine nodded slowly, bunching the pant leg up over the bandage. "Vanessa was surprised. I hadn't told her what had happened to you, only about your leg injury. But when she saw the brand..." She stopped working. "I noticed she worked a little more carefully after that." I watched her expression change, a stab of pain taking over her features for a moment. "Her brother was killed by Rochester in a bombing a few years back and she has never forgotten."

Somehow I felt better knowing that I had been worked on by someone with their own personal agenda of revenge, even if she was relying on me to do it.

Finally dressed I took the last unused wash cloth and hobbled to the bathroom sink, drenching it then wringing it out over my hair to transfer some of the scents that way. I dried it hastily with a towel then tied it up into a small bun. I came out of the bathroom, trying to stand up straighter, my knuckles white around the cane handle. My leg stung like fury.

"Do I look like I have come back from a spa?" I

tried to smile, but nowadays such an action was against my general nature.

The doctors looked at each other. I knew they could see what I had seen in the mirror—my face was pale, dark circles under my eyes. I looked like I had been ill, and at times I had. My smiled faded quickly.

"It's all right, I'll put some makeup on you on our way back," Catherine said confidently.

I watched Catherine give her friend a hug and step back as we said our goodbyes, Dr Malley approaching me, hand extended. I took it and nodded in thanks. There were tears in her eyes and I now understood she was desperate for this procedure to take.

The sooner I recovered, the sooner I could get back to what I did best. If avenging the doctor's brother ended up the end result, she would not gainsay it. Knowing what I did now, if the procedure worked the way Dr Malley predicted, I felt I owed her nothing less.

But my revenge would come first.

Home Coming

Catherine and I talked in the car on the way back, knowing the men would watch for signs that we had bonded during our time away. I was covert in many of my answers—there were things even Tomlin didn't know.

Catherine warned me that she would need to examine my leg right away when we arrived. Since I had been walking on it and then gone through the uncomfortably long car ride home there would be a risk of swelling. Usually patients would be in the hospital for a week with their leg elevated after the procedure.

It was time I couldn't afford.

Catherine got out first when the car pulled up to the doors of the school, her loud hello indicating we weren't alone. StPatrick was there to greet us, cautiously curious to see how my trip away had gone.

From my view in the car, I saw his eyes spark when the woman stepped out, jubilation at her return. For a moment it made me wonder whether the Headmaster and lead doctor's relationship was purely professional. Tomlin skidded to a stop beside him seconds later, his training sweats showing he had run all the way from Ops.

Their faces fell when they saw me.

"What the hell happened?" StPatrick asked in concern and anger as he look large strides to my side to help, my difficulty of getting my leg out of the car's doorway obvious.

Tomlin rushed over as well, letting me put my full weight on him as I got out.

"Oh, she'll be fine," Catherine said convincingly. "She just tripped on the stones going into the hot springs, took a nasty fall. There's a lot of bruising and she strained the muscle so I bandaged her up. I'll take some x-rays as a precaution, but it's nothing we can't fix."

StPatrick drew himself up to his full height before her, his fists clenching. The affection that had been there moments before was all but wiped clean. I hadn't realized how nervous my being away would make him, although, considering the last time.... "You should have been more careful," he growled.

I was surprised by his anger, but I now possessed knowledge about our kind, I already knew a lot about the school. Even as a cripple, I was still useful to him as a teacher and a possible successor—and a threat in the wrong hands.

"You're right, we should have," I said, trying to

diffuse the situation. I gave in to Tomlin's insistent help and let him pick me up. "I truly regret it now. I was just careless."

You are never careless. I shut my mouth as the word slipped, hearing my other half for the first time in days. I didn't welcome the obvious observation of my slip up.

StPatrick put a hand on Tomlin's arm to halt him and looked into my face looking for a lie then, suspecting something. His look passed through my eyes like he had the ability to do. We stared at each other for nearly a minute and I struggled to keep still, not looking away.

In my mind I replayed my own truths, the only way I would be able to get through the charade. I did regret the deception, and the inability to come clean.

After the minute was over, the man removed his hand and visibly eased, the tension disappearing. "Let us get you inside then."

Tomlin carried me to the infirmary and placed my feet down on the floor near an empty bed, the doctor scooting the men out before any more questions could be asked. Once the door was closed I dropped my cane and collapsed against the bed, my hands rushing to grasp just below my knee. I broke into a sweat, my emotions true once more. I gritted my teeth against the pain.

Immediately, Catherine took a pair of scissors to the bandages, not bothering to unwrap them, hissing against the swelling. "It's fine, we anticipated this," she said, a bit of panic in her usually calm demeanor. "I'll start you on an IV for pain and one for the antibiotics and the swelling will go down."

It did, after a worrisome few days. The doctor justified my convalescence by saying that I had fractured my bone, my remaining real bone, and needed to stay in bed. Elevating my leg above the bed level and covering it loosely with a gauze bandage she kept me blissfully content with drugs.

It was a welcome respite.

I woke up on the second day. Between the pain meds and the lack of rest I had experienced directly after the surgery, I was exhausted. I had fallen into a fitful sleep, feeling the plastic crawl its way, expanding and adapting, pushing aside and knitting muscle and bone. Added to the pain was the numbness of my leg as it rested, elevated above the rest of my body.

It was an uncomfortable sensation.

When I woke up, I rubbed my eyes, feeling someone watching me. I opened them wider, shielding them from the sunlight beaming in with my hand.

"You lied to me."

I focused on the sound of the man's voice, raising my head. "What?" I asked, making out Tomlin's shape. I reached out for a glass of water that was at the far end of the nightstand, waiting for him to hand it to me. When he didn't move I swore, stretching my arm and shifting my position. Pulling inadvertently at the contraption holding up my leg, I squeaked, then gave up, leaning back. "What are you talking about?" I snarked at him.

He nodded toward the foot of my bed. "You looked right into my eyes, and you lied."

I glanced down and froze, seeing the gauze pad that had been covering my leg moved aside. The tiny stitches were visible over the expanse of my skin. "What did you do?" he asked stiffly.

I looked away. I couldn't explain it in a way he would understand.

"I would have expected you to keep this from your students, even the team," he sounded defeated. "But from me? What about StPatrick, does he know?"

I shook my head slowly, unable to cloak my own deception.

He took a deep breath. "Why?" He looked like I had beaten him, his shoulders slumped, wrinkles in places on his face I had never noticed before.

"I had to," I started quietly. "I have to do more, Tomlin. I have to get back to what I was before. You don't know what it's like, to be so close to being yourself and yet immensely far. I love teaching," I continued, "but my soul is pulling me toward the missions, toward so much more."

He interrupted then, reaching for the glass of water and passing it to me while sighing. "I know," he admitted, "I've only been off the missions for a few weeks but I know what it is like to be held at arm's length, wanting to help but not being able to. I want to scream every time my people leave here in black without me."

I took a sip. So he did know, then.

"I am not happy you did it," he said, speaking as I opened my mouth to object. "But, if it works, this will change a lot."

I shook my head. "Not really, it just means I could get back on the team. If StPatrick lets me, that is."

"He will," Tomlin said, considering. "But you're wrong, it will change everything. We've been without experienced leadership—you have that. You are able to inspire and convince and manage while others can't. And you're one hell of a tactician on your feet. We work well together. The team needs you." He reached over, taking my hand in his. "I need you."

We stared at each other in companionable silence, observing the momentary peace in each other before the next challenge, like a calm before the storm.

Consequences

"You lied to me," an angry voice came from the doorway as the door slammed shut with a bang.

I jumped at the sound and looked up from the book I was reading, sitting straighter in the bed as I saw StPatrick approach. He was irritated, his mood emphasized when a male nurse came in with my chart and he ripped it out of the man's hand, jabbing a thumb toward the door. The younger man looked startled and paused, but ultimately turned and left in a hurry.

I sighed, closing the book. "Yes, apparently its been going around."

StPatrick jerked open the chart, reading. I knew he had been a field medic years ago, so no doubt he would be able to decipher whatever information he wanted quickly. "Don't be a smart-ass," he snapped.

I shut my mouth. He was legitimately angry and I knew this was a time to be quiet and take orders.

"So how did it work, exactly?" he asked, putting the chart at the end of my bed and leaning over the footboard. "Did you and the doctor just wake up one morning and say, 'How can we bullshit StPatrick today?'"

I shook my head but the man cut me off before I could speak. "Catherine told me about the procedure long ago. We discussed it and I said it was out of the question."—The man's face was growing red and it occurred to me I had never really seen him angry before.

"But the procedure worked," I protested.

"I do *not* care to be made a fool of." St Patrick was curt. "I had my reasons to say no, you should have respected that." His words were full of venom and I suspected there was no acceptable opposition to his argument.

"I do not particularly care how you pulled it off. Of course, in the end it is likely you will get what you were after—you will be back in uniform and ammoed up, barring any complication with your physicals." He was staring at me, his eyes boring through my skull. "I expect you to work...hard. There will not be any accommodations made for you, no kid gloves. You will have to pass whatever evaluations I deem necessary, and that includes a detailed psyche work-up," he grumbled. "For you, of all people, that should be torture and hell to pass."

I paused until I was sure he was done. "How soon can I get back, then? I'm sure after I get up again I can start working immediately," I trailed off as the man's face grew red once more.

"I do not think you understand," he snapped. "*You* are not going to work for me, with *my* teams until I am sure you are ready. That means I am going to have you worked up until you are tired of the doctors, exercised until you wish I had let them take that damn thing off." He motioned to my leg and stood straight, pulling at his suit jacket and straightening his tie.

"I am going to make your re-training hell. The tests will be so gruelling that if you *do not* quit, I will know you want this badly." Any smile I might have thought of spreading was just a memory. "You could have been seen, captured again, killed for good. What is more you could have gotten our head doctor injured—or worse. No matter how well-laid, your plan was irresponsible. The doctor has already received her punishment, now it is time for yours."

I grew stiff. "You didn't fire Dr Catherine, did you?"

He glared at me. "You two wanted to make a decision that would affect this place, I had to as well."

He walked over to the door, turning before leaving. "As of today you are on report. You will have a soldier trailing you to make sure you stay in place. You so much as sneeze out of line and I will know about it. You will get back on a team when *I* say you are ready, but you will *never* be Captain under my command again." He spun on his heels and left, a cold chill lingering in the room.

The scary thing was I knew he meant it.

Uphill Climb

StPatrick was true to his word. Once the new lead doctor cleared me I left the infirmary, returning daily for therapy. It was exhausting—the doctor knew about our kind and that I could afford to push myself. For hours, he would drill me on equipment, letting me stumble and fall but never letting those indicators be enough to halt the time there.

He acted as a drill sergeant, his orders direct and unrelenting as I heaved and pushed and pulled, the sinew in my limbs trembling during my therapy. Always trailed by a soldier at a distance, I would get out of the exercise room soaked with sweat, falling into my bed and asleep before I even had the chance to shower.

Tomlin had been approved to return to duty and we saw little of each other, him often finishing his duties as I limped back to my quarters, red-eyed and unsociable.

We suspected our schedules had been arranged to make mingling difficult as an extra punishment and motivation for my rehabilitation. He didn't agree with StPatrick's decision to make me work for my position back on the team, nor about my demotion. After the first two weeks of retraining, I couldn't help but agree with my commander.

In fact, we had a heated discussion about it which ended with Tomlin's face red and swollen in anger. I just sat there on my bed at the end, unable to argue anymore.

As for Doctor Catherine, she too was demoted, sent to work in the clinic with the younger children. Whether she would be able to earn back the man's trust was left to be seen. I had no doubt the romance I was sure existed between them had cooled as well.

Despite the hours of being yelled at by the doctor, the therapy did me good. My leg hurt much of the time with its continued healing but it was something I became accustomed to. As time went on I grew sturdy on it, the limp becoming slight and more due to the stiffening from the plastic fibers.

Eventually the man ordered more practical exercises, passing on my invigoration to instructors and students talented in hand-to-hand fighting. A master of martial arts was brought in, bringing as much passion as discipline. Unbalanced at first, I lost over and over, my ego bruising more than my body.

Gradually I grew stronger, the turning point of my failure coming on suddenly.

It was as though a switch clicked—one day I was

untutored and floundering in my actions, the next I was passing through the routine defensive steps without fail. I was staying upright and putting down every move the black-belt could throw at me.

The day after, I won a match for the first time.

After that I was more confident of my moves, and the trailing soldier—a hard-faced eighteen-year-old man with aspirations of his own team—informed me practice that day would be in the gym. I didn't think anything of the change in venue—it had happened before.

We entered and I was taken aback to find the dohyo, the sumo mat we used often in our group practices, had been set up, and a crowd was growing. StPatrick was there, sitting down in front within a cluster of chairs, Tomlin looking concerned on his left. I hastily took my towel from around my shoulders and tossed it on the ground, reaching up to tie my hair in a half-bun out of the way.

Kicking off my socks and shoes, I went to the mat and fell to my knees, head bowed in respect as the master had taught me.

"I was told you have healed nicely, that you have gotten strong. Some have suggested you have completed your retraining." StPatrick's voice cut off the chatter behind him. I looked up at him as a smile of amusement formed on his lips. "Prove it."

I knew this was my test, that if I succeeded here I

would be allowed back where I belonged. I just didn't know how far my commander would take it.

The doors opposite me opened, a man coming in with soldiers flanking on either side, guns drawn. I straightened my back. I sucked in my breath. It was the man who had aided in my death so many times in the past, the muscular man from Rochester's complex. I could tell they had worked at getting him in, his dark face showed bruises from a previous fight, the guards looking even worse for wear.

His eyes met mine and there were hateful sparks in them.

I remembered from my days as a prisoner that he had given me all the leeway he could afford to a fellow soldier. He had tried to give me some measure of dignity in my deaths. Even so, he had gone through with them, something I would never make an excuse for.

The guards took off his hand and ankle cuffs quickly, leaving the man unhindered. He reached up with one hand, rubbing his throat with his enormous paw, reminding me unkindly of the time he had strangled me to death. My expression hardened—the man had truly become Rochester's since I had left.

"You know the conditions." StPatrick nodded to the man, whose muscles were tensed, ready for a fight. "Kill her and you go free."

My other half rose in victory. *Yes, a fight. A real test, finally.*

Tomlin startled in his chair, others around him shocked by the words as well. I was not surprised at all—how else was my commander to gauge my ability and determine if I was ready unless I was able to carry through with a real fight with real consequences.

I glanced at StPatrick. I could tell with one nod that he knew what he offered. The muscular man either had to perform some vile act of murder, mutilating my body to keep me in death—or, he would never leave this place. Having been at several of my trials before, the muscular man must have known as well.

The muscular man nodded once and I did the same. I was prepared to do whatever I had to.

He won't leave this room alive. We will be the ones to go free.

The six-and-a-half foot muscular man stepped onto the mat, watching me as I remained kneeling, my hands balled on my knees. He didn't jeer, didn't speak. He always had been a man of few words.

Closing the gap, he stepped toward me and reached down, grabbing my hair in his right hand, twisting it painfully.

I could hear the arguments beyond the mat, the offense growing.

I stared into the man's face as I put my hand around his thick arm, my eyes squinting in pain as he lifted me off the ground. I could see the hint of humor there, the sick possibility of my final death in his hands. My other half rose within me, arms outstretched, fingers straining toward me as though a match fighter pleading to be tapped into the ring.

My training, both what I had received for years when I was a teenager and that which I had learned just recently, flipped through my brain in fast motion. I brought my right fist up, bringing it down squarely with my bony knuckles on the sensitive crook of his arm, my left foot coming down on his thigh where the femoral artery lay.

He cried out and dropped me at once, his own body stumbling backward. The minute my feet hit the ground I gave into my other half.

I snapped.

Yelling, I ran at the man, my pent-up rage taking over. In one jump I had my fist to his head. I saw in his eyes the image of his body holding mine down under water.

He reached up for the injured spot. It allowed me to grab his arm, throwing my own body over his in a move I had imagined for Rochester. His arm twisted painfully across his back. I wrenched my shoulder downward with a heave hard enough to hear his shoulder pop.

He cried out. I shoved him, letting him lurch forward with his massive body weight. Spinning around, he glared at me. His left arm dangled loosely by his side.

Putting his other hand on his shoulder, he squeezed and manoeuvred the joint. I could hear a revolting series of crunches as bones moved somewhat into place, at least enough for the limb not to be a liability anymore, his expression impassive.

We stared at each other for a moment before the man came at me again. I fell to my knees, punching at his midsection in the soft tissue areas between the stomach and side. The muscular man hunched over slightly, grabbing around my torso from above. He flipped me so my back was to his shoulder, my legs above his head, my head down by his knees, and gave me a shake. He pulled my spine taut as I bent backwards.

I kicked his back with my legs as I bent myself further, my open palms reaching upwards and around to smack him on either side of his head.

Disoriented, he lost his hold on me, then caught me from behind before I hit the ground. He adjusted his hold, his powerful arms now wrapped around my chest, squeezing hard. Still upside down, I felt the creak of my own bones as he increased pressure.

Gritting my teeth I brought my legs into position, my thighs going around the man's neck, my calves interlocking behind it. I felt the blood rushing to my head. Successfully cutting off his air supply, the man swayed, wheezing for a minute before I felt his grip loosen.

It was all I needed.

Knowing I couldn't topple the man easily, I let my legs go, using his body as leverage as I flipped forward, righting myself.

I faced the man, instituting a series of kicks and jabs the master had drilled into me. Trying to retain his balance, the muscular man threw in a few lost-cause punches himself, their contacts barely felt on my skin. Hitting him hard once again in the head I watched the man slump to his knees, blood dripping from his ear. He gazed up at me in a stupor as his face contorted, raising his fist to get in another jab.

Do it!

My other half urged me with wild eyes, relinquishing some of its hold on me.

The punch never hit me. I took his momentary disorientation to get in a hit again to his temple.

Deflecting his arm, I grabbed either side of his lower jaw below his ears with both hands splayed, looking up at the audience behind the man as he wobbled. StPatrick lifted his chin the tiniest amount, enough that I took it as permission.

I felt my other half step back, my hands once again mine. This was more than StPatrick's test. My other half wanted to see if I was capable as well, if I was ready to return to battle as the cold-hearted killer I now needed to be.

I am.

Wrenching my hands, I heard the sickening crunch as the man's bones snapped.

The audience was silent as the muscular man's

body hit the ground with a hard thud. His eyes were wide and his head was turned at an unnatural angle. It was then that I noticed a small mark on the man's bicep. Reaching out with one of my big toes, I moved his sleeve, revealing the brand. A crude image of a stag, the antlers wrapping circular round the entire image.

It matched my own.

Over at the chairs, StPatrick was smiling, speaking with Tomlin as reality came back to the room. The guards rushed over to haul the man's body away while I stepped forward to accept my consequence. Whether it would be punishment or acclaim, I wasn't sure.

Breathing hard, I sought to catch my breath, my ribs aching. I stepped forward toward the men who were now approaching and collapsed on my knees again.

Tomlin knelt down, a comforting hand on the side of my face as he rubbed my cheek with his thumb. I hissed, starting to feel the sting of the many pummels to my temple. A veil of red came over my eye and I realized I was bleeding heavily from a cut above.

Only a slight head wound. They bleed a lot.

Students, all soldiers, filed in around us as they discussed the fight in excited, muted tones, looking from one another back to me. My mouth hurt and moving my tongue around I felt a loose tooth. Letting it be, I spat out a mouthful of blood onto the mat and wiped my split lip with the back of my arm.

Tomlin pulled a few errant sweaty locks off my

forehead as he snatched my towel from the hands of a student nearby. Pressing the towel to my bleeding head, he gave me a thankful smile.

Behind him, StPatrick nodded once—only once—in acknowledgement, which I returned.

I was ready.

Mission bound

I recovered quickly, although a concussion, bruised ribs, cracked knuckles and several lacerations had me laid up for a few days. Tomlin used my downtime to his advantage, spoiling me with breakfast in bed, issuing massages at his discretion, and bringing me up to speed on the missions. I repaid his kindness with an affection I had not been able to express since my procedure, making use of my exercise-built arm muscles and now exceptionally strong leg.

I was sitting on my bed days later, tying the laces of a new pair of boots, when a rap came from outside my room. Tucking in my laces as regulation required, I looked up, recognizing the suit before I even saw his face. I stood at attention, straightening and standing tall, my hands by my sides. "Sir," I acknowledged.

I had developed a deep sense of respect for the man since my fight. He had allowed me to both prove myself to the team as well as get some closure in only the way our kind could. While a few like Tomlin were appalled at the public show of fight to the death, I understood what StPatrick did as well—the muscular man had been a loyal minion of a mass murderer and by all rights was a murderer himself. His days has been numbered either way.

"As you were." The man came closer to the bed. I sat again and finished with my laces, reaching over to shrug on my shirt over my tight grey-black tank top, tucking it into my pants.

"You are healing well," he said, tapping his own forehead to mirror where my stitches lay. They were almost ready to come out, the skin underneath fusing nicely. He smiled. "Big day, first one back."

I paused, my hands halfway up my buttons, and nodded. "Big day."

He has news.

StPatrick looked me over as I finished doing up the last two buttons, fixing my collar and cuffs. He held a hand out so I could precede him, closing the door behind us as we started out into the hall. I walked stiffly, nervous for the first time that I could remember.

A lot of baggage came with this return after a year and a half—my capture, my return broken and beaten, my recovery and erstwhile teaching, the fight....

The eradication of the first of our murderers.

"I have arranged for you to be on Tomlin's team," he said as we hurried down the hall. "While I do not usually condone soldiers that are in a relationship being on the same team, we need our most experienced on this mission and there is no denying you two work excellently together."

Students that were in the hallways stepped sideways, stopping to make way for us, watching. The news of my return to the team had spread somehow. While most students, like when I had begun at the school, had no idea of our true nature, there was no denying the people in grey-black were doing something special.

At the entrance to the hallway leading to Ops, looking like just another large set of double doors, we stopped. StPatrick passed a card to me from a pocket inside his jacket. I swiped it on the reader, hearing the click of the lock releasing that used to be so very familiar to me. I pushed the door open and stepped through.

Expectedly, the hallway was empty, another façade of wooden doors in case the regular students were able to look through the entrance. It was for the last door that I headed, the one with 'School Operations' on the plaque above. Using the card again I entered the elevator.

I was standing at ease, my feet shoulder-width apart and hands joined behind my back, looking down with StPatrick two steps to my right when the doors opened onto Ops. Quickly, those people who so religiously kept our operation going looked up and, upon seeing me, ceased what they were doing.

Silence fell over the vast room like a blanket, the

only sound the quiet beeps and ticks of the computers.

Raising my sight, I looked over the room, not showing any change of emotion despite the smiles that were beginning in my direction. It wasn't that I was unhappy about returning, but the seriousness of the recent state of the world was sobering. As well, being part of the team meant the possibility of death. Even though I was immune to most forms of the permanent state of inevitability, the same could not be said for most of my young teammates.

There was also the unwelcome chance that my own life may meet its end—this time, for good.

If our death means the destruction of Rochester and his people, we should embrace it.

I left the elevator and ignored the whispers around me as I took a deep breath and made the long walk through the underbelly of the school to the briefing room. It was where the team spent most of its time when not training and it was where I knew I would find them now. StPatrick stepped forward, opening the door to the briefing room and entering before me.

"That would leave us too vulnerable." Tomlin was arguing with a subordinate when I stepped inside, my boots scuffing lightly on the concrete floor. His back was to us but as each of his team looked past him toward us he turned, our eyes locking.

Holding his pointer a little tighter, Tomlin nodded to his commander and me, standing up straighter. Nodding back in response, I hurried over to one of the empty seats among the others. They shifted in their chairs, as though being in my presence was uncomfortable. The other soldiers were no doubt wary of me, having seen either my return from captivity or my redemption from the fight. Neither spoke positively for my mental state.

They don't trust us yet, but they will.

Regardless of the mood in the room, Tomlin took control once StPatrick left. It came effortlessly to him, leading our squad, and I quickly found that since I had been on his team years ago, he had grown to be a great captain. I was distracted, watching him negotiating tactics and discussing strategies.

"What do you think?" I heard at one point, my head bowed over the blueprints I was making unrelated notes on, my pen scratching furiously. When no answer was given, my head bolted up, looking to the front of the room. Tomlin was looking in my direction, his eyes piercing me. "What do you think?" he repeated. "Would it work?"

Not willing to give a guess on something that could affect any of the soldiers' health, I stammered, glancing frantically at the board behind him for some clues to the strategy in question.

"She wasn't paying attention," one of the older girls jabbed verbally at me, unimpressed and angry.

I closed my mouth and looked down. I had no excuse. Months of being away had made my mind slower somehow. I felt disconnected from the very people who, at one time, had been my own claim to life.

I heard Tomlin snap at a few soldiers who had begun to banter on the matter, ordering silence. "It's late and we are all hungry and tired. Let's adjourn for the night and meet back around..." he paused, considering, "0500 hours. I want to have a concrete plan by tomorrow night."

I sat still, looking down at my hands resting on the table as the scraping of chair legs on the floor was heard, a scuffling of boots and swishing of material as the others left. I couldn't help but feel as though I had made a mistake, and considered that maybe I had been invited back only due to my presumed instability— perhaps they thought it would intimidate whoever we would be up against.

You know who we are going up against. Your insanity will only stroke his ego.

A large hand came to rest on the table in my sight-line. "No one expected you to be back to full speed the first day." Tomlin's sympathetic tone was endearing. His hand lifted, turning palm-up and extending. "Come on," he invited, "let's get some sleep. We only have about six hours."

Reluctant at first, I put my hand in his and stood, letting him lead me. I glanced over my shoulder as we left through a different doorway than the others. "I made sure to have quarters within ops for while I am on missions," he explained. It made a lot of sense—if anything were to change with the timeline during a mission he would already be accessible and ready to go.

He slowed his steps as we left the briefing room behind and walked down the short, quiet corridor. His back lost the rigidity of command as he neared a series of simple doors. "It's actually a room meant for the use of all the captains but nowadays our missions always occur at different times so...." He opened a door to his left, leading me inside and closing it again.

He stopped and turned, stepping closer to me. "I can't even tell you how happy I am that you are here with me on this."

I shook my head. "The private was right, I wasn't paying attention."

He stepped even closer, reaching down to intertwine our fingers. "Perhaps you need something to jog your tactician skills, something to hone your focus." He leaned in and I instinctively swooned, closing my eyes and bending backwards as my lover's fingers stroked my cheek.

I bumped into the wall, feeling its hard surface holding me fast. I felt his soft lips, parting slightly to dart his tongue over mine. As his kissing became more urgent, my own body responded, leaning into him and pulling away in playful suggestion.

He lifted my arms.

My hands pinned above my head, I arched my back as my lover nibbled my earlobe. Growling slightly, I kissed him harder, pressing him back. Determined to stay in control, Tomlin forced my hands flat against the wall, moving his fingers out of mine. He held my wrists hard in place above my head while his other hand started to fumble with the buttons of my shirt.

Instantly, I drew in a surprised breath, bombarded by flashbacks of the water trial in Rochester's complex. The muscle man's face swam in my vision as I felt the weight of his hand on my wrists above my head, his legs straddling my body, his other hand on my chest. Then the vile guard, fumbling with my shift as his hand worked on the zipper of his pants, his greasy fingers on my skin.

I wrenched my head away from Tomlin's insistent lips and made a noise, clamping my mouth shut.

Startled, Tomlin threw himself back from me. I dropped my hands to my sides, sweat breaking out on my palms and forehead as I reeled in the memories, locking them away again. Silent tension between us, I shook my head to clear the visions. "I'm sorry."

My lover's face fell, catching a glimpse for the first time of what it had been for me to be Rochester's captive. We had never been so aggressive in our lovemaking before—in that moment, I knew it would be a long time until we were again. Tomlin went to his knees before me, hugging me hard around the waist as he shuddered. He didn't say he was sorry for what had befallen me, he didn't have to.

I looked down at the grown man showing silent

homage at my feet.

I tugged at his arms to bring him off his knees and stand before me once more, his height a full head and a half over me. My eyes reflected in his, both watery with the threat of unshed tears. I brought his head down to mine, kissing him gently, and continued what he had started, working on the buttons of my shirt.

One by one, we shed our pieces of clothing, letting them lay where they fell. The fact that our impeccable dress would get wrinkled was not a concern at the moment—that could be dealt with later.

Like two beings never meant to see each other again our mouths devoured each other, lips growing puffy from the aggressive kisses.

As each piece of clothing came off, the skin underneath was christened by the other's lips, an exquisite torture as the process continued through the many layers of grey-black garb.

Relishing in the taste of each other, Tomlin grabbed my buttocks as I hopped up, wrapping my legs around his naked waist. My arms around his neck, Tomlin ravished my own, my moans egging him on for more.

He carried me slowly to the bed, a long double. The room had never been meant for roommates, let alone lovers. Placing me on the quilt, he broke his mouth away from my skin long enough to reach over for a button on the nightstand, activating the fireplace.

Surprised by the sound, I looked sideways at it between moans, bringing myself up on my elbows to see better. "A captain has to have some comforts," he grinned.

I smiled back, my eyelids heavy in both arousal and exhaustion. I sighed in pleasure as he put his large hand on my chest, forcing me to lay flat on the bed, and drew his fingers over my flat stomach and battle scars now littering my torso. His expression over my naked form was rapt, observing me like he had never done during our love making before.

I looked over him too. His chest was lean and chiseled with muscles, his upper biceps corded, his skin largely flawless except for the marring scar on his right side from his only death.

It made me self-conscious of my own marks: a pocked circle from being shot in the chest, lines on my wrists and forearms, numerous constellations of scars from badly made stitches, and cuts and contusions over my face and arms from my time at the complex.

Instinctively I drew up an arm to cover my front.

My lover grabbed me by the wrist, bringing the scars on the inside to his lips as he lowered himself onto me.

"You are beautiful, every mark, every dimple," he said tenderly, joining our bodies together gently. Unlike most others, he knew the gravity of each piece of healed flesh and could see in each scar the humility and beauty of their distinction. Drawing his lips over the uneven lines of my wrist was strangely sensual and my body arched at the intimacy of it, inviting him in finally.

With quiet understanding we moved together in perfect rhythm.

Minutes later, Tomlin cried out, collapsing on me with his release, my rapid breathing echoing his. He drew himself up on his elbows, one hand reaching up to play with my damp hair, wiping loose tendrils off my sweat-glistened skin. "I didn't mean for it to be that quick but that was...."

"I know," I panted, my expression forgiving. "But we do have all night...."

He grinned as he rolled onto his side, taking me with him.

Plans Made

Tomlin and I strode through the doors into the briefing room, seeing the other soldiers already there. We weren't late—it was generally a rule that one would try to get to the room before the captain appeared.

All eyes were on me as we entered and I raised my chin in reply. I had nothing to apologize for and if the others were bitter or jealous or angry by our decision to spend the night together, that was their business. For ones such as our kind, I had learned there can be little pleasure sometimes in a vast world of hurt.

I would take whatever consolations I could.

Regardless of the late night in which we had attempted to relieve each other of any and all painful memories, Tomlin and I had gotten up early enough to order a quick breakfast and fix up our uniforms. Nothing was out of place, no wrinkle in evidence due to the quick work of a little heat by the fire. The fact that our eyes had a few more wrinkles of sleep deprivation was another matter but not one that would affect our performance.

In a way Tomlin's joking the night before had been correct: thoroughly cleansed of helpless and murderous thoughts for the moment, I felt purged, my mind thinking clearer and faster. It was more focused on the task at hand, which at the current time was to execute our mission and rid the world of yet another evil.

Knowing the mission objective now, I thought briefly to the night before. At some point we had been lying next to each other, me on my back, him on his side, our limbs interlocked and sweaty with our love making. Tomlin had brought two fingers down, making an invisible line from between my breasts to my navel, then to my side as it trailed down to my hip and lower.

There, it paused.

Frowning, his hand stayed still on that one scar which would never be forgotten.

"He will always be between us, won't he?" Tomlin asked, his fingers over the brand that I had received while in my captor's custody, marking me his.

Only his for now, while he lives.

I put my hand over Tomlin's, drawing his fingers off the area as I lowered my voice. "Just until this mission ends, then we will both be free."

"So that's it, then," Tomlin clapped his hands together once loudly, bringing me out of my reverie. Some of the members smiled, happy to be done. Others merely nodded, understanding the challenge that lay ahead. "Well, we all know our parts." He glanced at his watch, and I did the same, 1800 glowing from the screen. "It's early. Go on, get some food, have a little fun and get to sleep—0500 will be here before we know it." He smiled reassuringly around the room. "We leave promptly at 0600, so no horseplay."

The soldiers gathered their tablets, their jackets now strewn on the backs of chairs, and started to leave. "That goes for you too, sir," a younger male said as he noticed Tomlin's gaze resting on me from across the room. Grinning, Tomlin thumped the boy on the back good-naturedly.

They seemed so young then, the children we were leading into this mission. Some were as young as fifteen, the oldest only eighteen. I forgot sometimes, hearing the advanced tactical speech and battle-hardened discussions, that they were only that—children. But the minute they put on their grey-black garbs they were no longer youth. Then they were what we had chosen to make them: soldiers.

To be sure, the choice was theirs as well. Like Tomlin and I and every member before us, each child had been given a choice at a certain time in their lives.

Some didn't remain, leaving because they could not handle the emotional and physical stress the job put on them. They were sworn to secrecy and sent back into the normal run of school life, no harm to them. Others didn't leave by choice, their remains brought back and buried in a secret cemetery outside the city.

Tomlin came up to me as I considered my teammates. "They will be fine," he said. "Their part in this should be mostly routine."

Taking me by my upper arm, he turned me toward him. "It's you I'm worried about. Are you sure you're ready for this?"

"Do I have a choice?" I asked. I was ready, more than ready for this to be over. If my discomfort made it possible, then so be it.

Once this is done I can really start my life.

Or we will at least be content in our afterlife.

He nodded toward the exit that would lead to his room. "Come on, I ordered dinner to be delivered to our room."

I went without argument—after that long of a day we could both use some food and rest.

After devouring the large meal before us, possibly our last good meal for some time, Tomlin laid a comforter in front of the electric fire. There we sat, stripped down to shorts and tank tops for sleeping, staring at the flames. The decisions one makes in the briefing room can weigh heavily on the soul. We, two of the most experienced soldiers at the school now, knew this all too well. One wrong move, one unanticipated act by the enemy, and all would change.

We could all die. The thought was humbling.

We did not make love that night, the act too tender

for what lay ahead. Instead we fell asleep there on the floor, the electric fireplace heating us as we lay with each other, his arm over my stomach and my arm over his.

Heavy Compromise

I woke shortly after dawn, carefully peeling Tomlin's arms from around me, covering him with a blanket from the bed. He mumbled, brows furrowed, but remained asleep.

Silently putting on my boots, I stole out of the room, another blanket wrapped around me for warmth. I had spent many a troubled night in the underbelly of Ops and knew which corridors to take so I would be relatively unseen. The few technicians who I came upon merely nodded seriously—they weren't shocked to find me there and would never begrudge a soldier of the sanctuary needed before a mission.

I found the bay door easily, opening it enough to stand in the luminescence of the teasing sunrise. Leaning against the doorframe I held the blanket around me, my breath coming out in puffs of crystal humidity in the cold air. I don't know how long I stood there, my fingers growing stiff from holding the blanket as I watched the sun rise over the wall behind the field of the school.

"I knew I would find you here," a voice came behind me.

I didn't look away from the sunrise. Its rays were just spilling into the complex, peeking over the rows of trees in the distance lining the wall perimeter. "Sir," I acknowledged, my voice tight.

"I will admit, I was a little shocked when I saw the mission plans come across my desk last night." He stood next to me in the bay doorway. "It is quite a risk you and Tomlin are taking. Are you sure you are up to it?"

We are, we have to be.

I pulled the blanket tighter, my bare legs freezing. "I don't think we have much choice, do you?" I was replaying the plans in my head, making sure we had not overlooked anything.

The sun was almost halfway up now. Here and there I could see signs of spring as the winter's frost dissipated. Green lily shoots were starting up through the snowpack in the gardens, water dripping from the roof as it warmed.

StPatrick sighed. "No. Not if we want this over." He came back to himself then, watching me. The sunlight warmed my skin, locks of my brown hair falling over my face, turning golden in the light.

"We should not be standing here," he said, the moment over.

I nodded and stood straight, backing up inside as

my commander closed the bay door. I sensed he too had spent many a morning in this very doorway. He understood needing to see beauty before the gore of a mission.

"If anything should go wrong...." He didn't continue, he didn't have to. In that tiny sentence was everything he didn't need to say. He wanted us to protect the others, to bring back whomever we could. He forgave us for anyone we had to leave behind. He wanted us to come back too, in whatever capacity, and to know he cared about us in case we couldn't.

He's saying goodbye.

"There you are," Tomlin's voice echoed across the hanger. I looked across at him, fully dressed in his soldier garb, a bulletproof vest and gun holster added to it. "The others will be assembling soon."

StPatrick drew himself to his full height and nodded. It was time.

There

It didn't take long for me to get dressed, the locker rooms beside the hanger having every piece of clothing I needed. Dressing quickly in the grey-black pants, undershirt and top, loose jacket and socks I laced up my boots regulation-style by habit. Splashing water on my face and drying it, I tied my shoulder-length hair into a tightly braided club out of the way. Once I added my own bulletproof vest, I looked over myself in the mirror.

At first I barely recognized the young woman staring back at me, my face older than it had been the last time I had worn the outfit. But there beneath the faint scar at my hairline were those same hazel eyes. Those eyes that I had pondered when I made Captain, observed in the reflective surface of my bars.

It had been only four years since I had wondered at my parents' reflection in my features and asked myself whether or not they would have been proud of me. Things were different now—I didn't have to wonder at all.

I took up the gun holster and headed out of the room, my boots echoing when I stepped into the hanger. Everyone was there, somber in resolve.

Only a few of the soldiers knew the whole plan, and even then we had kept back some details. The success in entirety depended on their legitimate reactions—surprise, shock, even immature experience.

Most of the soldiers quieted down as I stepped past them to take my place next to Tomlin. While I was not a captain anymore, this mission depended on my memory and my tactical hunches and it was generally accepted that I was his second-in-command.

Tomlin watched me strap the gun holster around my hips, securing the piece around my thigh. "Ready lieutenant?" he asked me, the other members doing a quick double-check on their gear.

I saw the ammo technician approach with a sharp knife and gun similar to the Berettas the guards at the complex had used. I slipped the blade into the thigh holster and added several extra clips into the pouch at my hip. I opened the gun's compartment to ensure the magazine was loaded, smacking it back in with a satisfying click, and nodded. We were ready.

It took hours to get to our mission target, longer than it had taken on return from my rescue. This time we were attempting to fly completely covertly. The large helicopter was quiet but was meant for short-term missions—the seating was cramped and limited. Comfort was not a main concern.

Most of the soldiers shut their eyes for the duration or, bored of resting finally, pulled out a deck of cards. Little else to do, a few talked of better times.

Tomlin and I stayed silent and awake, the only interaction between us when the helicopter started its descent into the rocky-cliffed beach. I felt his warm hand against mine and looked down to see our fingers interlocked. My pale fingers stuck out in contrast against the black fingerless glove I wore, preparation for what lie ahead.

I raised my eyes to his, both sets showing concern, holding each other's gaze. My lips reflected the soft smile that was on his own mouth. In that look was everything we needed to say. In the copter, the soldiers had gone quiet, witnessing our intimate moment. While no one approved of us being together, it was a brief moment of humanity that all needed. Like always, we never said goodbye. There would either be time for it later or not.

As the rails touched the ground we let each other go, unbuckling from our seats. Tomlin gave out instructions as per the plan and turned back to me as I opened the door, the blades winding down as the engines shut off. Tomlin tapped my shoulder to get my attention over the noise. "You ready?"

I'm never ready.

We are.

"See you up there," I yelled over the blades, jumping out.

My first challenge was to get to the complex. Surrounded by sixty-foot cliffs on three sides, the fourth was bordered by a beach, leading nowhere but back to the ocean. It seemed the only way was up. Taking a deep breath I approached the rocky wall and chose my path, placing my hands.

Carefully planting hands and feet, I made my way up the cliff, thankful I wore the leather gloves. Where my own skin was exposed I could feel the burn of tiny cuts, sliced by barnacles stuck to the rock face. Over and over I moved my palms, gripped with white-knuckled fingers. Over and over my boots scraped sideways, upwards along the sheer rocks.

Reaching over the top of the cliff finally, I heaved my body over, kneeling for a moment to catch my breath. Feeling my arms and legs quiver from the climb, I prepped myself for the next stage, patting my weapon to make sure it was there, also a small pocket on my holster containing locator chips and my knife on my thigh. I pulled small ear buds from a pocket, placing them in my ears, the better to avoid damage and the less pleading of the enemy I would need to hear if it came down to it.

I am ready.

Standing quickly, I rushed toward a large rock jutting out from the smoothed pathway I was on. I stood behind it, glancing out. There I could see the beginning of the building, its exterior camouflaged to disappear into the rock. A guard, dressed in black pants and a blue buttoned shirt, was standing outside tapping a cigarette against his hand, debating.

Another guard gestured for him to go and turned back into the building, closing the door. The first shrugged, putting the smoke in his mouth as he stepped closer to my cover, feeling around in his pocket. Stepping past me, he pulled out a lighter and lit his cigarette, his back to me. I watched the man from behind, debating how to disperse him.

In the end, my knife applied pressure to his neck easily, the spray of arterial fluids kept neatly behind the large rock. We couldn't afford any witnesses.

I wiped my knife on the back of the man's shirt, his cigarette still smoldering. Smudging it out with my boot, I stepped around the rock, moving my head back and forth to crack my neck. At the door I noticed no handle. I knocked lightly three times, my knife still in hand.

"Took you freaking long enough," a man's voice snarled as the door opened. Looking up, he followed the path of my boots to my grey-black pants up to my top and face. He swore. "How in the hell—"

I leapt toward him, covering his mouth with my hand. Driving him back against the wall, I spun my blade in my hand and plunged it deep into the man's gut in one quick motion, giving it a twist for good measure.

This one I watched die, having remembered his face as the man who had tried to molest me. If I'd had time, I would have let him die slowly while I told him all the horrible things that I could do to him. Instead I gave him a quick death and left his body in a pile.

We should've unmanned him for all the women he likely did rape. We should've inflicted the same beating he gave us.

We should've made it last longer.

The thoughts of torturing the man haunted me.

Again wiping my knife, I took a transmitter from my pouch. Twisting the tiny dial I stuck it to the wall seam, hoping it was on. With no indicator lights, the tracker was discreet but difficult to use.

I took the guard's weapon, placing it in the door jamb to keep accessibility for the rest of my team I knew would be arriving shortly. We had planned it that way, after all.

Looking down the hall, I glanced between the two choices. Standing tall, I tried to remember the crudely drawn blueprints, ultimately choosing the left path as the most direct. I continued in this way, choosing my directions carefully, leaving the transmitters and hoping my team was right behind me. While stealth was needed to get in, we had expected that very quickly our presence would be noticed and therefore just getting inside the complex was key.

Otherwise it is just me alone on a killing spree....

I shook my head. I had no reason to doubt. Tomlin was in command—of course he would follow our plan, of course he would lead the team to safety.

I was almost to my destination, attaching another transmitter to the wall when I heard whispers. A click sounded around the corner. My eyes grew large as I realized what it was.

I dove to the ground and covered my ears as the blast exploded. Bullets flew past me. I waited until the shrapnel had finished then took my gun slowly from my holster. The safety was already off.

Inching up on my belly, I looked around the corner. As the smoke subsided I heard a guard advancing, almost right on top of me. I aimed high, shooting him upward through the groin as he spun around at another noise behind me. The reinforcements must have arrived.

Ah yes, a good battle. We have missed this.

The next man yelled and dove for me as I struggled to my feet. My balance was disturbed by the blast despite the ear buds I wore. He brought the butt of his gun across the shoulder of my vest, still unable to see fully through the clearing smoke. The move smarted, having deflected off the vest, the butt hitting my jaw instead. I grunted and raised my weapon, but the distance was too short.

We grappled, him losing his weapon first, then I lost mine. Putting one hand on my throat and one on my wrist—that could, in theory, reach my knife—he pounded me hard against the wall. He was lifting me by the hold on my throat, my feet now inches off the ground.

Claude. I recognised the gruff expression and harsh features of the man.

My vision was sparkling, black dancing across my eyes as I gasped. I winced as the air was forced out of me then gritted my teeth in focus. I brought my other hand up, the heel pushing against the bottom of my attacker's chin.

When I felt Claude's grip on my throat loosen slightly, I took the advantage, bending my legs. I lifted my boots to the man's thighs and heaved. Just enough force, he fell backwards and lost his grip entirely.

I fell against the wall, using it to land upright on my feet. Taking in huge breaths, I felt consciousness return to me in full. I saw the guard right himself, clenching his fists as he narrowed his eyes and stepped toward me once more. Pulling out my knife, I threw hard.

Claude's body landed with a thump as more people could be heard, a lot more arriving, probably through the levels above. I swore as I picked up my gun and turned to retrieve my knife, buried deep in the man's skull. I considered leaving it there, but chances were I would need it near the end.

Plus, it is a nice knife.

Quickly, I placed a boot on the side of Claude's face as I pulled the blade out with a sickening sucking sound. I didn't bother to clean it this time—it would be covered in more gore before too long.

I heard the click behind me before I saw the muzzle of the gun pointed my way. The smoke had left a haze in the hallway, vision made more difficult by the dim lighting and red alarms that were now flashing. I glanced to the side, turning slowly, and froze.

Just past the gun, holding the weapon firmly in two hands, was my companion. She wore one of her usual pretty dresses. I took that as a sign that she was not meant to be in this fight. Looking at the gun, I recognized it as a guard's and saw the first man's body near her.

She must have decided to try to help.

Squinting, she looked into my face. It was the first rookie mistake when it came to trying to kill your opponent, the gun wavering as her eyes grew large. She started to smile, the gun still pointed but lowering. I heard the sound of footsteps and wished she had stayed wherever she had come from.

I am running out of time.

"Lower the gun," I said, my voice raspy but firm, taking a chance by raising my own. My throat was a bit sore from the last guard's attack, but I forced my voice through the pain. Her smile faded and she shook her head as she leveled it at me again. I noticed both hands on the weapon getting slick with nervous sweat.

My other half wanted to urge me on, but it hesitated, perhaps for the first time. So, it was fond of her too.

"You're speaking," she said, her eyes softening in gladness, and my heart ached at her compassion as I considered where I should hit her.

"I do a lot of things now," I said, stepping closer. "Lower the gun, I don't want to hurt you."

"I—" The muzzle lowered a bit then she shook her head again. "—I can't let you do this. Please, just turn and leave."

I wanted to laugh at her, the tickle there at the back of my sore throat. But ultimately I hardened, knowing she was asking me to spare *his* life. I closed my eyes for a moment in regret. "Last chance, lower the gun." I was close enough now that if she did shoot it would hurt a lot, the barrel almost against my chest.

I don't have to kill her—I could just incapacitate her. I could knock her out to keep her out of the way and safe.

We can't. She is his. You know we can't.

"Your name?" I asked softly then, my voice shaking for a moment, my resolve firm but regretful.

"What?" She looked at me, confused.

I took a deep breath. "What is your name?"

The woman smiled. "Ilyana."

I heard the unmistakable sound of live weight being thrown against a door as more guards yelled their way through the complex, barred from entering the hallway. My luck ran out. As the men burst through the doorway, pieces of the door flying out, I swore, seeing my companion's finger tighten on the trigger in surprise at the sound.

Goodbye.

In a split second decision, I pulled first.

I didn't wait to hear her body hit the ground.

I knew she was dead—I had aimed for her forehead. I never missed. *Never.* I had wanted it to be a quick kill, not something that would cause her any pain. I paused, wondering at my humanity. Right now I could not be upset, even though my hands shook from the act I had just performed.

I have to be a soldier. The best soldier.

The shaking stopped.

I sprinted for the intersection I had come from, taking cover from the bullets of the guards that were now spilling out of the doorway. I stumbled over the bodies. I closed my eyes, listening, my gun raised beside my head.

My companion had been my brief kindness in a world of pain and discomfort. She had made living, and dying, easier. And I had just killed her.

"Report," Tomlin's voice came beside me. I opened my eyes, seeing the team there as expected.

"Six, from what I can tell, basic weapons, nothing I can't handle." I pointed to an adjacent hallway. "That's the way to his office, one hall over. Massive wood doors, you can't miss it. Go on. I'll be there in a few minutes."

Leave us, Captain, this battle is ours.

Tomlin hesitated, the other soldiers' guns drawn. They were waiting for orders, ready to shoot.

"Go!" I yelled at him over the shouting of the guards around the corner. "Just leave me an extra gun and rounds and I'll meet you."

My lover reached behind, pulling a gun from his backside. He came close to me, pressing his body to mine as he slid the weapon into my holster. "Aim true," he said softly into my ear.

If only we had more time. My other half leaned toward Tomlin.

Tucking an extra clip of ammo in my belt, my captain waited for my nod. He signaled to the others and took a step back. In one movement, I spun around the corner, shooting wildly at first then taking deadly aim. As the team ran behind me into their desired corridor, I felt stings as I was hit. A bullet landed in my left thigh, another grazing my upper right arm. I pulled the other gun out with my opposite hand, continuing my solo attack. The first gun dropped as it ran out of bullets.

It didn't take long, the assault on the guards. Only so many defenders were at this part of the complex, although I had no doubt reinforcements had already been called and were on their way.

Within what seemed like seconds, it was over, the bodies in a heap. I granted myself one last regretful look toward the pink dress in the corner, then turned and ran.

Endings

I skidded to a stop outside Rochester's office, gulping deep breaths through my irritated throat as I calmed my heartbeat. The door slightly ajar, I could hear the conversation inside in full swing.

"Surely you would not have me believe she is not here with you?" Rochester's deep voice questioned.

"That doesn't matter right now," Toms said in response, his voice unwavering.

"Oh, but I think it does. After all, we would want your lover present when I have you all killed for this intrusion." I could hear the enjoyment in the criminal's voice. "Come now," he urged, "go over your earpiece or watch-speaker or whatever technology you hold and tell her to join us."

I closed my eyes and took one last deep breath, reaching up to remove my ear buds and throw them on the floor. Turning the corner, I pushed open the door with one hand, stepping in.

The room was the same as it had been, as I hoped it

would be. Our plan was based on such consistencies. Wood paneling surrounded the space, a roaring fire in the fireplace on one side, his desk in the centre back, rows of filled bookcases lining every edge. On the walls were authentic artworks, a statue of armor standing tall beside Tomlin, it's metal plates and sword polished to a shine.

"Ah, there you are!" Rochester grinned widely, his arms outstretched. One of the soldiers closed the door behind me, locking it. The rest of the soldiers' guns were trained on him, the bodies of several guards strewn around the room. "My," he said, partially amused, "you have been busy."

My eyes flickered momentarily to the mirror above the fireplace.

My face was sooty from the earlier explosion, my chin and arms smeared with blood, my jacket disposed of somewhere along the way. The hand that held my gun loosely at my side was black with grime. My vest and pants were shiny with sweat and gore from my victims. The only indication of my own injuries was in the torn fabric on my arm and thigh, a bit of red peaking from beneath.

I stepped into the room further, waiting behind Tomlin and two of our people. "You're not leaving here alive."

The man burst into loud, booming laughter, echoing in the space. "You of all people should know better. I have more guards—better ones—coming as we speak.

They will have you surrounded before you know it."
We were silent and still as he continued. "Besides, who
is going to kill me...you?"

I can.

We will.

I stared hard at the man, resolving to show no
emotion. "Yes."

"Pfft." The man waved a hand my way. "You do
not have it in you to do cold, hard murder. When you
were insane from isolation, that was another matter.
Such a piece of beauty, watching a lovely young
woman kill with her bare hands." He chuckled. I could
hear two of the soldiers behind me shuffle uneasily.

And now look what I've become.

Rochester caught the motion and smiled wide. "But
that was another time. I bet until today you haven't
killed at all since escaping here."

"She has," Tomlin's voice came immediately.
"Seen your muscle man around lately?"

My other half grinned.

"Victor?" Rochester's irritation showed through
then. We had called his gambit with an unexpected
response. "He went out on an errand and never came
back."

"He won't be, either," Tomlin said then, forcing a
smile and glance in my direction. I stood still.

"Well." Rochester was frowning now, staring at me
for the lie that went deeper into my soul. He couldn't
see any, and I knew it. But I was staring back at him

and his own truths bled out to me like the red liquid through the clothes covering the death wound my other half so longed to deliver. He was confused how he missed such an important detail as his man being eliminated. "That's another matter then. Present your terms."

I watched him for a moment before stepping past Tomlin and the two guards in front of me. Stopping just in front of them, I still held at my thigh the gun Tomlin had given me earlier.

Rochester gestured to my attire and weapons. "Come now, is this how one takes a surrender? I thought you would respect terms of war better than that."

I hesitated, then holstered my weapon and flicked on the safety, loosening the belt.

Tomlin made a strangled protest as the weapons hit the ground, the other soldiers beginning to look nervously at one another when I reached up and ripped off the velcro straps that were holding my vest. The item fell to the ground at my feet.

Tomlin stepped forward. He grabbed my arm just below my wound. "Do you think that is a good idea?"

I hissed in pain, yanking my limb free.

"Your guns are all on him, what can he do, really?" I responded, staring ahead at the villain and stepping forward.

Tomlin returned to his position, raising his small rifle and aiming carefully, a new resolve on his face.

"You *are* lovers, then." Rochester grinned again, seeing something in our exchange that no other would. "I thought so."

He turned to Tomlin. "Kudos, my boy, I doubt you will ever find anyone else so...stimulating." He took in a deep breath, his hands on his hips as he considered us. "And what a pairing, if I suspect you are afflicted with the same...talents as our dear girl. Just think of the possibilities." He paused, cocking his head. "Think of the potential in the children you may bear, even now."

It was a tactic we hadn't anticipated, although we knew Rochester liked to play mind games. In that moment, Tomlin's determination wavered, shown only by the slightest shake of his gun as the thought of me bring pregnant with his child seemed to enter his thoughts. He had obviously never considered the result that our intimacies could have, never thought about the possibility of me bearing his child.

I had. How could I not?

It changed what we had to do. In that instant, it had altered our mission.

I knew it.

Rochester saw it all even faster than Tomlin thought it, using the disorientation to his advantage. Even before I could yell out, the mastermind had spun me around. My back was against him, his wide frame behind mine as he held me still with his arm across my collar-bone. His hand gripped my shoulder. My hands went to his arm, trying to dislodge him. I stopped resisting when I felt the blade at my neck. Pressing slightly, it nicked me.

Tomlin pursed his lips as he and the other soldiers retrained their guns.

"Here is how this is going to go," the large criminal behind me said with a new maliciousness. "You are going to put down your weapons and open the door for my guards. *Then* I will release her."

"So you can kill us all? No, I don't think so," Tomlin replied, picking his way slowly around to find the best vantage point. Unfortunately, the large fur jacket Rochester always wore hid much of his figure, and he had ensured our bodies were pressed together as close as possible. Aiming to kill the man behind me was a guess at best.

"Only the young ones," Rochester said, his breath hitting my ear. I tried to shift, to put some distance between us. "I will, of course, spare you two. There is nothing I could not accomplish with a whole army of your offspring by my side."

That thought was unbelievable in itself, but if anyone would do it, Rochester could. The idea that it was a possibility was horrifying.

I interrupted, my words small so as not to move my throat too much. "Your guards are dead by now. Our reinforcements took care of that." I smiled through my pain, knowing what I said was true. It was part of the plan, and I had no doubt it had been carried out.

"That is impossible, your little school does not have

the resources to train that many, not effectively," Rochester spat out.

"Not our school, no." Tomlin's lips curled into a smile.

The man moved his hand to encompass my throat as he shifted, considering. "The other vigilantes? But...that is impossible." The blade pressed harder on my throat as the man tensed. It sliced a little more of my skin. I felt a warm liquid trail down the hollow of my clavicle.

Taking a word from Rochester's speech to me long ago, knowing it would mean more to him than to anyone else, I spoke out, raspy, "They haven't been coddled, either."

I turned my head slightly, seeing my captor's eyes grow wide. At my lover's tightening of his finger on the trigger, Rochester snapped at him, "I will kill her before you get the chance."

"If you are so smart, you should know a slit throat won't kill her." Tomlin stepped closer, his rifle still drawn.

I made a small noise as Rochester pressed a little harder with the blade, the sharp metal popping through my skin further, making the cut wider. "No, a cut throat would not." He pulled me closer to him, adjusting his hand on the blade so it was angled for a deep impact, his lips next to my ear as he spoke, "But beheading would. I believe you know a little something about that, hey boy?"

I felt the blood drain from my face at the words. Tomlin's cheeks grew red. Rochester's knowledge of how the captain's mother had been killed only made it more of a possibility that he had been involved.

Considering the man for a moment, Tomlin raised his chin, staring into the criminal's eyes. "Do it," he said loudly to the others. He lowered his gun to the ground. The younger soldiers hesitated, but followed their orders, putting their guns down on the floor and straightening up. As the last soldier—the one who had teased Tomlin about horseplay the day before—stood up, he began the steps toward the door to unlock it. It seemed to be in slow motion, the events now, as I looked at Tomlin with tears in my eyes.

"Aim true," I said softly.

In a move quicker than I had even known Tomlin to be, he spun around, ripping the sword from the statue of armor behind him with both hands. He plunged the metal blade deep through my chest, aiming upward. I slammed my eyes shut. My head involuntarily snapped up.

Rochester's mouth gaped. He realized too late what had happened—that the death blow had penetrated the both of us. He looked behind him.

In the mirror, I could see the tip of the blade glint in the firelight. It was visible over his shoulder, red with both our blood. The tears were running freely down my face as Rochester's hand dropped off my chest. He reached for the sword grip to dislodge it. I blinked once in confirmation, Tomlin reaching the grip first. The fingers of one hand around it, he used the other palm on the pummel for stability as his hands shook. They stabilized as he glared at the man behind me. He twisted the blade a half turn, shoving it home.

My eyes grew wide and my own mouth opened, a small trickle of blood forming in my throat. The weight of Rochester's body took me down with him. He was dead before he hit the ground. I knew, no breath coming from his lips, his body a limp mass.

Hot wetness spread over my backside as I saw Tomlin bark an order to the soldiers. They secured the room and regaining their weapons. He threw himself on his knees near me, his hands fluttering over the sword but not touching it. I nodded, feeling going from my extremities as the blood pumped out of my body in rhythmic waves.

Tomlin wrenched on the sword once to remove it but it was caught on bone and organs, the blade dull from disuse. I cried out, the pain significant. Calling out, two of the older soldiers came over, lending a hand in holding the body behind me while the sword was pulled free. In one fluid motion it slid out of my chest and was flung aside, clattering across the room.

My hands went to my chest shakily as Tomlin pulled me away from the vile man who had once dictated a whole life between us. I took in deep gasping breaths, blood seeping through my fingers as I tried to smile at Tomlin reassuringly.

Resting my head in his lap he let his tears flow freely. It had been a possibility in our plan all along—not with the sword but his gun. I had told him to bring the rifle, something he never carried, so the bullet would pass through me into the man should this situation arise. I had predicted correctly that given the chance Rochester would gladly bloody his hands with my death, especially if it meant saving his own life.

I grew colder by the minute as shouts were heard outside, the doors thrown open to admit the others.

Grey-black clad soldiers spilled in, older militants, men and women of varying size and shape and skin color, bound together by this common goal. They laughed in praise as they saw Rochester's body, his eyes still open in surprise on his death mask.

They fell silent as they noticed Tomlin sitting on the ground, my body stiffening in his arms. My breath came short now as a medic rushed over, hands coming to examine the long, thin slice in my chest. I tried to lift a hand to push him away—there were others who needed his attention more, who could use it at all.

Tomlin raised his hand in halt to the man and shook his head, looking miserable. My time was almost over.

Final Changes

No one ever tells you what it is like to die. Worse yet, they don't tell you the consequences when that state fails to remain.

I thought I had received my final reward, that sweet taste of the heavens the philosophers and religious leaders boasted of all those thousands of years.

As I took my last breaths on the ground, my head nestled in my love's lap, the words "I love you" died silently on my lips before I did. My heartbeat became infinitely slow, the sound of it in my ears louder than anything else in the room. I reached up to stroke the tears that streamed down my handsome lover's face, but stopped when I saw the blood covering my own hand, dropping it limply back to my chest.

So much blood.

I could feel it pump out of me with each heartbeat, soaking my back and chest as it exited both sides. My body grew cold as ice, my limbs numb and useless. Eventually it became difficult even to blink. Still, I forced my eyes open, wanting Tomlin's face to be the last thing in my memory.

I don't know how long it took me to go, time seeming endless as a world of unspoken affections and conversations lay between my love and I.

My heart beat twice. The lights grew bright and began to overtake my vision. Seeing a white light I felt my heart throb only once more.

I don't remember my time while I was dead, only a sense afterward that I was ever waiting for the next event. It was neither boring nor exciting. It just was.

Unlike the other times, sensations hit me like a tsunami cresting over a peak when I awoke, a smash of wave upon wave of hard truths. The white light got excessively bright so that my eyes stung painfully. My ears pounded with noise that reverberated through my skull. My muscles spasmed excruciatingly, any effort to move them choppy and uncoordinated. At first, air eluded me, and I gasped in the oxygen as though it were water, choking on it.

I flailed, and screamed, and begged.

Catherine told me after that I had been delirious. She said I had screamed out that he was going to kill me, begging them to stop him. They all knew I was speaking of Tomlin, my last known murderer.

It had taken three rounds of sedatives and four nurses to restrain me in an attempt to prevent me from hurting myself or others. Even then, I had acted so wildly that one nurse had wound up with a bruised eye socket, another a broken nose.

I had been dead for five days, the longest period I had ever experienced of that state of un-living.

Of course, Tomlin was there to witness my reanimation. StPatrick told me later that the young man had come back from the mission miserable and angry and sad beyond what most humans could usually take. When I screamed out unknowingly and he heard it, he took it as an accusation and dismissal.

Nothing could be further from the truth.

Still my lover avoided me after that, leaving in haste. When I got out of bed the next day, despite the doctor's orders to rest and heal from the sword wound still closing in my chest, I dressed in a set of dark scrubs I stole from the nurses' cupboard and went to find Tomlin, to explain what I could.

He wouldn't see me.

Not meeting my eyes, the young soldiers who had been on our mission shook their heads and offered apologies that he was indisposed. After the second day of trying, I gave up.

I visited StPatrick instead, giving him my debriefing, what I remembered. He said to give Tomlin time, that his wounds too would heal. I was doubtful. I knew the young man had determined we were over.

My commander told me what had happened in the five days before my life had been restored, that the other vigilantes had returned with our team early the next morning after our victory. They had let themselves be debriefed just as the others did, lending their version of the tale.

He told me he had opened the hanger to the group so they could spend a night together, the old and young. It was important that our children, our soldiers, knew life after the school existed and that there would always be allies. So they shared a night of storytelling, healing both in the telling and in the hearing.

He told me the vigilantes had approached Tomlin that night about leaving with them and that the man had refused.

The other soldiers had taken the time to also bury their dead, five in total. Taking advantage of StPatrick's offer to have it done in our private cemetery a handful of the vigilantes and our own had gone, their boots sloshing in the wet grass as they said their goodbyes and paid respects. Despite the fact that the casualties were low, it was still a hard point in the victory.

He also told me what had happened during the mission. The vigilantes had arrived on schedule, taking the top of the complex and moving down as my people moved from the bottom up.

No guards had been taken alive as prisoners—anyone who worked in that capacity had already sold their soul to the devil, their bodies branded as proof. Their gruesome defence of the complex had proved it. The various maids and prisoners had been assessed, some returned from where they had been taken long ago, the others flown back to a facility for rehabilitation.

I later remembered what Rochester had told me once, that his people would always be his. I was glad then that our people hadn't tried to take survivors from among the guards.

When the vigilantes arrived at Rochester's office, they were surprised at the efficiency with which our team, hardly more than a band of teenagers, had acted. The deed was already done, the criminal's body cooling, his blood staining his precious Persian rug.

The more-experienced soldiers had raided Rochester's office, taking back items the man had collected illegally—precious artwork and beloved trinkets of soldiers past that he had murdered. Within the bookshelves they also found disks, hundreds of disks cataloguing his operations and events within the complex. They found records of the victories against the vigilantes. StPatrick said there were other disks too, but did not disclose their content. Suspecting what they may have contained, I shuddered and let the comment pass.

He didn't mention Tomlin or I, sitting on the floor waiting for death, but I knew the truth, had seen the older soldier's faces fall and sympathetically place hands on my lover's shoulders as the light had descended on me.

Rochester's death had left several unanswered

questions—how he had known my mother and if he had killed Tomlin's. I meant to ask StPatrick about any information on the disks, but somehow that past seemed irrelevant now. Maybe one day I would seek the truth, but for now I was content to be oblivious.

When StPatrick's long-ago friend Outou approached me the following day, joining me briefly for my morning stroll on the grounds, I knew what he would ask before he did. I looked once across the grounds at Tomlin, knowing the answer Outou sought would take me farther from where my heart said I needed to be. It didn't matter—my answer was already yes.

So when the vigilantes left later the next morning, I went with them, my rucksack filled with the few world possessions I had. I didn't know what purpose I would fulfill in my new role, but Outou had promised that my talents would be well utilized, that I could be of great use. I so longed to be useful.

Our world changed after that mission, the nation becoming dramatically more peaceful. Whether it was due to Rochester's dissolved influence or the fear the other villains had of their own demise by our hands, we could never tell. To be sure, we were busy—drugs and child slavery and violence existing on every corner of the earth. But the threat was never the same.

As the vigilantes' helicopter took flight, I looked

through the side window, listening to my new comrades eagerly talk of home. I didn't know where that was now for me exactly, but I was willing to try to forge a new one.

As I viewed the building in its entirety, I couldn't help but think of my time with it as my home, from child to early adulthood. My memories were filled with gladness and heartache and pain and victory.

I wondered what the future would hold for someone such as me—I hoped I would find my place, continuing to be useful in the new home I now travelled to.

Somehow, I felt the school was still important within my life, that I would come back one day.

We will be back. To return will mean the continuation of something even greater.

I saw StPatrick raise a hand in goodbye and returned the gesture, Tomlin a half-step behind him, a grim expression on his face. He didn't move, didn't lift his hand. He only looked away.

Still, I could not help but suspect that our lives had not crossed for the last time, and all of us would be better for it.

I did the same, focusing on the interior skeleton of the helicopter, the faces of my new comrades. All I knew was, for now, we were all alive and that if the opportunity presented itself again I was prepared to die. After all, dying was not necessarily permanent.

For now we would have to live as we could, knowing at least that some of us could come back again and again. For those who didn't, they had the sweetest lives of all.

Did you like what you read?

Join my enewsletter list for promotions, specials, and new releases at:

www.rebekahraymond.com

Also connect with Rebekah Raymond:

Twitter:
@RRaymondAuthor

Facebook:
Author Rebekah Raymond

Watch for the next instalments in the Life's Series:

Life's Hope

Seleah hears the devastating news from Tomlin with the resolve of a child who has grown too much to return home. But when she decides to come back, her course is altered dramatically. Her resolve is to stay the independent soldier she envisions herself to be, but her soul has other plans...

Tomlin wants her, *needs* her to return for good. But what will he sacrifice to ensure she stays?

Life's Legacy

Arkem has been living in his parents' shadow far too long. When he is given the chance at freedom and faces his own demons, he falls down into remorse and anger. Will Arkem be able to battle free from his counterpart's hold to become what he was once again? Or will he be damned to a life of never-ending pain and sacrifice?

45891313R00189

Made in the USA
Charleston, SC
06 September 2015